WAKING MAGIC

WAKING MAGIC

THE LEIRA CHRONICLES™ BOOK ONE

MARTHA CARR
MICHAEL ANDERLE

DISRUPTIVE IMAGINATION

Copyright © 2020 (as revised) Martha Carr and Michael T. Anderle
Cover Art by Jake @ J Caleb Design
http://jcalebdesign.com / jcalebdesign@gmail.com
Cover copyright © LMBPN Publishing

LMBPN Publishing
PMB 196, 2540 South Maryland Pkwy
Las Vegas, NV 89109

Version 3.01, June 2020
Version 3.02, August 2020
eBook ISBN: 978-1-64971-010-9
Print ISBN: 978-1-64971-011-6

From Martha

To everyone who still believes in magic and all the possibilities that holds.

To all the readers who make this entire ride so much fun.

To Louie, Jackie, and so many wonderful friends who remind me all the time of what really matters and how wonderful life can be in any given moment.

And finally, a special thank you to John Nelson of the Austin, Texas Police Department who patiently answers all of my questions. I hope I made you proud. Thank you for your service.

From Michael

*To Family, Friends and
Those Who Love
To Read.
May We All Enjoy Grace
To Live The Life We Are
Called.*

WAKING MAGIC TEAM

Thanks to our JIT and Beta Readers

JIT Beta Readers

Joshua Ahles
Paul Westman
Kimberly Boyer
Peter Manis
Keith Verret
Erika Daly
James Caplan
Micky Cocker
John Raisor

If I missed anyone, please let me know!

Editor

Ellen Campbell

CHAPTER ONE

Detective Leira Berens was getting impatient. Murder suspects shouldn't get to call the shots.

"You're going to need to come out sometime, Arthur." Leira yelled from where she stood in the weed-filled, postage-stamp of a front yard. She was giving the suspect five minutes to think it over but then she was going in and getting him.

The five minutes was just to make her Captain happy. Happy Captain, happy life.

"Fuck, Arthur, it's us or the Mexican Federales," she yelled again. She squinted into the hot Texas sun, trying to persuade him. "I hear our hospitality is better." She turned back and looked at the small house. "It's not going to be pretty if we come in there."

"He's coming out," said her partner, Detective Felix Hagan. "He's out of options. We're the only ones who won't shoot him," he said looking around at the neighborhood. "Or worse."

Arthur was a punk kid in a local upstart gang trying to take over territory in Austin. He had killed a man in a Tijuana bar fight. Normally, not an Austin problem.

Tough luck that the dead guy was a member of the Latin

Kings. Even worse luck when the Kings picked up Arthur's best friend who quickly told them every secret, including a few about Arthur.

They had cornered Arthur in a biker bar on South Lamar and Arthur chose to shoot his way out of there. A kid fresh out of college, not much younger than Leira took a bullet to his neck.

Unintended consequences.

He bled out in a minute making Arthur an Austin P.D. problem. Now, everyone was looking for Arthur.

Leira glanced down at her watch. The face of the watch shimmered and blurred for a moment. Gold sparks shot out in every direction. She froze, staring at her watch.

"Shit," she whispered. She looked around quickly before looking back at her watch. "Not again." Two days of watching things lose their shape and glow like the fourth of July had her unnerved.

Too young for a stroke, right? Fuck, I hope so.

Worse idea, she was going crazy like her mother, Eireka Berens. She was sent off to the padded rooms at thirty-two when Leira was just ten years old for talking about entire worlds that no one else could see.

Leira shook her head and looked again. The dial of the watch cleared. Let it go. One more minute.

"You getting antsy? Youth," said her partner, with a snort of laughter.

Leira glanced at him and back at the run-down bungalow. She was giving him the look he had nicknamed the dead fish the first week they rode together. Leira thought of it as more of a blank stare.

"Don't be an asshole, Felix, just because I can still see my shoes. Old age is making you cranky." She brushed her bangs off her sweaty forehead.

"That would bother me more if you were wearing grown-up shoes." He smirked at her Merrell Vapor blue and orange thin-soled running shoes. It was the most expensive thing she ever wore.

"Somebody's got to be able to run after the bad guys." The young detective crossed her arms over her chest and didn't look in Hagan's direction. He let out a laugh. He liked his young partner even if she was impossible to read. Frankly, he saw it as one of her better qualities even if he could never tell if she was trying to make a joke or just stating the obvious.

It didn't take him long to also realize Leira didn't like chitchat and never hesitated to shoot.

More reasons to like her.

She wasn't much to look at despite the curves and skinny pants she favored, and flawless ivory skin with a face framed by thick, short dark hair that curled around her face.

Men tried asking her out back when she was a student at the University of Texas, but no one ever got her way of looking at the world.

She liked being able to reason things out and leave feelings out of it. Life was a lot easier that way.

But not being willing to tell a guy what he wanted to hear accomplished jack shit for her dating profile.

"Damn house looks like it's being held together by the paint chips." Leira was still aiming her semi .40 at the front door. "Okay, enough of this," she growled, taking the front steps two at a time. "Arthur shouldn't get to eat his last meal as a free idiot in peace."

"I'll make sure to tell the Captain you paused before doing your usual foot through the front door." Hagan followed her up the stairs, his .45 raised, quickly scanning left to right.

Leira turned, her back to the door and kicked backward, splintering the old wood as the door swung open, banging against the wall. She swiveled and whispered, "Going left."

Hagan nodded, slipping down the narrow hallway to the right toward the bedrooms.

"Clear!" Leira called out from the kitchen, looking out toward the back porch.

A plate of half-eaten mac and cheese was on the kitchen table. Leira kicked a fork, making it slide across the floor. "Arthur, your last meal was powdered orange cheese," she called out, looking around. "It's poor choices like these that got you to this point in time."

A loud crack rang out. Detective Hagan let out a deep, strangled scream. "Stop! Stop goddammit!" he yelled.

Detective Berens wasn't sure if her partner was yelling in pain or out of habit. She ran down the hall in time to see Arthur squirm through the window in the back bedroom.

Hagan was collapsed on the floor holding his shoulder. Blood was seeping through his fingers. "Go, get him!" he yelled through his clenched teeth. "Get the little fucker!"

"Call for a bus," she yelled over her shoulder. She slipped easily through the window and took off after Arthur as he leaped over the chain link fence into the next yard.

She vaulted the fence, already running as she closed the distance between them. Arthur looked back to see where she was and was surprised to find Leira right on his heels.

He tried to bring the pistol up just as she punched him hard in the face. She caught him mid-stride, tackling him as the pistol flipped end over end in the grass.

"That's for Hagan," she spit out, wrenching his arms behind his back and closing the handcuffs tight around his wrists as he squirmed on the ground.

He spit out grass, twisting around to look up at her. "You broke my fucking nose, you bitch!"

"Yeah, you're having one hell of a bad day." She jammed a knee into the small of his back.

"What the hell? You taking steroids?" Arthur whined. "How did you get to be so strong?"

Leira secured his gun and pulled him up to his feet, pushing him back the way they came.

She dragged him down the alley to the small house and right up to the window, shoving him inside through the same window.

He landed with a thud. She easily crawled through and stood over him.

"Damn, lock me in the car instead. Why you have to do me like that? Never use a door?" He rolled over and tried to stand.

Leira ignored the bitching and shoved him back to the floor. "Shut up and stay there."

The sound of sirens was getting closer. "Move and you have a bigger problem." Leira went to the bathroom and pulled a dirty hand towel off a plastic circle hanging from the wall, hurrying back to the room.

"Hagan, you okay?" She handed him the towel, trying to look him in the eyes. "Here, press this on your shoulder. It's the least questionable rag I could find in this place."

"Damn, Berens, you sound like you're worried. Makes me think I might be dying if you're concerned." He grunted, his face twisting in pain.

Leira gave him the dead fish look.

"Much better," he smiled. "Now I know I'll be okay."

"Get a room," Arthur sneered. Leira turned to him and delivered a swift kick. She stood there waiting to see if he had anything else to say.

He gave off nothing more than the occasional whimper until a couple of uniforms came to take him away.

"Feel free to bounce his head a couple of times when you tell him to duck getting into the backseat," she said, as they marched him out.

The paramedics rushed in, hovering over Hagan. "I can walk my own damn self out. Don't give me crap about policy."

He struggled to his feet as the two medics helped him down the hall.

"I'll meet you at the hospital." Leira followed them out and got into her car, turning on the lights and siren.

Leira waited at the hospital until Detective Hagan was stitched up and relaxing with green jello in his own room.

"This is the life." He lay back in his bed trying to fish out a square of jello with one hand. Leira managed a smile.

"All the paperwork we're gonna have to fill out for a flesh wound. I better enjoy this." He shook his head, slurping the square of jello off a white plastic spoon.

"I think the flesh wound is supposed to be the good news. I gotta go." She smoothed out the blanket at the end of the bed, "Your wife on the way?"

He looked up and shrugged. "Yeah, damn boss wouldn't let her off any earlier without clocking out. My fault, just a little. I told her all I got was a scratch. Go, before she sees me and the yelling starts." He gave her a wink and slurped another green square.

Leira slipped past the nurses' station where Rose Hagan was demanding to know why her husband had to stay overnight.

She thought about stopping to say hello but when she turned to head in that direction the desk lost its shape and the gold fireworks started again.

"Damn, it's bigger," Leira whispered, frozen to the spot. She reached back for the wall to try and orient herself.

"Oh no." The middle section of the station had disappeared altogether. The center of the oversized circle turned a watery gray. Her eyes grew wide and she instinctively rested her hand on her gun.

Someone, or something in the giant murky space was looking back at her. "Not happening," she whispered, stepping forward to get a better look.

The gold fireworks around the edges hummed. Hell, they snapped, crackled and popped. "This is a hell of a hallucination," muttered Leira, putting out her hand to see what would happen.

Curiosity was always her go-to even when caution was the sane choice. But sanity was clearly checking out, so why not go all in?

Whatever it was felt large and squishy, more solid than she expected.

"Hey!" A startled nurse tried to right a tray of small paper cups filled with medications, bouncing around on the tray. Leira's hand was resting on her boob.

The nurses' station was back where it belonged, and the opening was gone.

No more sparklers. Just low fluorescent lighting.

"Sorry about that." Leira quickly removed her hand. "Was trying to point at something." Making something up on the fly always ends badly for me. She tended to stick closely to the truth, but she had never faced trying to explain her own crazy before.

"Next time, ask before you touch," the nurse ordered.

Leira gave her the dead fish look. "Not really my type," she said, trying to make a joke.

The nurse narrowed her eyes. "You should be so lucky."

"Into... men..." Leira told the nurse's retreating back. The nurses at the desk let out a laugh. Leira nodded and waved, feeling her face grow warm as she headed down the hall. "Crap."

She found her way to their unmarked patrol car, a green Mustang, opened the door and sat very still behind the wheel, waiting to see if something else was going to happen.

Nothing did.

"First step of going crazy is making an ass of yourself." She took some deep breaths and blinked a few times, hard, to see if she could conjure up the image.

Nothing. She tried again. She needed to be sure. Blink. Blink.

"So, this won't be like I Dream of Jeanie. Okay, either I sit here or try driving." She started the car, listening to the engine's low rumble. "Always did love a challenge. Steady as she goes, brain. Let's see if we can drive home in one piece."

She pulled the Mustang onto the one-way street, tightening her grip on the wheel, turning up the music.

"I am not my mother, I am not my mother."

Damn headaches.

From behind her there was a hum and a pop. A pinhole appeared between the cars in the first row, widening until it was large enough for the two tall elves to step through. Swirls of light surrounded them, making them invisible to the few people parking their cars or walking through the parking lot.

"She can see us," said the older of the two Elves. An elven crown held down his straight, silver hair that was tucked behind pointed ears, and flowed past his shoulders. His words sounded like a stream of music floating on the air.

"It would appear so," the younger Elf replied. He raised a long, slender arm, trailing thin streams of colored light with every movement and traced a half circle in the air with his right hand. A baseball-sized orb of violet light with a glowing yellow center bounced in the air in front of them.

"Go," sang the Elf.

The violet ball zipped down the street in the direction of the Mustang that was turning a corner a few blocks away. The light slipped under the back fender and stayed there, glowing softly as the car drove out of sight.

"She's well suited to our needs. A detective, right?" asked the royal Elf.

"They call her a homicide detective."

"You know what it means, don't you? That she can see us? The energy within her is strong. Stronger than it should be in a human being. Stronger than it's been in this world for thousands of years."

"Thirteen millennia ago." There was a short pause. "That

could prove to be a problem," the older Elf mused, looking around at the buildings and vehicles lined up on the street.

"First the murder, now this girl can see us. Something is not right," said the younger Elf.

"One thing at a time. Be glad she can see us. We need her help." His face spasmed with anguish. "My son is dead long before his time. Someone will need to pay for it."

"Time is running short for answers I fear, your majesty."

"Then let's get on with it."

The younger Elf sang a single loud note. The hole widened again and they stepped back into the glowing portal in the middle of a parking lot.

No one in the lot noticed, but they all suddenly thought of the same song.

"La, da, da, da," sang an orderly on his way into work. "Ode to Joy, beautiful symphony. Wonder what made me think of that?"

"Ode to Joy? Nah, man, that's the theme to Die Hard, dude," said his friend, humming the same tune. "Best Christmas movie ever. Was thinking about the same song. Weird, huh? Coincidences. Gotta love 'em."

"Yeah, you and me." The orderly smirked, pointing at the other man. "We're like twins."

A low hum behind them went undetected as the hole disappeared and a last spray of gold flashed and sparkled on the dark pavement.

CHAPTER TWO

L eira pulled up in front of the small blue house on Rainey Street and waved to the people on the front porch next door. They were already drinking. Most of the colorfully painted houses on the street were bars and happy hour was just getting underway.

The strings of white lights hanging from the porch were already on, even though the sun hadn't quite set. Even the neon sign Estelle mounted above the roofline was lit.

Leira went through the tall gate marked private and weaved through the painted metal tables and chairs on the oversized patio to the small guesthouse in the back.

She had rented the place when she was still in college and saw no reason to move once she headed out into the real world, especially after her grandmother disappeared.

Her grandmother had vanished without a trace. The unsolved case became Leira's motivation to become a cop and work so hard to make detective.

There had to be a reason and someday, she'd find it.

Besides, the rent was the right price these days. Free in exchange for stomping out bar fights, which were a rarity anyway, and occasionally bringing her coworkers home for a drink.

At least as far as the patio. Estelle liked having cops around her business. She said it kept away a lower element.

The patio was already filling up with people getting a head start on this evening's buzz.

"Hey, Leira." A regular lifted a cold Shiner Bock in a salute. Leira waved back but kept moving. "On a case?" he called out, but Leira ignored him. She wanted to get to her small sanctuary and figure out what the hell was happening to her mind.

She wasn't anti-social, she just wasn't social at times.

She slid in the key, and turned the knob, sliding her purse off her shoulder as she stepped in. "Home, sweet home." She quietly pressed the door closed behind her. She reached over to shut the wooden blinds that overlooked the patio and dropped her purse on the red velvet easy chair to her left. Her grandmother's favorite reading chair.

Leira took a deep breath, still pressing her back against the door.

"Can't be happening," she whispered into the darkened room. She bit her lower lip, willing herself to get it together.

She picked up the framed photo of a much younger Leira with her mother and grandmother. Everyone with the same dark green eyes, smiling at the camera.

"How can everyone call me Lucky Leira with a family like this?" She traced the image of her mother with her finger. "One locked away, one disappeared without a trace and now there's just me."

Leira started to sigh but caught herself and slapped her hand hard on the wall.

"Enough! Damn, Berens, sentimental much? She carefully replaced the picture and brushed her bangs off her forehead.

I could use a drink. She turned on a small lamp with seashells around the base. Another relic of her grandmother's. There was so much more in storage.

She stopped to look at herself in the mirror by the door.

"Another shirt ruined." She pulled off the dirt and blood streaked button-down shirt. "Damn, that was a rough day at the office."

She went to her bedroom just off the living room. The small cottage was square with just four rooms. The living room was the largest of them, and the kitchen was just big enough to fit a round table and four chairs in the center with a few feet of clearance on every side.

The bedroom was even smaller but Leira liked it. Big enough for a bed and a dresser, with a small closet on the far side of the room. She made her way to the hamper and after another look, dropped in the shirt.

She unholstered her gun and retrieved the grey metal lockbox from her wooden childhood dresser. She pressed the combination, placed the gun inside and shut the lid firmly, listening for the solid 'click.'

'You survive the chewing out?' she texted Felix. Three bouncing dots appeared almost immediately.

'By the skin of my teeth,' he texted back. 'Go enjoy your evening, Berens. I'm good. Going to watch reruns of Golden Girls on this broke-ass TV and fall asleep.'

'I'll bring coffee in the morning'.

'And a cruller. But don't let Rose see it.'

Leira smiled her crooked smile and pocketed her phone.

She went back to the large oval mirror hanging by the bedroom door and leaned in to get a better look. Not bad for someone who never wears makeup, she thought, rolling her eyes. Or at least, good enough.

She looked down, straightening her favorite Wonder Woman t-shirt, feeling some relief. No bloodstains had seeped through and ruined one of her favorite t-shirts. That's something else to be grateful for.

She crossed the living room in a few steps and opened the front door, pausing on the threshold and waiting for the usual greetings. She liked the ritual more than she was willing to admit.

"Leira!" called the woman just coming onto the patio from the main room. Several other patrons turned their heads to look.

"Leira!" they shouted in unison. She stepped down and shut her door, not bothering to lock it. No one who knew her would be dumb enough to try breaking into her place. Anyone who didn't know her would get stopped a dozen different ways by as many people before they got the door all the way open.

"Come sit by me," said Mike, a regular, patting the seat next to him. He was sitting at the weathered and faded long wooden bar. Battered old license plates from Estelle's travels decorated the sides. Clusters of tiny white lights hung in bunches overhead.

Leira grabbed a stool as the bartender popped the top off a tall neck and set it in front of her.

"Boone River lager," said a man in a coat and tie on the next bar stool. Leira didn't recognize him. Not a regular at Estelle's. "Little lady has taste." He gave her a wink as he held up his glass.

Leira frowned, sizing him up before turning her back. Not in the mood.

"Aw, come on, don't be like that. It's Friday! It's even happy hour. Let me buy you a drink." He pulled his barstool closer to hers.

Leira knew his type. Relentless. She turned and scowled at him. "Look asshole, this isn't Match.com. You're not going to score here. You're in the wrong bar. Try Rodeo Pete's on 6th Street. You'll have a lot better luck with the tourists." She turned back to say something to Mike.

There was a heavy tap-tap on her shoulder. She looked in time to see a larger finger tap her again. There was a gunmetal gray Rolex on his wrist.

"Seriously?" Leira gave him the dead fish look, but he wasn't getting it. People were turning around, some of them moving their chairs closer. They were ready to jump in and help Leira if it became necessary. It was never necessary.

Leira felt the crowd grow tense. Time to help everyone ease out of this and calm down.

"Look, dude, you're in the wrong establishment." Leira scooted her t-shirt just high enough to show him her gold shield. "Last time I'm telling you, nicely or otherwise. Try Rodeo Pete's but dial it back a little or even beer goggles won't help you score. I don't care how much you try and wallet-slap the honeys."

"Feisty, I like it. Come on, one drink." He smiled, dimples appearing in his cheeks, as he held up his hands in mock surrender. He stood up and waved at the bartender, holding up two fingers, but the bartender looked at Leira to see what she wanted him to do. She shook her head, no.

"Okay, I get it. This is your place." He sat back down on his stool. "Look, I'll buy your beer and you don't even have to give me your name." The dimples appeared again. "I'll be right over here, minding my own business, Officer." He tilted his head to the side.

Leira frowned. "Suit yourself." She turned back around and took a sip of her beer. The first few sips of a cold beer on a hot Austin night were always the best.

Mike leaned in and whispered, "I think that's called harmless flirting."

Leira looked up at him through thick, dark lashes. "Maybe? I'm not in the mood."

"Doesn't mean you need to treat everyone like they're about to be charged with something." He gave her a smile. "I've known you since you moved in, what is it? Over four years ago?"

Just after my grandmother disappeared. It was how she broke up time.

"Have to look out for you, you know. Estelle's rule number

thirty-one." He took a quick sip. "Look out for Leira, which we would all do anyway, by the way."

He took a long swallow of his gin and tonic, catching a piece of ice and crunching it.

"Long day. Felix got shot. He's okay." She said it quickly, holding up her hand to head off the potential words of comfort, or worse, a hug. "Just needed some stitches and a night at the hospital. Still, long day." She tilted the bottle to drink in the last of her beer.

"Another?" The bartender was already leaning into the cooler.

"Sure, one more." She wasn't ready to go home just yet, even if it was just a few feet away.

"Hang out with us for a while. You should be around some kind of family." Mike shrugged, giving her a smile. "I'm afraid we'll have to do."

"You guys are more than enough." She smiled, resting her arms on the bar. "Hey, I'll be right back. Watch my beer." She slid off the stool and headed for the comfort of her own bathroom. One of the perks of living behind a bar.

"She always so hard to get along with?" The pickup artist was watching Leira walk out.

A meaty hand clapped him on the back, making him spit just a little of his drink, dribbling it down his chin.

"That's Craig." Mike nodded at Craig, who still had his hand on the man's back. "He's another regular here. To even be considered a regular here, you have to want to be a part of Leira's Society. That's what we call ourselves."

"Didn't catch your name?" A woman with blonde hair cut in layers pulled her chair closer. She held out her hand, letting it hang there, waiting.

"Bob," he replied, trying out his dimples again.

"Lucy... Bob." She shook his hand hard and gave him a smile that didn't make its way up to her eyes.

"Not that Leira knows about our little society," said Craig,

15

brusquely. "We'll make that our little secret." It sounded more like a command.

"He's an old Marine." Lucy tilted her head toward Craig. "Abrupt is his only style of conversation."

"Take a good look around, Bob." Mike held out his arm. "Everyone here tonight is a part of Leira's Society."

"Except for that couple, over there." Craig pointed at a middle-aged man leaning over the table smiling at the woman who was showing him pictures on her phone. "First date, I suspect. Too much talking to suit my taste. They're clearly, still enjoying each other's company." He looked pained. Lucy laughed and poked him, brushing a long, blonde lock of hair off her shoulder.

"What are you, like a fan club?" Bob was still smiling, but he sounded nervous.

"More like a family." Lucy drummed polished pink nails on the bar top. "An over-protective, Texas-sized family."

"See that tiny little woman in there?" Craig pointed at Estelle who was showing someone to their table.

"The grandmother packing a gun?" Bob's eyes widened. He took a large swallow of his drink.

"That's Estelle. She leads this merry band and is the head of the society. No one bothers Leira here," Mike proclaimed.

"No one," Craig agreed, slapping Bob's back again.

"Rodeo Pete's?" Bob hurriedly pulled a twenty-dollar bill out of his wallet, and slapped it on the bar.

"Good idea," said Lucy. "Here's a pro tip. Take an Uber. No parking on 6th Street after nine. They tow whatever's still parked there and let everyone wander in the streets."

Bob smiled stiffly as he backed off his stool and left quickly, weaving through the now-packed chairs till he got to the door.

"You know, she might actually figure out how to like a guy if y'all stopped running everyone off." Lucy watched him go, finally swiveling on her seat.

"He wasn't good enough for her," Craig insisted. "Besides, you know the rules."

Lucy arched an eyebrow and tapped Craig on his shoulder. "He was acting like a guy, and he wasn't that bad looking. Leira could use the practice."

Leira stepped up behind them. "You chased him off, didn't you?" She ignored Lucy's comment. She knew they all thought of her as dating-impaired. Maybe they were right.

"Damn girl, you're like Batman in those shoes. Sneak up on anyone." Craig pulled out a bar stool for her.

"Thanks for doing that." Leira paused, letting out a sigh. "I'd remind you again that I can take care of myself but tonight, I kind of appreciate it."

Craig and Mike exchanged a look.

"Her partner got shot," said Mike, "but he's doing fine," he added, as Leira scowled at him. "I'd have told him eventually," he said, sheepishly. "Rigorous honesty." He waved at the bartender. "How about I get the next round?"

"You owe Craig a few beers, anyway." Lucy scooted her chair back to her table, waving at the women seated around it. "You can send mine over here. Leira, you can come sit with the girls, if you want."

Leira sat down on her barstool and turned toward the bar as a man took the seat next to her.

"Hey there," he said, with a smile.

What is it with tonight?

"Damn, girl, whatever it is you're doing, let me in on it," Lucy yelled from her seat. "All the good ones are making their way over to you tonight."

"Semi-good ones," said Mike.

"Okay, big brothers, maybe step back a little. At least for my sake." Lucy tried to get the new guy's attention, smiling at him. He didn't take his eyes off Leira.

"I think I'll take this one to go." Leira picked up her beer, taking a long sip. She could feel a tight soreness in her shoulder from where she had landed on top of Arthur and to her relief, the remnants of pain were easing. "I'll be fine." She gave him a reassuring smile to seal the deal.

Bad choice. A look of concern passed across Mike's face. Damn.

She waved as she turned to walk away. No looking back. Tonight, I have a feeling they'd follow me.

She opened the door to her cottage as another shout went up. "To Leira!" It was followed by a lot of clinking glasses and the sounds of laughter. Leira braced herself and turned, raising her beer in the air.

"Till tomorrow," she shouted, her usual farewell. Craig at the bar smiled broadly at her, raising his glass.

"Or later tonight!" someone shouted back, causing another ripple of laughter.

"Gotta' love a routine," she muttered to herself, pushing open her door.

She curled up on the couch and took a sip of her beer, tucking her legs underneath. "Ow!" She sucked in air through her teeth and carefully set the bottle down on the floor as she pushed down the waistband of her form-fitting black pants. A bruise the size of a quarter was forming on the curve of her hip.

She gently pressed the green and purple spot. "Have to stick my landing better the next time."

She let go of her pants and was reaching down for her beer as the room exploded with gold light. It was streaming everywhere, sparks shooting out to the sides.

Leira ducked and rolled to the floor, knocking over her bottle. "Fuck me!"

She covered her head with her arms, waiting for the rest of the blast. The beer was pooling around her right knee, soaking through her pants.

Nothing happened. The room was so quiet she could hear the beer as it dripped from the bottle onto her rug.

"No!" she yelled, squeezing her eyes shut, willing herself to not go crazy.

Go crazy like my mother. No! Not possible!

CHAPTER THREE

Leira was not used to the feeling of panic that washed over her. Her heart was beating fast – too fast – and she was finding it hard to catch her breath.

Instincts kicked in and she forced herself to make an assessment of the room.

Come on, Leira. Enough.

She opened her eyes and looked up, ready to at least try and take down whatever was in front of her.

A hole had opened up in the middle of her small living room, exactly like the one she had seen at the hospital. The air around it shimmered, and she could feel the pulses of energy it gave off as they moved through her body.

Two tall Elves stood just inside the opening looking out at her. Pointed ears, long white hair, long leather tunics and tall boots.

"Elves… One of you even has a crown. Straight out of D and fucking D." What is happening?

She looked at the edges of the large rip in the air, hanging in the middle of her living room.

"Not human," she shook her head. "Freakin' elves."

There was something familiar about all of it. Something tugging at her. In a flash, a memory came back to her and she shuddered.

My mother's goddammed crazy stories. Never about little green men or the government out to get her, oh no. "Tall beings that could bend light. That's what she said. No fucking way."

"She's under duress."

"Standard for the first meeting"

"Goddamn Light Elves!" she shouted, "That's what she called you." Leira shook her head hard and backed up on the couch. The shorter of the pair looked surprised and hesitated, putting his hand on the other one's arm, pulling him backward. "Correk, give her a moment."

"As you wish, your majesty."

The large leaves pushing in behind them, swayed and moved with the sound of their voices. Leira ducked down to get a better look at the dense forest behind them. "I've never seen anything like that. I dreamed up this?"

"Now," said the king, stepping into the room. Correk was close behind him."

"Oh no you don't. No one comes in here without knocking first." Every muscle in her body was tense and she stood up, rocking back on her heels. Her brain searched for solutions. The gun was still in the lockbox in her bedroom behind her. "Plan fucking B."

She reached for the metal bat she kept under her couch and in one fluid motion she grabbed the bat, rolled within striking distance and swung at their ankles.

Knock these fuckers over like bowling pins.

The older elf sang out loudly and made a sweeping motion. They easily rose high enough to avoid being struck by the bat and hovered in midair. Leira let the bat rest against the floor, her mouth hanging open.

"Crazy comes with a lot more details than I realized," she

muttered, glancing around while still maintaining her situational awareness. "Like I'm inside the fucking movie."

The king stretched out his arm and whistled a low note. The bat in Leira's hand began to vibrate and she tightened her grip but her arm was shaking violently.

"Stronger than I imagined," he said.

"She's absorbing the energy," Correk observed. "But how?"

"No, it's more than that. She has powerful inner strength. An energy that's coming from within. She's a natural…"

Leira bit her lip and pulled back as hard as she could on the bat. For an instant, the vibrations settled down.

The Elf waved his hand again, creating a circular symbol of light and the bat finally pulled itself from her grasp and flew to him. Leira fell backward from the momentum, landing hard on her tailbone.

"Can you be beaten to death by a hallucination?" She wondered if her brain could slip over the edge and supply an answer.

The younger Elf rolled his eyes, looking annoyed.

"That seems about right. I go crazy, I come up with annoyed aliens." She got back on her feet, scowling at the Elves.

"I don't think we qualify as aliens," said the king. A breeze from inside the portal blew into her face, carrying the sweet scent of flowers. The king adjusted the bow strapped to his back. "We're not from this world, but many of our kind have lived here for a very long time. We're more like distant cousins."

Correk took the bat from his companion and gave more of a huff than a sigh.

"You're fully formed images. There's even smell-a-rama." Her mind was swimming as she reached out to poke one of them. "You're even beautiful," she said, awe in her voice. "I knew watching Star Trek late at night would come back to haunt me." Her finger moved closer to the younger elf, who pulled away from her.

"Let her touch you. She needs to know we're not an illusion." The king turned around and light from the forest behind him glinted off the crown on his head, showing off the details of twisted metal shaped into vines and leaves with a ruby in the center. He closed the portal easily, sparks dancing across Leira's living room floor.

Correk pulled back anyway and raised his hands, rolling them around in a circle.

"No fireballs in here," ordered the king.

"The boss has spoken. Wonder what it means that I wanted royalty in my delusions." Leira touched Correk's arm, wrapping her hand around his wrist, squeezing it.

"I assure you, I'm real." His words came out in a rush of music.

Leira froze. They aren't actually speaking. They're singing...

"What's going on? I can't carry a tune and I'm not this creative on a good day. Shouldn't my insanity be limited by my ability to dream you guys up?" Her questions came out in rapid fire and she eyed the bat again. Correk followed her gaze and moved the bat further out of her reach.

"Did you just read my mind?" She tapped the side of her head, looking at him from different angles.

"No, you were staring at it," he sang.

"You're not crazy," the king added. It was the most beautiful string of sounds Leira had ever heard. "We're really here. You can call me Oriceran."

"King Oriceran," the younger Elf clarified. "And yes, we're Elves... Light Elves."

"Trust your senses. You can see us, you can touch us. More importantly, we're not here to harm you."

"While I'm glad to hear I didn't dream up something that wants to kill me, I'm going to need more proof to be sure I'm not nuts. This isn't the first time you've appeared and I'm the only one who reacts." She looked back and forth at them. "That's not a good sign for me."

"Fair enough. How can we help you with this, what… a test?" the king asked.

Leira hesitated. Every idea that came to her could be explained away. There was no way to know for sure if she was losing her mind.

She held out her hands in frustration. "I've got nothing," she admitted. "No idea how to prove it."

"Then let's get on with things." Correk crossed his muscled arms across his chest. "Time is passing in your world and a killer is getting further and further away."

"Killer? Hell, I dreamed up a case, too?" A crooked smile coming across her face. "That actually makes more sense. I'm working even as I go insane. No rest for the wicked."

"You're really going to need to put that aside if you're going to help us," the king said gently. "The entire sane or insane argument." He lifted his hand as if he was about to do something.

"Wait, I have an idea how you can prove you're really here." Leira stood very still, staring at them.

The Elves waited but Leira didn't say another word, just leaned in toward them. She opened her eyes wider and raised her eyebrows. The king finally got the message.

"We really don't read minds. It's not a talent we've acquired, just yet. You'll have to tell us."

Correk rolled his eyes again.

"Good to know." Leira gave the dead fish look to Correk. "You can't do everything. Magic has limits."

"Okay, on with it," sang the king. "What's the test?"

Leira took a deep breath and held it, making them wait. She almost couldn't say it out loud.

"Find my mother's ring." Leira's voice cracked and she pressed her lips together, trying to hide how much she was hoping they could do it.

The ring had been lost for years and was the only piece of

jewelry she had that belonged to her mother. She still felt the loss.

"Easy enough," the king said.

"Party trick." Correk gave her that same arched eyebrow, standing over her.

"Do you have a name?" Leira glared at him. She was getting annoyed, even if she was hallucinating him.

He sang the notes again, but she couldn't make out what he was saying.

"What the hell was that?" she asked. "Wait, that's familiar. Do it again."

He sang it again, holding the last notes.

"Hold on, that's the theme from Die Hard." She laughed despite what was happening to her. "Best Christmas movie, ever." Leira and Correk said it in unison.

"Yes, I've heard that before," he said. "Not my first visit here."

"He goes by Correk." The king had leveled out his voice, making it audible for Leira.

"Was that so hard?"

Correk started to say something but Leira cut him off. "The ring?" The spark of hope she felt was dimming. A pang of loneliness settled in her chest. Next step to going crazy.

"Can you picture it in your mind?" the king asked.

"Child," Correk sang, sounding annoyed.

"Keebler," growled Leira.

"Not a cookie, and we don't live in trees," he said. "Those Keeblers are a strange cross between a Wood Elf and a Gnome and I assure you, have nothing to do with Light Elves. Although, neither one of those species has ever made cookies either."

"How would you know about Keebler...?"

"Picture the ring," the king interrupted. He took a deep breath and swept his hands across his chest, trailing gold light. Symbols appeared in orange and yellow flames that briefly hung in the air

25

before melding and reshaping themselves until they finally formed into the shape of a box made of light.

The king looked pleased, relieved even. He sang something Leira couldn't understand, his face close to the glowing box.

The box began to spin faster and faster, moving around the perimeter of the room bathing everything in a rosy glow and filling the space with a high-pitched moan that was almost unbearable to Leira.

She struggled to keep her bearings and felt herself swaying from side to side.

Zip! Woot!

A continuous stream of glowing orange light appeared in front of her. Inside of the stream was every memory she had of the ring, right up to the day it was lost.

Leira watched fascinated, remembering all the good times with her mother. Then came the dread as her mother started to get worse, finally giving Leira the ring for safekeeping. It was just before the orderlies took her away. She tried to look away.

Plink!

The spinning stopped abruptly, and the light disappeared. Something small and hard dropped at her feet. Leira looked down and saw it. Resting against the tip of her sneaker was a platinum band with two sapphires flanking an emerald.

"Not possible," she whispered. It was her mother's ring.

She bent down slowly, hoping this illusion would last. Tears welled up in her eyes as she picked up the ring and slid it onto her finger, and back where it belonged. She wiped away a tear with the back of her hand and blew out the breath she didn't realize she was holding.

"Not a crier, Berens," she said, balling her hands into fists. She looked up at the Elves, who were waiting patiently for her.

"Was the conclusion of the test satisfactory?" asked the king.

She held her hand out in front of her and looked at the ring from every angle.

"I can feel it there. Cold metal." She pressed the ring into the palm of her other hand and felt the sharp prongs. "I'm not sure I care if I'm crazy or not," she said softly.

"Good, then let's be going." Correk put his hands together, a light appearing in the palm of his hand.

"Wait," said the king. "She has to agree to go. We don't kidnap anyone."

"That's a fucking positive. Where exactly are we going?" Leira studied the younger Elf. Threat, not a threat?

"Our world, on the other side. To Oriceran and our kingdom where the Light Elves reside." The king was talking calmly, but he was growing impatient. "We need you to help us solve a murder."

"You have the same name as your entire planet?"

"We're Light Elves," said Correk, as if that was all the explanation needed.

"Who was killed?" Leira easily slipped back into detective mode.

"My son, Prince Rolim." The king held out his hand to Leira. "Take my hand and you'll learn everything you need to know, and then some. Trust me."

She hesitated. "I never have been very good at turning down a good mystery. Fuck it, I'm in." She put her hand in his and glanced back at her bedroom. "Maybe I should get my gun. What the hell..." She felt a warmth course through her veins. Glowing symbols of every color appeared, crawling up her arm, just under the skin.

Correk looked at her arm, surprised as he finally let the bat fall to the ground. "Who are you, Leira Berens?"

Correk put his hands together again, a ball of light growing between them. He sang into it and pulled his hands apart, letting a portal open around them, filling her cottage and swallowing up her world, until she found herself surrounded by a lush, dense forest.

"Welcome to Oriceran," the king smiled. "Come, there isn't much time. The memories fade with every passing hour."

"Memories of what?" Leira followed the two Elves down a worn dirt path in the forest, ducking under a tree branch. She looked around in amazement at the new world almost tripping over a root. The forest overhead was full of noise, rustling the dense foliage letting in the occasional stab of light. Her mother's ring picked up the light, flashing on her finger. "What rabbit hole did I fall into?" muttered Leira.

"Memories of my son's murder." The king looked back at her. "More will be revealed, but we must hurry."

She was in a single line directly behind Correk. "Say your name for me again, Correk. You know, sing it." She was moving more easily along the uneven ground. All the years of running were paying off.

"I told you my name." He sang it for her again.

"Yeah, I know, theme from Die Hard. Guys in my world are hung up on it, too." She scrutinized him, looking him up and down. "You look like a Bert. You know, like Bert and Ernie. Same high forehead." She leaped over another oversized tree root, landing easily on the other side. Correk took note of her agility.

"Frankly, on you, it's more of a seven or eight head," she said.

"That's a new one to me. What's a Bert and Ernie?"

"They're Muppets."

"What's a Muppet?"

"You know what a Keebler is, but missed out on Muppets? Okay, whatever. It's an oversized doll and someone puts a hand up their…" she said, jabbing the air. "To make them talk."

The Elf rolled his eyes. "My real name is Correk." He spoke it slowly without singing.

"You still look like a Bert."

"We're past the Wood Elves kingdom," said the king as they entered a lush, mossy clearing. "We can use magic again without being detected. Get us home, Correk before someone sees the detective."

Leira looked up suddenly at the king, her eyes narrowing. "I'm not allowed here, am I?" She glanced between the two Light Elves. "You're breaking the rules. It must be worth it."

The king's face looked strained. "It is, but it's already complicated. We don't need to make it worse. Let's go, Correk."

Unnoticed, a cicada flew along above them, part organic, part machine. The whirring sound it made blended into the forest's constant background noise of chirps and howls. A bird took flight overhead, the light shining through its translucent wings and changing color as it moved. Leira's eyes grew wide, her head tilted back. "Amazing…"

"Keep your eyes on the ground, Detective." The King came and stood next to Correk.

Correk leaned close enough to Leira to whisper. "I'm not a Muppet." He held his hands together near his chest, pulling them apart. Violet symbols made of light appeared in the air.

"Uh oh, I've pissed off Bert," Leira whispered, as the ground abruptly dissolved around her and she felt a small lurch in her stomach.

The cicada hovered for a moment longer after they were gone, circling once before turning toward the deep recesses of the forest to report back to other forces.

CHAPTER FOUR

D on't panic.

Leira found herself standing high in the air, floating above a wide green valley, nestled near a mountain range. The forest was far below her in the distance.

Her heart was pounding, and she was making herself take long, even breaths. The king and Correk were standing near her, unconcerned. "Did you get your wires crossed, Bert?" There was an edge to her voice.

"We're inside the castle. Relax. You have nothing to worry about." Correk went back to speaking quietly with the king. There's no walls, no floors. There isn't even a table or chair. She lifted her foot and tapped her toe carefully in the air. There was something solid beneath her.

Reassuring.

Leira was still frozen in place, not willing to move any further.

"You look distressed." The king said it as a statement of fact. "We'll make sure you get home safe and sound."

She stared back at him, not sure what to say. "The...ground..." she stammered. Everyone turned to look at her, confused.

"Where the hell is it?" She pointed down. "The ground, where's the damned ground?" She waved her arms, but that felt too much like she was flapping wings. She stopped, arms still out, fighting the urge to curl into a ball.

"I've got this one," said Correk. He touched his fingertips together in elaborate patterns, and the floors became visible, flowing out from the corners like liquid before turning into solid marble. The center of the floor was inlaid with a cursive O in the same style that was on the crown the king was wearing. It was bracketed by a mosaic design of Irish wolfhounds sitting at attention.

The liquid continued to flow up toward the sky, forming walls and leaving space for windows that stretched from the floor to the ceiling. An oversized crystal chandelier blossomed from the ceiling, while the room seemed to furnish itself. Everything glowed around the edges.

"We do like the glitter." The king looked up, admiring the chandelier.

"I quite prefer to do without any of it," said a female Elf, as tall as Correk with pale white skin and long, flowing dark hair, wearing a crown similar to the king's. "It really spoils the view to have to pretend we have floors and walls."

"Leira Berens, this is my wife, Queen Saria," said the king.

"Pretend?" Alarmed, Leira quickly tested the sturdiness of the floor by stomping her foot this time. Best to find out now if she was about to fall to her death.

The floor held.

"Well done," said the king. "Very brave, that's a good sign. You face things head on." He gave her a smile that quickly faded. "That will serve you well with the task at hand."

"You're staring." The queen fixed her deep green eyes on Leira. "It's as if you've never seen an Elf before. That can't be true." She arched a perfectly shaped eyebrow at the king and said, "Surely you've noticed."

"How long do we have left?" asked the king, ignoring the queen's words.

"Three hours, no more," Correk replied.

Leira ignored him to take a moment and study the room. She let her fingers graze cut glass pitchers that sang melodies when she touched them, admired gold framed paintings that came to life as she looked at them, and carved wooden trays with leaves growing from the edges.

Everything is so beautiful.

She turned back to Correk who was standing with his arms crossed against his chest. Okay, he's annoyed. It's like a default mode for him. "What happens in three hours?"

"The memories will be lost," Correk urged.

The king cleared his throat to catch Leira's attention. She was staring at a prism dangling in one of the windows. The sunlight was shining through it, casting an image of a blue reindeer on a nearby wall.

Its broad antlers were refracting in the light.

Leira touched the prism and as it moved the images changed. She was mesmerized as first a gold antelope, then a white wolf and finally an emerald green dragonfly danced on the wall.

"She's enraptured by a child's toy." The queen shook her head, pressing her lips together. "This is who you're entrusting with finding our son's killer?" Her voice was sharp and full of pain.

Leira snapped out of it, pulling her hand away from the prism. "I'm here to do a job. I get it." It doesn't matter if I'm in grownup fucking Disneyland. I'm here to investigate a crime. "Singleness of purpose."

"Indeed," Correk replied, frowning.

Leira gave Correk a good dose of side eye. Not happy. Not my problem. You called me. "Let's get on with it, then. Time matters, even over here." She added on top her best dead fish look.

"Better," said Correk, holding open a tall door. Leira strode through confidently, as Correk tsked loudly. The king and queen followed but Leira hesitated. Which way to Space Mountain?

The queen looked back, scowling. "Perhaps we should lead the way for the fearless detective?" She stepped in front of Leira, waving her arms to show the floors in front of them. "All of this opening and closing is a tiresome nuisance." She flicked her wrist, her long silky gown sliding across the floor. "A short-term necessity."

"I could always just go home." Leira stood still, waiting for a response.

Correk cleared his throat, suppressing a smile.

The queen turned to look at her and Leira held her gaze, not backing down. She cocked her head to one side, waiting to see if the queen had anything else to say. No one else moved, waiting to see who would win.

"Very well," said the queen. "Have it your way. Let's get on with it." She waved an arm over her head, her sleeve fluttering as the walls and floors behind them dissolved completely. "There, that's better," she said. She flicked her wrist, completing the spell as the rest of the castle disappeared again. She didn't bother to turn around to see Leira's reaction.

Bitch wanna play, thought Leira. Okay, you're a grieving mother, I get it. I'll give you this one. Leira focused on the queen walking in front of her and the surrounding peaks in the distance. Don't look down.

They made their way through the castle as rooms became briefly visible. Elves appeared, busy at work or lying down, resting, or practicing magic. Leira couldn't help herself and kept looking in every direction, momentarily forgetting there was no structure and then snapping back to her new reality, steeling herself again.

The queen made a series of swift motions and a dark cloud appeared, lightning and thunder cracking and rumbling. She moved swiftly into the cloud as it enveloped her.

Leira hesitated before following her into the dense, grey mist.

At least I can't see what's not underneath me anymore. Leira moved deeper into the cloud, the darkness clearing as swiftly as it arrived. She found herself walking into the center of a room with smooth, granite walls, and a gleaming marble floor.

On the far wall, a fire burned in a marble bowl.

A young Elf lay in the center of the room. A male who looked to be about Leira's age. His skin was a pale white and he was dressed in dark green robes that twinkled with light. A braided necklace with a diamond-shaped lavender stone pendant hung from his neck. On his head was an Elven crown. He looked like he was asleep, but Leira knew what she was seeing.

This was their dead son.

"This is my son, Prince Rolim, of the Oriceran Light Elves. I keep this room perpetually shrouded." The queen touched her son gently. Grief crossed her face and she seemed lost, but only for the moment. "No one enters this room without my express permission, no one," she said sternly, looking at Leira.

Leira was already taking mental notes. "Message received. Tell me why I'm here. Here, specifically. Is this where he died? It looks like you already cleaned up the crime scene." She looked at the perfectly laid out prince. "There isn't much, if anything to learn here."

The queen scowled at Correk.

"Is he supposed to be my handler?" asked Leira. "I don't do well with babysitters. If you want me to work a case, let me work the case."

Correk stepped forward but the queen held up her hand.

"Let me do what you brought me here to do or return me to my world and we'll call all of this a weird dream brought on by a seriously bad breakfast taco." Leira stood in the center of the room with her hands on her hips, waiting to see who would blink first.

It wasn't going to be her.

"Fine..." The queen waved a hand in annoyance. "We're wasting time."

"Look, why do you need a homicide detective from Earth in the first place? I'm a damn good one, I get that. But still. Why can't you figure this out and take care of the guilty party with a swoosh of your hands?" Leira waved her hands in the air mimicking the queen.

"Stop!" Correk snapped. "A little respect."

She turned to Correk. "You're going to have to decide if you want protocol or solutions. I can't do both. Frankly, I can't do the first one at all, but if I know you don't want solutions at least we'll know how to proceed and we can cut this short," she said. "Bert here seems hung up on niceties."

"Bert?" asked the king, frowning.

"Come closer." The queen held out her hand. "Some things take direct contact."

It wasn't until Leira got closer that she saw the tears in the queen's eyes. She is barely containing her grief. My bad. My very bad.

Leira grabbed her hand tightly and a series of fiery symbols materialized on the queen's arm while the room faded and changed.

Leira was standing in yet another room made of the same granite walls but open to the sky. There were glass domes on pedestals around the room, each of them illuminated from within.

The king and queen and even Correk were gone. The prince was alive and standing there, arguing with someone who looked more like a human form of trouble from her world.

A male, late thirties I'd say, average height. Dressed in worn brown cowboy boots, work pants and a long-sleeved khaki shirt over a t-shirt with the faded image of a T-Rex on the front. He's a cross between a hipster and a geek and could be from anywhere. I'll bet he fades into backgrounds everywhere he goes.

35

He was doing his best to look nonchalant. Not working.

"Hello?" Neither one seemed to hear her. There was a low buzzing sound in her head.

"This is only a memory." It was the queen's voice. Leira could still feel the warmth of her hand, even if she couldn't see her. "Elves retain the last hour of their lives for four days after death. This is the fourth day." Leira could hear the grief in her voice. "Normally, it brings comfort to those who remain."

"The images only project a few yards from the body." It was Correk, somewhere off to the side.

"This is more than just images," said Leira in awe as she looked at the prince. "He looks... alive."

"Yes, he does," said the queen, a catch in her voice. "Pay attention to the details. We wasted precious time selecting you and we can't be sure how strong the images will remain."

Prince Rolim was holding something. Leira moved closer, still holding on to the queen, to get a closer look.

"That's a pin with the family crest," said the king. "We are in the royal relics room. This room is kept hidden at all times. Objects that contain potent magic within them are kept here, especially these items."

"Why these?" Leira was watching closely and saw a look of surprise and anger on the prince's face. He clearly didn't know the man who was greedily looking around the room.

"Many of these relics were made stronger. Elves over the centuries have gathered together and imbued certain objects with some of their own power. It's a kind of safekeeping, meant for future generations or when more power than a single Elf can provide may be needed," said the queen.

"Even royal power," the king added. "Keep watching."

The man licked his lips, barely paying attention to the prince.

"How did you get in here?" the prince demanded. "Who helped you? Who are you?"

The prince pocketed the pin, making a series of small

motions, fiery symbols appearing in front of him. They formed a large ball that showed images of the man in front of him, crossing over into this world. "Your name is Bill Somers. You're trying to steal a relic from my world."

"I found a relic. It's what I do, I uncover things. Dig them up. I'm an archaeologist, by trade. Translates to finders keepers in my world." He sounded determined but Leira saw his hands shaking.

"You're a common thief. You've taken a powerful relic from this room. It belongs to me." The prince towered over the man, clenching his fists.

"I can't do that. I'm going to need it," Bill said, nervously. "I'm on an assignment and this pretty necklace will need to go with me. I've waited much too long to prove this world exists."

"What slime," said Leira, watching Bill try to justify what he was doing.

"Give me the pendant in your pocket," Prince Rolim ordered, holding out his hand.

"You can't take it from me, can you?" Bill's voice was relieved and delighted. "I have to give it to you. Well, well. So, you have rules too. Good to know."

The prince gestured and a dagger flew to his hand.

"Hold on now." The nervous smile returned to Bill. "No need to get touchy. I get it. It's your plaything. No reason we can't both walk away feeling like we got something, is there?" He had both of his arms up, as if he was trying to let the prince know he was harmless.

"Stop," Leira said quietly, knowing her words were useless.

Somers began to twitch. His anxiety was clearly growing, making him dangerous and unpredictable. Leira watched helplessly, gripping the queen's hand tighter as she took a step forward to try and stop what she could see coming.

But a wave of light pushed her back.

"Stay where you are," the queen said in a low voice. "The

memories will only let us so close. You can make them break apart by getting too near."

Leira stopped struggling, watching Bill offer to give back the pendant, bargaining for something else in the room.

"What about a different stone? A magic crystal?" he asked, reaching into his pants pocket with a shaking hand. "Something that can do a little levitating. Or, how about a pretty one that can help me read minds. You have something like that?"

The prince stayed where he was, his hand outstretched, his anger clearly growing.

"Humans are all the same. Selfish. Nothing in this room belongs to you," he spit angrily. "These aren't trinkets you can steal and then justify it all later. Give me the rock and we'll deal with how you got here. And who helped you."

A braided gold necklace slipped out of Bill's pocket and dangling from the end was a piece of lavender rock, held in place by gold prongs.

"That necklace," said Leira. "I saw it on the prince's body."

"It's the twin to the one that was stolen. Another relic that was in the same display case. We put it on him for a reason. Nearby objects can take on energy from traumatic events," said the king.

"Like a murder," said Leira.

"Yes," the queen said, "like a murder. Having this one on my son's body has helped make the memory stronger. It might even buy us time, if we need it."

"I know that kind of rock. I've seen something like it before," said Leira, trying to remember where. She felt the queen squeeze her hand tightly. The end must be near.

"How can you stand to watch this?" Leira felt her heart beating harder.

"I have to." The queen's voice came out in a rasp. "My beautiful son was only one hundred and twenty-five years old. In our years, that makes him the same age as you. He had hundreds of years left to live." She tilted her chin down. "There should have been grandchildren to continue our line, the Oriceran line. All of that was taken from him by a human."

Somers dangled the necklace in front of his chest, his arm close to his body, a sheen of sweat on his face. Leira's eyes swept the scene, taking in every detail.

The archaeologist kept talking, buying himself time. He snuck glances at the door as if he expected someone to rescue him.

"He has an accomplice," Leira said, softly. "Even with all your magic, we're not that different. A crime plays out pretty much the same way."

The prince lunged forward to grab the necklace out of Somers' hand. Somers held the necklace against his body and stepped back, losing his footing. He fell against a display case, knocking another relic loose. The prince saw his chance and lunged at the thick chain, grabbing one end of it. Somers' eyes widened and he pulled back, shoving the prince with his other hand as he tried to regain his balance.

The prince pulled on the necklace again, and Somers stumbled into him, struggling to keep his hold on the necklace, clutching the prince's arm with his other hand. Somers let go of the prince, pulling something out of his pocket, even as the prince held him close, trying to wrench the necklace from his hand. Leira leaned to the side, trying to see what Somers was holding. She heard the queen gasp and Leira shook her head. The end is coming.

The pair struggled, twisting and turning, making it hard for Leira to see exactly what was happening, until it was too late. The prince staggered back, a dagger deep in his chest.

The anger drained from the prince's face, replaced by surprise and pain. He looked into Bill's eyes, finally letting go of the necklace.

The queen's grip tightened, almost twisting Leira's knuckles.

Leira ignored the pain and focused on the memory playing out in front of her.

"What? No!" Somers looked down and saw the blade of the dagger buried to the hilt in the prince's chest. He let out a startled cry, still holding on to the prince.

Prince Rolim tried to pull away, to lift his arm, as if that would help. He opened his mouth to speak but only a gurgle emerged, followed by a thin stream of silvery blood. Leira heard the queen sob quietly.

Focus, it's just a memory that's already played out. Do your fucking job. Leira watched Somers, looking for clues.

Somers panicked and pulled the knife out in one swift motion pushing the prince back, watching him teeter for a moment before falling. He fell to the floor barely alive, his eyes still open, staring up at the sky. The pendant finally in his grasp. A shimmer of light surrounded him, growing dimmer.

Somers stood for a moment, turning his head to see if anyone was coming.

He never called for help.

"No, I didn't mean to," he said with a shudder, as he panicked and stepped over the Prince's body. He reached down at the last moment and tugged the relic from the prince's hand, pocketing it.

The shimmer of light around the prince faded till it was gone.

There were tears in Somers' eyes as he moved toward the door. At the last moment he turned and snatched some of the smaller artifacts in the room, filling his pockets. He looked back one last time and muttered, "Sorry, I never...you shouldn't have..." and fled.

The images faded and the room changed around Leira, back to its present state. The queen was staring at the spot where her son had fallen as she let go of Leira's hand. The low buzzing in Leira's head finally stopped, making the space eerily quiet.

She waited, not wanting to break the silence.

CHAPTER FIVE

"That was a lot to take in," Leira finally said, trying to keep her focus. "I've never been present at the 'before' part of a murder investigation."

Correk looked at the stricken queen and quickly created a chair of light, catching her before she fell.

"Take Leira to the place where we think the killer escaped back to her world." The king's voice was heavy with grief. "Answer any of her questions. Give her whatever she needs." He knelt by his wife, taking her hand. The queen was twisting in the chair, looking back at her son's body.

"Yes, your majesty." Correk gave a small wave to Leira. "Follow me."

"For what it's worth, the prince was wrong about one thing." Leira didn't move, still picturing the last images.

"Come. Now." Correk's tone was stern, but she didn't budge.

"About what?" asked the queen, tears shimmering on her face.

"The selfish part. Not all humans are selfish. Some can be very kind. It's just that when you get a bad one, or a pathetically weak one, they don't have limits on the harm they cause. Makes people like me necessary."

"We have the same kind of evil in our world." The king gently kissed the top of the queen's head.

"If that's the case, why do you need me? I can't do any magic." Leira ignored the scowl from Correk. Hagan would get it. I have to ask even if it's painful.

"Precisely." The queen held her gaze. "The killer used no magic, left no trail marking his evil. Magic won't solve this crime. To make things worse, he appears to have gotten away cleanly to your world. It's difficult for us to travel there without being seen. There are rules about all of this." A sob escaped from her throat.

"Enough," the king said firmly, eyeing both his wife and Leira.

"I'm sorry," said Leira. "If you want me to solve…" She didn't get to finish the sentence.

The dark cloud abruptly reappeared, growing around her and just as quickly pulled away. She was standing in the middle of the sky once again, the valley far below her feet. Her stomach lurched and she tripped forward, still surprised to feel a floor beneath her when she couldn't see one.

"Can we stand on actual ground?" She wanted to shut her eyes. "I can't concentrate hanging around like this."

"As you wish," said Correk, drawing symbols in front of them. Leira finally shut her eyes to cut down on the nausea, and opened them again to find herself transported yet again. "Much better." She was standing in a garden of neatly trimmed low hedges and paved walkways with stone benches lining one side. She fell toward a seat and put her head between her legs.

"Think what you want," she said, her head still down, squeezing her eyes shut. "I'm not puking today."

She opened her eyes and saw his leather boots stop in front of her.

"I can wait," he said.

"Sit down next to me." She patted the bench seat next to her. "Don't stand in front of me like that." She put her head in her hands and took in long, even breaths. Finally, she was able to lift her head.

Correk was watching her patiently.

She looked up at him, "That's kind of creepy, Bert."

"I'm letting the name thing go for now," he said, a slight frown on his face. "Ask me your questions."

"Why me, would seem to be the most obvious one." She gently rubbed the side of her temples.

"You're a homicide detective, a good one."

"And?"

"And Bill Somers escaped to your hometown of Austin. We believe he's moved on already, but you will be able to follow him. He has no reason to think he didn't get away with his crime."

"What are you going to do with him when I find him?" She slowly took another deep breath.

"You're confident you'll find him. Good. We'll try him. We're not Kilomea."

"I'd ask what those are, but I have a feeling that's a rabbit hole of information."

"They're ugly, large creatures built for warfare. They live in the northwestern part of the land." Correk pointed to the west toward the mountains.

"We're going there with all of the crazy, magical things, aren't we?" Leira made herself sit up, leaning back against the seat, blowing out air. "Okay, go ahead. How many kinds of beings are there in this world? At least the ones who can talk, cause trouble, look kind of human."

"There are about a dozen," said Correk. "To start with there are the Witches and Wizards who keep to themselves. Many of them belong to an Order that serves a group known as the prophets. There are Dark Elves who live on the other side of the Great Forest, and the Wood Elves who inhabit parts of the forest and watch over it."

"The king mentioned them when we arrived. He was trying to avoid them," said Leira. "Are they dangerous?"

"No, there's a treaty. Those days have passed. He was trying to avoid letting it be known we willingly brought a human over to this side."

"Against your rules. I'd do a better job if I knew what they are, at least the main ones. Is there a chance I can get a list of them?"

"There's not enough time," said Correk. "You'll be back on your world soon and then you will be able to go back to what you know."

"Fair enough. Come on, let's walk around the grounds." Leira stood up slowly, feeling better. "I do better when I'm moving."

"Very well, I can show you more of the grounds." Correk stood up, his arms crossed against his chest. "These are the royal gardens. This is a maze."

"Not much of a challenge. You can see over the top."

"It's really for the young Elves' amusement. We can make our way to the queen's garden, among the enchanted trees and talk there. No one will be able to hear us."

"No transporting." She pulled on Correk's arm. "We can just walk there."

Correk looked her up and down. "It gets easier, but we can go at your pace."

"I didn't say I need special treatment," said Leira, annoyed. "Tell me more about the Light Elves."

"Our line goes back almost to the beginning of this world's existence."

"Almost, but not quite. This place is like a paradise." said Leira.

"There was only one other race of Elves that were older than Light Elves, but they haven't been seen for thousands of years. The Jasper Elves were powerful magicals, but the last of their kind died out in a war that engulfed this world for a generation."

They walked down a grassy path between tall trees with enormous roots. Correk saw her looking at the trees. "We're passing through Golden Chestnut Grove. They grow to be over two hundred feet tall and can be found all over the kingdom."

Leira heard the sound of high-pitched voices and scratching inside one of the trees as they passed.

"Can't be oversized squirrels. What is that?" she asked, scanning her surroundings.

"You mean that sound? Those are Ashgrog dwarves. Smaller than the dwarves that live along the rivers. Generally harmless, if left alone."

"Understood," said Leira. "Stick to the path."

"Stay close to me and listen well. That should be sufficient." Correk adjusted the buckles on the front of his jacket.

"Once I'm back in my world, will I be able to find you if I have more questions?"

"That may prove difficult."

"Because of that no contact with sweaty humans rule."

"Because opening a portal is illegal and sometimes deadly." Correk stopped walking and waved his hands to draw symbols in the air. "There are moments in time when crossing is far less risky... and legal."

"When you can cross over to Earth with no problem. No fucking way..."

"Way. Our worlds have come together before. There are moments in time when our worlds line up and gates open letting both sides cross back and forth easily. Like a giant portal but stable and they stay open for thousands of years, slowly closing again. A full cycle takes twenty-six millennia, or if you want to be exact, 25,800 years. We call one complete pass a Great Year."

"Let me guess, the last time the worlds came together was right around the time the war wiped out the other Elves."

"Correct. Humans didn't cause all of the mayhem," said Correk. "Everyone played a part in the war the last time the gates were fully open. Humans from your world and magicals. That's why councils were gathered, rules were created, and powerful spells were cast enchanting everything to make sure history didn't repeat itself."

"That was the last time my kind lived in this world." Leira's eyes grew wide watching a Light Elf walking a large, thin dog with wings fluttering along its back. The Elf gave Leira a nod and tugged gently on the leash, the dog responding with a trill that sounded more like a bird.

"Not at all. There are humans still living on Oriceran. Many chose to stay here when the gates closed."

"Come on, let's keep going. I can't stand this stationary thing."

"You're a very restless creature."

"Also not something all humans have in common. A lot of us are referred to as couch potatoes."

"Furniture made out of food," said Correk. "Hmph. We would just call that lazy."

"That could also work. I don't suppose you guys have something called sarcasm. Never mind." Leira took a deep breath, feeling herself relax. "What is that scent? Something familiar about it."

"I don't know why. It only grows on this side of the veil, on this world. It's moon haldi blossoms. They only bloom when our moons are out together, like tonight."

"So familiar." *Where do I know it from?* "Any other creatures in particular I should know about before I go? I am leaving soon..."

"Within the hour, I would imagine."

"Good. I want to get back before morning on my side. I don't want anyone to notice I've been gone."

"That won't be a problem. We need to get you back to your world."

Leira gave him a sidelong glance. "Before anyone finds out you took me through a portal, I get it. Too many explanations. Hey! What was that?"

46

A tiny creature with a shock of green hair standing straight up on its head darted in front of them and into the nearest golden chestnut.

Correk threw out his arm, stopping Leira in her tracks. "Don't move! It's a pesky troll. Look away! If you play with one of those damn things, it'll follow you! If you actually help one? Two moons! It'll bond with you, causing trouble, getting into everything. That's just the beginning of your troubles with a troll."

"Two moons? That's the best you've got? No fucking way." Leira gave him a crooked smile. She held up her hands in front of her. "I'm looking away. Don't get twisted."

She stole glances as they got closer to the tall metal gates and the entrance of the queen's gardens. "You sound like you have some troll experience. Bad memories?"

"You think this is funny, but a troll's a nuisance that you can never shake. It'd be like having a permanent boil on your skin that always festers just enough to irritate."

"Very good visual." Out of the corner of her eye, she saw the tiny troll no taller than five inches, scamper over a root. The troll cackled, green hair and white fur vanishing into the trees. "Looks like a little doll I had as a kid," she muttered. "Same wild hair and lack of clothes. I used to tie bandanas around mine."

Leira caught Correk glaring at her and she looked away again. "Okay, okay, no helping trolls. Nasty, troublesome boils."

She dug her hands in her pockets as they passed under the intricate metal O above the wrought iron entrance.

"Tell me about where you live. Is every Light Elf an Oriceran?"

"Very perceptive," said Correk. "Or a good guess. Every Light Elf belongs to the House of Oriceran, but the name is only given to the king. It would have been Prince Rolim's one day. It was given to the first king back when this world was still young."

"What do you call these?" asked Leira, bending down to smell a blossom.

"Roses," said Correk, rolling his eyes.

"No fucking way. Same thing." She stopped in her tracks. "That's it. I've smelled that scent before in my world. It was on Enchanted Rock. It's everywhere in the spring. It grows like a weed on a massive quartz cliff just outside of Austin. Hey, that necklace is from there, isn't it? That piece of jewelry comes from my world. Wait a minute. Magic...exists...in...my...world."

"Well done, Detective. I was wondering how long that one would take you." Correk turned by a large stone gargoyle spraying a mist into the air.

"You could have told me sooner. What else are you waiting for me to figure out?"

"I have my orders. Answer any of your questions."

"But offer nothing."

"I will tell you whatever you want to know about the murder."

"So be it. But I smell secrets and I'll find them all out, you know. It's only a matter of time."

Correk looked at her with a calm smile that gave away nothing.

They walked by tall slender reeds of green and red that ran along an iron fence. "Think of a question," said Correk. The reeds swayed as he spoke, bending toward him.

"Those are beautiful. It's like they're motion activated," said Leira, smiling. "Hey, they move for me too," she exclaimed before noticing his face. "No need to make that face. I'm sure there's plenty here that would ignore me."

"We should head back," said Correk, more than a little troubled. The grass responds to her voice. How is that possible?

"A little moving grass couldn't have done that to you." She looked from the gently moving grasses to her Elven escort. She narrowed her eyes, putting more of the puzzle together.

"We should go," he said, settling back into his usual irritable demeanor.

That's an act. "Can I create magic?" Leira asked on a hunch.

"That remains to be seen," said Correk. "Not today."

"You're an annoying riddle, wrapped in an enigma. All right, I get it. Not why I was brought over here, at great risk." The dense forest loomed on the horizon.

"Questions," said Correk.

"You're all business. Is there a timeline for when this Bill Somers needs to be found?"

"Yes, before the next double moons appear."

"What happens if I don't deliver him before then?" She paused a moment and tapped her lip. "Not sure I want the answer to that one."

"Then the power the prince stored in the relic will go to Bill Somers and give him certain powers in your world, if he survives it. Most humans can't handle that kind of an energy pulse."

Dammit. "I was right. I didn't want to know. How often do your double moons appear?"

"Once a month, much like your own full moon. But one has already passed. You have less than a week left."

"Before all hell breaks loose," said Leira.

"Yes, a momentary flash of hell."

CHAPTER SIX

The cicada whirred and spun toward its destination, the wings flapping and the gears turning till it arrived at the Silver Griffins waystation on a far edge of the woods. A tall witch named Mathilda stood outside of the small thatched building barely big enough to hold the cot, a chair and a small painted cupboard on the wall. She held out her wand, swirling it in ever tightening circles, pulling in the organic listening device.

The leaves rustled in the thick stand of old growth trees, disturbing the family of wrens in the crook of the branches. Out tumbled the cicada into the open, leaning too far to the right and leveling off quickly, homing in on the witch.

"Well done," said Mathilda, guiding the bug toward the plastic box full of small holes with grass and moss along the bottom. She gently shut the door and swirled the wand again. "Communicate est princeps," she commanded. A compact trail of light swirled around her head, soaking up the sound. "Silver Griffin number fifty-four reporting. The Light Elves brought over the detective from the Austin region through a portal. They've given her an assignment to track the Prince's killer. Awaiting command guidelines."

The light spun around the witch's head faster and faster, creating an illuminated beehive and lifting her hair straight above her head till the trail vanished in a pop and the air settled down. Mathilda opened the door to the waystation and pulled out the one wooden chair left there for operatives with the Order of the Silver Griffins. She carefully set the cage down on the ground, smiling contentedly, watching the cicada chewing on a leaf. "I need to get back before carpool," she said, checking her watch. "It's my turn to do pick up. These last-minute operations..." She watched the ferns nearby lean toward her as she spoke and she smiled, sitting down in the chair and leaning back. "I love this world. Always reminding me to take notice of what's right around me. Nothing like Ohio. Warmer too. Fine, have it your way." Mathilda took in a deep breath of the air that smelled like almonds and vanilla. Her stomach growled and she shut her eyes falling into a nap. The wind blew through the trees and a few leaves shook loose, landing in the witch's lap, but she didn't stir. The cicada crawled around its cage, poking at the holes.

It wasn't long before there was a sharp crack in the air and the gold stream of narrow light returned, snapping Mathilda out of her reverie. It danced around her head, twirling back into the beehive barking orders. "Lacey Trader, Silver Griffin number two. Message received. You can stand down and return home. Bring the device with you." The light fizzled into a thousand dots of light before fading altogether.

"Hmph, could have told me that a half hour ago." Mathilda looked down at her watch. "Damn, missed carpool. Roy is not going to be happy about that. Oh well, life of an agent." She put the chair back in the waystation and opened the cupboard, rummaging around in the snacks. "Granola... not much of a snack. Oooh Twizzlers, now you're talking. Thank you whoever passed through here last. I have to remember to bring those Twinkies. They'll last forever." She bit off a piece, tucking the rest into her pocket and picked up the cage, cooing at the cicada.

"You're not a device, are you? You're still a living thing. Well, kind of..." The witch swirled her wand, creating a ball of light and opening a portal to a quiet corner of her backyard in suburbia. She stepped through, carefully closing it behind her before calling out. "Roy! Sorry I'm late. I had to work!"

The Gnome prophet appeared at the entrance to the Light Elves library inside the castle, cautiously raising his hand and giving a wave to the other Gnomes walking in and out of the stacks replacing books and checking on a title. They were his cousins from a different region of Oriceran. He was slightly taller in stature at almost four feet and his kind were used to dark tunnels in the mines under the mountains. The two groups rarely mixed, if ever.

The flatland Gnomes were the librarians of the Light Elves library, appointed to be the guardians and they took their oath seriously. They were no more than a few feet high, each wearing a small suit and a black bowler hat they kept pulled down to their ears. Their faces were set in a perpetual scowl over large, bent noses and their oversized feet were bare.

They were said to be from the last Gold Age, well over thirteen thousand years ago and were prized for their ability to keep secrets, no matter how long, no matter who was asking. The library was conjured to their exact specifications and the vault at the back contained all the mysteries of every kind of creature in Oriceran.

A small red poppy was affixed to the band of each Gnome's hat and acted as an early warning system. One of the flowers on the nearest hat hissed at the prophet and folded its petals back to reveal sharp teeth. The librarian frowned glanced up at his poppy and looked over at the prophet. "What are you doing in here?" he asked, sharply. "We have no record of an appointment with a prophet!"

"I beg your pardon. I didn't make an appointment. I have a last minute request."

"Last minute?" The Gnome stood up straighter looking back at his comrades who repeated the statement with the same amount of incredulous growling.

"Last minute?"

"Last minute?"

"Last minute?"

The sound went back row after row like a strange echo.

"No one comes in here without an appointment." The librarian furrowed his brow. "Not even a prophet. You have no sway here."

The prophet carefully counted the number of heads that kept appearing out of the aisles to get a better look at the intruder. Eight, nine, ten...Short staffed today. Noted. Always the middle of the week, middle of the day. He glanced to the far away wall at the vault barely visible in the distance that read, Nevermore across it in bold lettering. The forbidden books. No one was standing guard around it at the moment.

Tucked in that vault were the forbidden books, relics and artifacts from ancient times written by a forgotten tribe that originated on Earth called the Atlanteans. They had died out around the time of the Great Treaty. It was rumored that within the vault was another, smaller vault that contained the darkest magic of all. All the objects inside were too powerful to be let loose. It was forbidden for anyone but the Gnomes to venture back there.

That included the prophets and they had tried over the centuries, many times. The prophets were feared because of their knowledge and power, as much as they were revered by everything that flew or walked or crawled on the land or swam the seas. That is, except by the Gnomes.

"No entrance!" growled the librarian, staring down the prophet. The prophet held up his thick, calloused hands in apology. "My mistake. I will not make it again." He quickly turned to leave, the librarian watching him go, wondering if that had been an amends or a warning.

CHAPTER SEVEN

Troll

Leira looked at Correk as they passed into the Golden Chestnut Grove, but thought twice about asking him anything else. She had enough details for now.

Just want to get back to the guest house and figure this out. Find a way to talk to Hagan about this without getting myself locked up… like my mother.

They passed under a long bough that bent down right above Leira's head. Moss covered the branch along with a trail of yellow blossoms.

"Beautiful," said Leira, reaching up to pull a blossom.

"You always have to touch things?"

"One of my more charming qualities."

A whoop of laughter rang out and she turned to see the tiny troll, staring into her eyes from the branch. He seemed just as mesmerized.

A gust of wind blew through the trees, rustling the branches and caught the troll off guard, blowing him down, tumbling ass over head. He let out a terrified squeal and Leira instinctively put out her hand and caught him, inches before he hit the hard ground. Reaching up, she placed him gently back on the branch.

He trilled appreciatively and rubbed against her hand.

"Oh crap! Shit! No!" she yelled, remembering Correk's admonition too late, yanking her hand back. She could feel Correk glaring at her.

"I wasn't going to let him crash land," she said, returning the look. "Little guy would have splatted on the ground. Am I screwed? Damn! Crap!"

"Swearing really has no effect on anything," Correk sighed. Leira looked back at the branch. No sign of the troll.

"It has a magic all its own. Trust me. Any chance I got away with that?" She gently shook the branch, but nothing appeared.

"You might be all right. Come on, let's get you out of this world. That should break the bond, if there is one."

"Never been so glad to leave a place and get back to my nest," said Leira, picking up the pace. "Do we have to go back to the woods, or can we say, bippity-boppity-boo right here?" She stepped over a branch.

"Why are you suddenly speaking in gibberish? That's not part of your language, is it?"

She held out her hand. "It's not mine. We call it the language of Disney. Very popular in my world."

"Doesn't appear in any of our books..." Correk said, puzzled.

"It's weird how easily I got used to hearing you say words, instead of singing."

"Another necessary enchantment. We're back at the edge of the castle."

"How does anyone ever know that?" Leira looked around at the vast empty clearing surrounded by the forest. "If I squint, I can just make out a shimmer, I think. The whole thing is invisible or what, nonexistent?" Her stomach gave a lurch.

"That's the whole point," said Correk. "You can't attack what you can't find."

"Which begs the question, how did Bill Somers find the castle, and that room, and so easily?" she said, ticking the questions off on her fingers.

"Indeed," Correk said. "That is a question you will need to answer, and soon. We need to head this way," he said, heading down an overgrown path. Leira hadn't seen the path until the Elf pointed it out.

"Someone betrayed you," said Leira, speeding up. Correk was moving faster through the woods. Leira looked down to make sure she didn't trip over any roots, jumping over a line of ladybugs the size of her hand, marching in formation and looked up to see him whispering something.

"You're casting something, aren't you? Covering my tracks."

"You're very good at your job, Detective Berens," he said, moving slightly faster.

"That's the first time you've called me that," she said, jogging to keep up. "What are you afraid of out here?" she asked, looking around. "Something has you spooked."

A chill ran down her spine. "You think one of your own kind helped Somers. That makes more sense. Only a magical could have helped him get in and out so easily." She stopped where she was and took a closer look at her surroundings. She was sure someone, or something was following them. She crouched down to get a better look. Something was moving through the underbrush at a rapid pace. There was a flash of green and a faint trill, nearby lilies bending briefly toward the sound.

In this damn enchanted land, it could just be the plants doing their own little dance.

Correk turned around and tapped on her arm and then headed further up the path. Leira started moving again, keeping up with him despite his pace.

"Everything is possible." Correk looked pained, a scowl on his face. "Even betrayal. Keep moving. I'm not worried about Light Elves knowing our whereabouts. Even the traitor, if there is a traitor, will know you were here."

"Then what are we trying to avoid?"

At last, they came to the clearing where Leira had first found herself in Oriceran.

"I realize your entire day is made up of question and answer sessions," said Correk, "but we're out of time."

"Warn me before you throw me back into my house." She shrugged, still putting the different pieces of the puzzle together. "The choice of a human killer was no accident." A frog hopped over her foot, looking back and letting out a sneeze and a sigh.

"I would agree but the murder was probably a surprise." Correk clasped his hands behind his back. "They were trying to bring over a human thief. At any rate, whoever is responsible was trying to ensure there would be no trail once he left this world."

"No magical trail, because if there was, you wouldn't need me. That's a lot of trouble to go to but it makes sense. You want to kill off royalty and live to tell the tale, you'd better do some planning. Who stood to benefit from the prince's death?"

He shook his head. "That's the puzzling part. No one. There was no other heir yet, but the queen can still bear more children.

Light Elves do not reach outside of their lineage for someone to sit on the throne."

"Someone was buying time, at least a century of time. What is it about this particular time period that makes all of this so valuable?"

"All very good questions, which you can spend time pondering back in your world."

"Getting the bum's rush. Forest has eyes?" Leira looked around, the trees above her head rustling.

"In our world, Detective, Elves don't deal in right and wrong. At least, not in the same way that humans insist on doing. So much judgment and emotion. We're more attuned to nature and nature doesn't know right or wrong. We deal in consequences. Having you here violates a treaty that's over thirteen millennia old, and at a very inopportune time."

"That's not the first time someone has brought up that exact measurement of time. What is it about that era?"

Correk raised his hands to start spinning light but hesitated, looking Leira in the eyes. "I'll tell you this much, and no more for now. There's a prophecy and everything hinges on that exact measurement of time. Not only for us, but for your world too. Whoever helped Billy Somers with his crime knows that. I fear those two things may somehow be connected. Find Bill Somers and bring him back here. Alive," he said, and rolled his hands in a circle, making different shapes with the light.

A portal opened up to Leira's living room, just as she left it. Home.

She stepped through, glad to feel the familiar carpet under her running shoes and see her familiar artwork on the wall. Most of it was by her mother.

Her mother.

"Wait!" yelled Leira, as the portal started to shimmer and fade, shrinking in size. "My mother! She's not crazy!" she shouted, as Correk waved an arm, shrinking the portal even further.

"Answer me!" she yelled, as the portal shrunk to just a handful of inches.

At the last moment, something popped its head through the small opening and cried out as if it was in pain, squeezing through with a 'pop,' and rolling like a ball, coming to a stop at Leira's feet, just as the portal closed.

She looked down to see the five-inch troll with wild tufts of luminescent green hair get to his feet and smile at her, laughing so hard it shook.

"Crap! This can't be good." Leira squinted at the small furry troll to get a better look.

The troll chortled and scampered quickly across the rug, bounding on to her sofa. It disappeared under the cushions, pushing them one by one on to the floor, coming out the other side and leaping high in the air toward Leira, catching her off guard.

She yelped as the troll dropped feet first into her pocket, turning around in a circle, making a loud squeaking noise. Leira gingerly peeled back the top of her pocket. "Teeth like that, have to wonder if you bite," she muttered.

The troll opened its eyes and smiled at her, cackling again as it curled up into a tight ball in her pocket, and drifted off to sleep.

"How much trouble could you be?" she whispered, watching its tiny back move with each breath. "Dig that hair." She smiled. "At least when Correk finds out I'll no longer be the only thing pissing him off."

There was a sudden knock at her cottage door, followed by a sharp bark. Mitzi, another regular, was on the other side and as usual, brought her schnauzer Lemon with her.

"One minute!" Leira called out.

She hesitated, not sure what to do. "I can't answer that. Lemon will sniff you out. What…"

She looked down in time to see the troll unfurl itself and its bright green eyes pop open.

Just like my doll. The troll climbed up, leaping out of her pocket and rolled down the side of her leg, landing right next to her, just as Mitzi opened her front door.

"Wait!" yelled Leira, not sure just who or what might be in danger, and whether she was responsible for the well-being of a troll. "Dammit," she whispered. "I have to protect something that's the size of a dog treat."

Mitzi pushed the door the rest of the way open, already coming inside. Lemon stood next to her yipping as loudly as possible, wagging her tail, ready to play.

From behind Leira's left leg, the troll let out a high-pitched jumble of sounds and shook itself all over till it practically vibrated, ballooning into a large furry animal that resembled an oversized dog, a streak of bright green hair down its back.

Leira was too shocked to do anything at first, the troll barking and growled, its ears pinned back close to its head. Leira lunged for the door, pushing Mitzi and Lemon back outside, slamming the door shut, leaving them on the other side, safe from whatever was about to happen.

She could feel her heart pounding in her chest and she turned to look at the large troll...dog?!

"No!" she said, as firmly as she could, wagging a finger at the troll.

"You got a dog!" Mitzi yelled through the door. "A very big dog! Why didn't you tell me? Is it a rescue?" Lemon continued to bark but it was now mixed with whimpering.

"Just dog sitting for a friend!" Leira shouted through the door.

"Nice green hair! Totally Austin," Mitzi yelled, Lemon's yapping growing louder for a moment. The troll leaned against Leira, smiling up and panting.

"Good, um, dog?" Leira whispered, looking through the peep-hole. Mitzi was still there. "I can't be totally crazy if Mitzi can see you too."

"Yeah, yeah, dog sitting. Just staying the night." She turned in time to see the troll shrinking back to his tiny body. "Oh geez," she muttered. "What was that? I'm in over my head and I don't have time for this."

The troll cackled and scaled her leg easily, holding onto her pants as it found its way back into her pocket, settling back in and shutting its eyes. A tuft of green hair poking out.

Leira looked down at her pocket and back up at her door. "Uh, sorry, Mitzi, another time."

"No problem. Let me know if you keep him longer. Have to get you some toys."

She waited until Lemon's barking got far enough away before turning the lock on her door. That move would make most of the regulars suspicious if they noticed.

She looked down at the green hair. "I don't suppose you come with an instruction manual?"

She gingerly walked over and sat on her couch. "Do you even understand what I'm saying? How do I get you to stay in one place? Correk!" she yelled. "Come back!" She immediately regretted the yelling, and cringed, waiting to see if anyone else would knock at her door... or worse, make the troll change into something else.

The troll shivered in her pocket. Leira blew out a breath as she cautiously settled back on her sofa, trying not to disturb it. She slid her hand carefully into her pocket, easing the sleeping troll out and stared at it. "I have too much to do and very little time to let you get in the way."

The troll let out a trill.

Leira rolled her eyes. "Well, hell." She stood up and carried the troll in the palm of her hand, cradling its little warm body as she walked to her closet and found a shoebox, dumping out a pair of heels she'd never wear anyway. She took a washcloth from the bathroom and put it in the box, tucking the small troll in, and put the box in the center of her bed.

As quietly as she could, glancing over her shoulder, Leira

unlocked the lockbox and got her gun, grabbing her keys. She noticed the beer stain was gone.

Score one for magical friends.

Taking one last look to make sure the troll was still sleeping she bit her bottom lip and thought about what to do next. Time to catch Bill Somers.

Catching people who would harm someone else was one of the reasons she got into the profession in the first place.

Asshole killers that crossed into other worlds and came back with magic to screw up her town? Yeah, I'm going to find him and bring him in.

Besides, even though the queen was a real bitch so far, she could cut her some slack. Even Leira wasn't that cut off from her feelings to know about the pain of a grieving mother.

At least, she didn't think she was.

Leira glanced at the box on her bed and sighed. "I don't want to know what kind of trouble ignoring a troll might unleash, so troll owner is going to have to fit into the manhunt. I'm talking to a sleeping troll." That's a new twist.

She looked down at her hand, at her mom's ring. "The moment I get you Bill Somers, I get mom out of the psych ward, and bring her home."

Leira fingered the sapphire and diamond ring. "There's still a few hours left in the evening. I'll start with Enchanted Rock. Who knows? I might get lucky and find the beginning of a trail." I'm coming for you, Bill Somers.

She left the cottage determined, heading toward the Mustang.

A few moments later the front door opened and she was back, muttering, "Leira, you're a goddammed idiot." She made her way into her bedroom and grabbed the box with the troll and set the lid firmly on top, heading back out the door.

Leaving a troll behind to tear up the place would not be a good start to finding the killer.

CHAPTER EIGHT

Leira drove up to the base of Enchanted Rock and parked in the crowded lot at the end, half of her car resting on the grassy field. It wasn't her first visit. Her grandmother had been taking her there for picnics and hiking since she was little. Mara Berens had been fond of telling her, as big as the base was, the lavender-colored rock crystal underneath the ground went on for miles. At night, hikers reported seeing ghost fires and locals thought the place was haunted.

Leira had always found the place strangely calming, but this was the first time she had been back since her grandmother had disappeared. She took a moment, gripping the steering wheel before getting out of the car. The troll let out a squeak from his box and a low mournful moan.

Leira lifted the lid and looked down at his little furry face. "I'm afraid that's the best I'm going to have for you on this trip. No happy thoughts. Any chance you can understand me enough to stay quiet in my pocket while we take a look around?"

The troll let out a soft trill and stood up, the washcloth draped around his feet. "I'm taking that as an agreement," she said, scooping him up and putting him in her pocket. At the last minute she dug around in the glove compartment and found a half-eaten bag of Cheetos, digging out most of the remains and stuffing them in her pocket. She felt the tiny sharp claws dig into the snack food followed by munching and slurping. "That's your bribe. There's more where that came from if you hold up your end. Not a sound."

She carefully patted her pocket and got out of the car to set out on the long hike. It was the equivalent of walking up a thirty-story building, winding around the giant rock. Fortunately, her habit of running a few miles most mornings helped her keep up a fast clip, passing most of the hikers.

Leira got to the top, cresting the hill to a rock formation called, the Council of Witches and took a moment to catch her breath. She felt a tingling and a buzz in her feet and loosened the ties, but it didn't help. She stood back up and her vision blurred, the top of her head feeling like it could float away. She sucked in air, holding it in, willing herself to stay upright as her eyesight finally cleared, but the buzzing remained and only seemed to be spreading through her limbs.

The young detective took a few careful steps out onto the rock, carefully picking her way past people who had spread out a blanket or were sitting in lawn chairs with a cooler next to them. She was making her way closer to the formation. Feels like I'm high.

A trio of young women were watching her closely as she made her way forward, one of them giving her a wink and a nod. Leira furrowed her brow, still feeling like the horizon was bobbing and twitching. The young woman looked surprised and smiled at Leira, confused, looking back at her friends.

The troll stirred in Leira's pocket, rolling around and punching the interior of the jacket. Leira made it to the peak with a vista overlooking the city in the distance and sat down hard on the ground, putting her head between her knees for a moment. She felt a hand on her shoulder and startled, looking up at the face of the woman who had winked at her. "First time here? It does that to most of us," she said, sympathetically, adjusting the UT sweatshirt and pushing up the sleeves.

"No, I came all the time when I was little. It's never done this before." She swallowed hard, her pocket still wriggling.

The woman stood back and crossed her arms over her chest. "No one's taught you how to regulate the energy through your body. Hmmm, that's teenager stuff."

Leira frowned and looked out at the view. "Yeah, well, I'm a little short on family."

"Oh, of course." The woman shook her head, finally putting out her hand. "I'm Linda." Leira shook her hand and felt the buzz pass through her to Linda's hand, calming down to a lower hum.

Linda pulled back her hand, her eyes wide. "Wow, you are really something!" She put her hands on her hips. "Try this. A short lesson to help you get off the rock without stumbling or falling." She smiled, brushing her brown ponytail off her shoulder. "First of all, stop fighting it. That only makes it worse. Let the energy flow through you and back out. The rest is kind of mental. You have to let it know you're in charge. You're calling the shots. There you go, breathe through it."

Leira kept taking long, even breaths, listening to Linda's voice as she carefully stood up on the rock. "What is this place?"

Linda took a long look at Leira, biting her bottom lip. "No one's told you anything, have they? Wow." She leaned in and whispered, making sure a nearby family couldn't hear her. "Welcome to one of the best repositories of energy for magicals in this area. This is where we come to get recharged. Most of us are elves or witches, but occasionally a stray human shows up," she said, nodding her head in the direction of the family with two little boys playing nearby. "Best to keep a low profile. Maybe you've had enough of the rock for one day?" She glanced back at her friends who were waving at her to return to where they were sitting.

Grackles flew overhead, letting out their usual loud, high-pitched caws, distracting Leira. The wave of buzzing returned, rolling up her legs again and she squeezed her eyes shut, making herself breath evenly. "I'm in charge, I'm in charge," she whispered. When she opened her eyes again, Linda was back with her friends, but Leira noticed almost everyone was stealing glances at her and whispering. Everyone but the family with two little boys.

Leira made two stops on the way home. The first was at Voodoo Donuts for a dozen assorted and the second was to check on Hagan. He was back home with Rose after only one night in the hospital. She put the troll back in his box, tucking the washcloth around him. He looked drunk from the rise and fall of the buzzing on Enchanted Rock and quickly fell to sleep, curling into a ball. There was sugar still clinging to the fur around his mouth from the one doughnut she had given him.

Leira put the lid back on the box, leaving it slightly ajar and got out of the car, grateful the woozy feeling had passed. She took the stairs two at a time and rang the doorbell of the neat bungalow, smiling through the glass as Rose came and opened the door. "How's he doing?" she asked.

"Cantankerous as ever. He won't go upstairs to bed. His favorite recliner was the best I could do" said Rose with her gentle smile. "Go see for yourself. He's still eating, so I know he's okay." She glanced down at the pink box in Leira's hands. "I suppose he's earned those, but don't tell him I said that."

Leira chuckled and made her way back to the den. Hagan was propped up in his favorite chair, a large pillow stuffed along one side.

"What are you doing here? I told you it was nothing."

"It was still a bullet. I came to check on you. I brought you these." She handed him the box and he lifted the lid, holding it close to his face and taking a big sniff. "Nectar of the Gods. Hey, there's one missing."

"It was a long ride." Leira shrugged and gave him a crooked smile. "You know you can take a few days off if you want to."

"It's just a goddamn flesh wound," he yelled, his face turning red.

Rose came in the room and sat down next to him. "Passed right through some auxiliary flesh," said his wife, Rose, patting his arm.

He grumbled but smiled. "She means fat. I'll be at my desk tomorrow, ready to go. Cleared by a doctor, no less. A pile of paperwork awaits."

Leira took a long look at her partner, happily biting into a Grape Ape. "Glad you're okay." She felt the hum return for a moment and curled her toes in her shoes, clenching and unclenching her fists.

"What?" Hagan looked up from the doughnut, still distracted. "Oh, yeah, I'm fine," he waved with the doughnut. "Go home, get some dinner. He looked up at Rose. "What are we having?"

Leira laughed. "I'll see myself out. See you tomorrow," she said, quickly making her way back down the hall and out the front door. She breathed in the cool early evening air and wondered, "What the hell is happening to me?"

Leira was worn out by the time she got home. Her mind was working overtime with everything that had happened in the past two days. Her body still felt like it was floating from the after-effects from being at the rock. "Feels like I stopped at the bar for a few shots and already have the hangover. Too weird."

She only made it as far as the couch, drifting off to sleep with the troll snoring happily from the inside of his box on the floor next to the couch. That night, she dreamed about magical Elves with balls of light, walking through portals, and plants that moved to the sound of her voice.

But Leira was a light sleeper and the sound of loud rustling in her closet, or her trash can tipping over kept ripping her out of a dream. It was when he rattled the front door that she finally leaped up from the couch to go find the troll. Again.

She glanced at the clock. "Five fucking a.m.," she muttered, rubbing her face. She found him in the recesses of her underwear drawer, turning in circles and settling down at last in a pile of cotton underwear. He was drifting off to sleep, curled up in a furry ball.

She put her hand out to pet the little guy as it shut its eyes and smacked its lips, satisfied to have finally found a nest.

At the last moment she remembered the sharp, pointed teeth and how fast the troll grew into an oversized version of a dog when Mitzi casually knocked on her door.

Nope, please keep all fingers and other soft and crunchy bits away from the mouth of sir lots-of-teeth. Leira quietly slid the drawer shut and went back to the couch, her gun nearby.

She grabbed a couple of hours of sleep before her alarm went off, startling both herself and the troll who angrily banged against the walls of her dresser until she let him out. He smiled up at her and blew a raspberry scrambling out of the dresser and taking off to explore the kitchen. "What early morning hell is this?" Leira rubbed her eyes and followed the troll into the kitchen.

The dim morning light shone through the blinds of the living room window as stood in the kitchen, stretching her arms over her head. The visit to Enchanted Rock was leaving its mark. Leira was left with a mild headache and a vibration in the middle of her chest that was still there.

She shook her head, trying to clear her mind.

"Something wasn't...right about that giant rock. Too many people just hanging out." That lightheaded feeling the whole time

I was there... like I was high...Ugh, I want to tell Hagan. Nope. Not yet, anyway.

Suddenly, a small green streak of hair zipped past her and her eyes opened wide, tracking the small varmint. "No... fuck! I've got to get to work!"

She lunged for the small miscreant, chasing it around the room. Small, like five inches small and almost nothing to grab onto, especially when it was moving in such a hurry.

The tiny creature was always in a hurry. "Come here, you pain in the ass! The weekend was hard enough already!" Leira ran to the bedroom and picked up the cardboard shoe box she was using as his bed just as it fell into pieces. The washcloth she had given the troll for bedding was in strips, shredded among the remains of the box.

"Good to know. Little demon can cause some damage." Leira ran back to the kitchen and caught sight of the troll using the trash can as a launch pad, barely making the edge of the counter, hanging by his claws as he swung a little leg over the edge. She lunged for him but came up empty, her fingertips just brushing the wild tuft of green hair.

The troll did a neat bounce, and a tuck on the butcher block countertop, weaving in and out of the different things on the counter without knocking over anything. Leira stood there impressed and frozen for a split second. It was all the time he needed to disappear again.

"Well, damn..." Her eyes narrowed listening for a sound. There was a crash from inside a cabinet. "Fuck!" she yelled, as the frustration returned.

"Fuck!" chirped the five-inch creature, followed by a trail of laughter as Leira scrambled to open the cabinet.

"Great, your first Earth word," she muttered, but he was already on to something else, followed by more drawers opening and slamming shut. She turned just in time to see a green streak slide neatly into her silverware drawer, claws appearing at the top, closing it tight.

She went and stood in front of the drawer. "I have to get to work, you little green pain in the ass!" She used her best detective voice, her heart pounding.

Damn, Enchanted Rock did something to me. There's still a buzz going right through me. She lifted her chin, her forehead wrinkling. That's it! Everyone there looked like they were absorbing something... Almost everyone. But what?

The sound of silverware banging together interrupted her thought. "Double fuck Monday mornings." She jerked the silverware drawer open. The troll stopped biting one of her spoons long enough to look up at her. There were tiny dents in the spoon from his sharp little teeth.

He jumped to the counter and banged headfirst into her honey pot-shaped cookie jar. He troll shook his head, dazed, teetering on one foot, his eyes not focusing very well.

Leira glanced at the time flashing on the microwave. "This is why I don't have a roommate or a pet." She ran to her bedroom for another shoe box.

Temporary fix will have to do.

"Hagan's coming back to the squad room today. Fuck, I'm talking to the troll." The troll stood still for a moment and looked up at her.

"Are you actually listening?" She arched an eyebrow, her hands on her hips and looked directly at the troll. "I need to be on time. Wasn't your behavior last night bad enough?"

She could still feel the remnants of a buzz. Maybe that giant rock is giving off some kind of odorless gas. "Hey!"

The troll leaped behind her coffee maker, pushing it toward the edge of the counter.

"Not the coffee!" she yelled. She lunged for the glass carafe, catching it just in time and flashing the troll an ugly look. "That's messing with my lifeblood." She caught a glimpse of herself in the mirror and ran a hand through her short, dark hair.

Wish I had time to throw some water on my face. Trying to catch a five-inch troll is a sonofabitch.

The troll crawled into a bag of stale popcorn, happily munching his way to the bottom, scattering kernels everywhere.

"You're cleaning that up." Leira put the carafe back on the counter. "Look... we'll get along a lot better if you never fuck with my coffee, my gun or my running shoes." She took a deep breath and let it out slowly. "Ever."

As she let out the breath, the troll popped up at the top of the popcorn bag. He relaxed, dropping his shoulders, and smacked his lips, rubbing his belly, lazily looking up at her.

"Oh no... Your emotions are connected to me?" She bit her bottom lip trying to come up with a way to prove her theory.

"Now!" Leira let out a roar, stomping her foot on the linoleum floor and glaring at the troll. He stirred in the popcorn bag, looking up at her, puzzled. "Okay, pretending is a no go."

She let herself think of Prince Rolim as the knife went deeper into his body and his eyes widened in shock and pain. The anguish on Queen Saria's face flashed in Leira's mind as she balled her hands into fists at her side and her anger grew at the thought of such a senseless death. Worse, the killer had gotten away and was somewhere here on Earth.

"Dammit," she hissed, curling a hand into a fist.

A surge of anger flowed through the troll and he stood up straighter, leaping nimbly from the drawer to the floor, getting larger at an alarming rate. Leira watching in wonder until the green tuft on his head was brushing the ceiling.

He let out a growl, baring his teeth, and stomped the floor in a nice imitation of Leira.

"Fuck me, it's true!" She looked up at him in awe. "You feel what I feel." The troll's head brushed against the oversized brass lamp that hung in the center of the room, sending it swinging and raining dust down on everything.

"Gross, this is not good." Leira covered her face with her hands and shook her head, trying to keep the dust from settling on her. "Who knew there was so much crap up there?" She reached for a dish towel to wipe her mouth, trying to ignore the gritty taste.

The troll growled again, a low rumble that rattled the dishes in the sink.

"That is intense." Leira stood still, keeping eye contact with the troll and assessing the danger. "You don't know this about me, but I don't run."

The troll growled, looking around the room for any approaching trouble. "Hang on, you're not growling at me... You're looking for danger... Damn, you're trying to guard dog me..."

What did that Light Elf say? Trolls bond with beings that help them. Bonding has to be a good thing. "I did save your life. That's good, right?" She looked up at the troll, towering over her.

"Clearly I'm starved for conversation. I'm chatting with a giant troll in my kitchen covered in old bug dust."

She sighed and tried to think of a happy place.

"Oh for fuck's sake," she muttered. "What's happy?" She glanced at the huge troll. "Hanging out at the bar? No, not really. Going for a run. Maybe. Damn, why has this never come up before?"

The troll felt her growing anxiety and screwed up its face to roar again. He turned in a circle, stomping his feet, and bumped into Leira. "Son of a bitch!" She stumbled into the lavender quartz countertop, banging her hip.

"Dammit! Okay, okay, I admit it." She brushed her hair out of her eyes. "My happy place is running someone down. A nice tackle and the sound the handcuffs make. There, you happy?"

The troll stopped stomping and trilled at her, cocking its head to the side. "I have my own personal Yeti. Look kids, Bigfoot…" A rumble passed through the troll's chest. Leira could feel it under her feet. "Okay, okay. Happy places."

Leira looked up into the troll's eyes, staring down at her. "Looking over a murder scene with Hagan. Knowing someone is lying during an interrogation and getting in his face. These are a few of my favorite things."

The troll shrunk down, shaking all over like a dog. Leira reached down to the floor and put out her hand. The troll leaped on, fitting neatly in the palm of her hand and promptly curled up into a ball.

"That wore you out," she whispered, as she watched him get comfortable. "Interesting. Thank goodness you can't say much besides fuck yet." She pursed her lips and shrugged. "And can't tell the world I'm happiest in the middle of mayhem."

She sighed as the troll opened one eye and looked up at her. She gave him a crooked smile and he trilled softly, closing his eye.

She looked around the kitchen covered in a fine silt. "This is going to be a long week at work. I'll clean this up later."

She walked to the couch and slid the sleeping troll into the roomy pocket of her favorite black leather jacket. The troll's head popped out of the pocket and he looked around the room, stretching his arms.

"Stay put!" She went to grab a pair of her underwear, stuffing them carefully into the pocket, tucking the edges around the troll. "Those can be yours now. No need to give them back. Not sure Tide is equipped to get out troll."

The troll closed his eyes and settled back down.

"At least we know your happy place now. Curled up in my underwear in a small, dark place. Turns out, the first word you learned was appropriate after all." she said quietly.

She went to her closet. "Because I am truly fucked. If you play nice on good feelings… hell, any kind of feelings are not my strong point." She searched through the clean pile, folded neatly next to her dresser. "Unless anger counts."

She changed into another pair of black pants and a shirt suitable enough for work, slipping on her favorite blue and orange running shoes.

She brushed her teeth twice trying to get rid of the gritty taste from the dust shower in the kitchen and gargled for good measure. The entire time she was making herself take slow, deep breaths, occasionally checking on the troll.

She slid carefully into her jacket, and felt the troll squirm around for a moment, adjusting in his sleep. Nah, that won't attract attention, she thought, as she watched her pocket move.

She scooped up her keys out of the pinch bowl she made in the second grade, headed out the door of the guesthouse, and across the quiet patio of the bar. Estelle's wouldn't be hopping again until the lunch crowd.

Leira went quickly through the gate marked private. The gate let out a loud creak and Leira made a mental note for the hundredth time to get something to fix that.

No one else would even notice the squeak. All the regulars knew that gate was reserved for her. They were the closest thing to family that Leira had left.

The mornings were the hardest time of day. Wide awake with a full day ahead and nothing to distract her. It was too easy to think about everyone missing from her life.

"A crazy mother, safely locked away, check. Missing grandmother, doublecheck." The troll grew restless in her pocket. She looked down at her jacket pocket. "It's my routine, okay? Some people drink coffee to get their blood going. I do this," she muttered to the little round green and brown ball of fur.

"Only problem is, mother may not be so crazy." She shut the wooden gate behind her till the latch caught, walking to her car parked right in front of Estelle's. She slid into the driver's seat of the Mustang and started it up, grateful for her leather jacket in the chilly morning air of what passed for winter in Austin, Texas.

She adjusted the seat belt carefully around the small bulge in her pocket and pulled out onto the street. "Mom, you'll have to wait just a little longer. First, we look for Bill Somers and that necklace. Clock is ticking."

The street was already teeming with people heading for a breakfast taco at the other end of the block. She never noticed the ball of light hovering just under her back fender, easily keeping up with her car as she headed to the precinct, keeping track of all her movements.

She told her tiny new partner, "need to make one stop." She turned onto 6th street and got lucky. There was a parking spot right in front of Voodoo Doughnuts. Good parking spots were nothing new for Leira. Lucky moments like that were always happening to her.

Kind of made up for all the really bad things that seemed to fall her way, too.

She checked the glove compartment, rummaging around till she found the twenty-dollar bill she kept tucked in there for doughnut runs. "Got to replace that."

Voodoo Doughnuts might be open every day, all day long, but they only took cash, no exceptions.

"Don't suppose you could stay in the car?" she whispered, looking in her pocket. She slid the troll out carefully, still curled in her underwear and rested him on the driver's seat. "I'll only be a minute, and there's a doughnut in it for you. Dooooooonut. Fried dough, sugar. Trust me, it's worth it."

Leira got out of the car and gently shut the door, nodding at the man walking out carrying two pink boxes, a broad smile across his face. She walked in the door and glanced up at the oversized plastic American flag that stretched from floor to ceiling across one wall as she passed the doughnut-tree sculpture and the colorfully painted columns and stood behind a guy whose spiky hair looked like it had lived through a rough night.

"S'up sweetie?" he said in a deep voice, his eyes only half open. He smiled, revealing tobacco-stained teeth.

Leira gave him her best dead fish look and he turned back around, muttering something under his breath. She wasn't much of a talker even under the best of circumstances and morning was never in that category.

She finally got to the front of the line and walked over to the cashier waving his hand at her, looking a little bored. "What'll it be?"

"Two Old Dirty Bastards, a No Name, a Grape Ape, three Maple Bars, three Raspberry Romeos, and two Mexican Hot Chocolate doughnuts." It was her usual order. "Two large coffees," she added, holding up her fingers. She fished in her pocket for the twenty.

"It'll be a minute on the coffee. Just started another batch," the short, stocky man behind the long counter replied. Leira liked him. He was always polite but never smiled at her in the morning and never asked how she was doing.

For her, it was the perfect morning exchange of pleasantries.

She sat down at one of the tables and started to read the newspaper clippings that were decoupaged on the tops. All of them were obituaries. Leira liked the ones that gave away something about the personality. He took off to study birds in the Amazon at eighteen. Another one read, had her own radio show that was heard across five states all through the forties and fifties.

That's a good obituary. She tapped the tabletop. It's about their life, not their death.

She glanced up at her car and was relieved. Nothing was moving.

"Leira Berens? Your order is ready."

She went to the counter lost in thought, carefully balancing the box and the coffee. It took a moment to register that people were gasping behind her.

"What the hell is that?" It was the dude who had been standing in front of her in line. He was eating a plain cake doughnut in front of the plate glass window, looking out at Leira's car. "What the...?" he sputtered, his mouth full of doughnut.

"No, no, no, no," whispered Leira. She hurried toward the door, zigzagging around the tables and the other customers who were turning to get a look.

She rushed toward her car watching the troll get larger, his face pressed against the window. He was baring his teeth and looking straight at the man in the window.

"Deep breath, deep breath," she chanted, resting the doughnuts and coffee on the roof and fumbling with the keys. "Happy places. How about think about arresting that guy?" She looked up to see a panicked expression on his face. His mouth hung open and half chewed bits of doughnut were dropping out.

"Karma whiplash." Leira smiled and got her door open, just as the troll shrunk down enough to disappear from view. She wrapped him back in the underwear and tucked him back into her pocket before resting the box on the passenger seat.

"Plain cake doughnut. Says a lot about a guy." She smiled as she pulled away, daydreaming about arresting sweetie-man.

The troll trilled softly as she cruised toward work, making good time.

She pulled into the back lot behind the low-slung Region Two substation, a newly built, two-story building of red brick atop white Texas stone.

She briefly considered and rejected the idea of leaving the troll in the car. "Not gonna try it. My luck, you'll bust out of the car and have a SWAT team on your tail with reports of a yeti." She kept glancing down at her pocket. "This town and that green hair though, someone might mistake you for a musician. Maybe. Hey, what the hell?"

Leira caught a glimpse of the violet ball of light as it bounced against the ground for a moment and zipped under her car.

She got out of the car and kneeled down on her hands and knees to watch the light recede into her engine.

"I know it's you, Bert!" She gave the underside of the car the middle finger hoping Correk could see her.

Her pocket started to wiggle. "Dammit! Deep breath! Deep breath!" She shook her head and sat back on her heels. "You put a damn tracker on my car. Way to trust, dude. Pull back or I'm off the case."

She looked under the car again and the light bobbed down where she could see it, disappearing in a small cloud of sparks.

"Thank you!" She got up and leaned into her car to grab the box of doughnuts and coffee, still arguing with Elves that were nowhere to be seen.

"Pull me all the way over to another world, another world!" She made sure she had her keys. "Ask me, no tell me, to work a damn case with a timer of just a few days, then don't trust me enough to just let me do my damned job!"

"You okay?" A man's voice called out.

Leira startled and bounced her head against the roof of her car. "Ow!" She squeezed her eyes shut. Her pocket began to jiggle furiously and was stretching to its limits. The voice was coming from directly behind her.

"Detective Berens, right? Something I can help you with?"

Leira picked up the doughnuts and coffee and pulled her head out of the car, turning her right side away and holding the box there. She was hoping it would hide the jerking, pulling and wiggling that was going on inside of her jacket.

At the last second, she noticed her underwear was hanging halfway out of her pocket, but it was too late to do anything about it.

"Officer Carlton, right?" She did her best to sound nonchalant. He had been a year behind her in the academy where he

earned the nickname Booger. Always hard to get rid of him once he was onto something. Served him well on cases, but he couldn't take a hint. "How's things?" she asked, hooking her heel around the car door behind her, pushing it shut.

"Things are good," said the officer, smiling at the pink Voodoo doughnut box. "Trouble in your world? Hauled into doughnut court. What are you making amends for, Berens? You forget to search somebody? Voodoo Doughnuts, no less."

"Just a goodwill gesture." She slid along the car till she could turn toward the building.

"Yeah, sure, that's why anyone gets up early to slog their way through the traffic on 6th Street and find a place to park. What'd you do, run the siren to get a good spot?"

"Didn't need to, Carlton, spot opened up right in front."

"Like magic, huh? You have the best luck of anyone I know, Berens." She turned away from him and picked up the pace, walking toward the building.

Happy places, geez, I'm running dry. How about if I try a song.

She hummed something she remembered from Kev Bev and the Woodland Creatures, a local band that had played at Estelle's more than once. Their music drifted back to the guesthouse and she would dance in the kitchen, sometimes even getting drawn back out to the patio to sit with the regulars.

"That is what my spirit needs," she sang softly, "I got something to celebrate, cuz God knows all my bills are paid... mmmmm," she hummed, hearing the music in her head as a trill came out of her pocket. "Workin' real hard just to get by. Where is my social life," she sang, doing a little two step. "That could be my theme song," she said, looking down at her pocket, the start of a smile on her face.

"Little bit of joy in the middle of trying to save the world, right?" Just as she got to the door, someone came out and held it open for her.

"Hey Berens, what'd you do? Doughnut court? Paying penance with Voodoo! You must have cocked it up good."

Leira ignored the ribbing and kept going, plowing down the hall with her eyes forward, straight to the detectives' room and her desk.

Detectives were grouped by division and housed in different parts of the city. A few were at the Main, like Robbery and some of Homicide, along with all the top brass on what was referred to as the Fifth Floor.

The rooms were classic government fare with green cubicles, ugly metal desks, ugly grey carpet with small maroon diamonds, and tech sprinkled here and there.

Initially, Leira had been offered a sector detective spot to work minor cases that didn't end up with other teams, like assaults that weren't family violence or robberies. It was a way to get to know the job before picking a specialty, but she had turned it down. She was already set on homicide from the day she showed up at the academy.

She kept moving down the hall, ignoring the gauntlet of hoots and inquiries, and carefully slid the box onto her partner, Detective Hagan's desk. He was swearing under his breath and typing on a keyboard with two fingers, filling out an incident report.

He turned to look at the box, then at her. "What are those for?" he asked, as she slid into her seat. "I know you never pull a boner, so this has to be about a favor." She shook her head. "No? Hmmm, then it's to say something I won't like. My least favorite kind of doughnut-offering." He took out one of the Maple Bars. Leira knew he would reach for that one first.

The Grape Ape would be saved for last.

"They're for the patient." Leira tried a smile.

"No patient here," he retorted. "But I'll take them off your hands, anyway."

"You do the weirdest thank yous, Hagan." Leira steeled herself and blurted it out. "I'm gonna ask for a few weeks off. Take all of my PTO at once."

Another detective lifted the lid on the Voodoo box. "Yum, Maple Bars." Hagan slapped his hand and slid the box out of reach. "Never touch another man's Maple Bars without permission." There was already a little icing in his graying moustache.

A ripple of laughter went around the squad room. Leira tried to rub the outside of her jacket in an effort to keep the troll happy without looking like she was really into leather.

"You mean the vacation time you've never touched? You're going to take it all at once?" Hagan gave her a sidelong glance as he bit hard into the middle of the Maple Bar. "You're not the tropical kind of vacationer. Too pale. Hell, your ability to spend time not working a case is limited to sleeping, eating, a little bowling and the occasional beer." He stopped chewing and tapped the side of his head, rocking back in the metal desk chair.

"That's what it is, isn't it? What are you up to Berens? Working a cold case without me? Seems kind of rude." He fished for another doughnut and pulled out the No Name, pausing long enough to swill down some of his coffee. "Have to admit, your tactics are solid. I applaud that. So, fill me in. What are you up to, Berens? Come on, we're a team."

"Mmmmmmm." The sound was coming from her pocket.

His eyes narrowed. "What the hell was that?" He looked to his side and at her feet. "Was that you?" he asked, eyeing her.

Leira hesitated, wondering if she could share this with her fifty-three-year-old partner. Another realm, portals between worlds, magical creatures. This might be over the line.

Hagan narrowed his eyes and stared at her. Leira stood stock still.

"This is serious, isn't it? Let's head out and you can tell me in the car. Come on, grab the doughnuts." Hagan licked his fingers and stood up, brushing off the crumbs, leaving a maple smudge on his tie. "Awww, come on. Dammit. This is how the wife finds out these things. Not good, Felix, not good at all." He licked a napkin and rubbed the spot as he headed for the door.

Leira took a quick look around to make sure no one was watching and lifted the lid of the doughnut box just high enough to tear off a piece of doughnut and slip it into her pocket. Two small, hairy hands grabbed her fingers and held on tight, devouring the morsel. She could feel the edges of his claws, but he was being careful not to press too hard.

"Yum," said the troll.

Leira scooped up the box and her coffee. "So, you can learn English, but one-syllable words at a time. Good to know. You should have all of my favorite swear words down by end of shift." She looked up in time to realize the Captain was approaching her desk.

He was the one responsible for talking Leira into becoming a detective. She proved to be good at standardized tests and knocked the civil service exam out of the park. It helped moved her up the line for a promotion. Captain Napora knew her grandmother's cold case was what drove her and had cautioned her more than once not to let it consume her.

With no leads to follow that suggestion had been easy to abide by. Maybe all of that was changing. First, though, she had to find this archaeologist and turn him over to the Light Elves.

Damn. My simple, orderly life is getting more complicated.

"Sir. Headed out with Hagan." She turned her back to him reaching across her desk for a file, her hand gently pressing against her pocket.

"Urp!" A loud belch erupted from the troll. She turned, red-faced, determined to look him in the eye. "Ate too fast, you know how it is."

He was more amused than anything as Leira gave him one last nod, ready to walk as fast as she could to the car.

"Uh, Captain," she said, looking back. "Do you have some time open later this afternoon? There's something I need to discuss with you."

"Yeah, sure, check with me after three. I'm sure I can find some. Slow down on the doughnuts, Berens. Voodoo can always make more," he said, arching an eyebrow.

CHAPTER NINE

Leira headed for the car, saying a quick hello to a detective coming in the door but she didn't give him more than a nod and a grunt. Let them think it was about a hot lead.

Hagan was waiting by the Mustang, still fiddling with his tie. "I've been cheating on the Paleo diet for months now without getting caught," he said with frustration.

Leira handed him the box of doughnuts and unlocked the car, walking around to the other side. "I don't think that's how a diet works. Besides, hasn't Rose noticed you haven't lost any weight?"

"She's lost a few pounds and is too happy to have noticed my utter failure yet. You know what? I'll drive today. I'm pulling rank, or age or whatever," he said. "Throw me the keys. How did you get this sweet ride, again?" He slid the box across the roof toward Leira as she tossed him the keys.

"Just got lucky."

"That should be your nickname, Berens." He pulled the seatbelt across his belly. "What are you doing?"

Leira was on the ground, taking a quick look under the car to make sure there were no flaming balls of light attached to the bumper. It wasn't until she stood back up again that it seeped out

MARTHA CARR & MICHAEL ANDERLE

of the engine, a violet ball of pulsing light, bobbing just under the car.

"Thought I heard a noise earlier. Just making sure there was nothing dragging."

"Make sure you get the doughnuts." Hagan pointed toward the roof. "Keep all valuables inside the car."

"Bringing you doughnuts kind of makes me your food pusher." Leira slid the box off the roof and got into her seat, putting her hand in the box. She pulled off another piece from an Old Dirty Bastard, sliding it into her squirming pocket.

Hagan started up the car, glancing over at her. "Can't help but notice that you're squirreling away doughnut for later. I do know how to share, somewhat. You can have a whole one, even out in the open, wrapped in a napkin if you need to."

She ignored him. "Where are we headed?"

"Remember that witness for the Leahy case who up and disappeared on us? The one who saw the robbery homicide in the Wag a Bag from behind the rack of Doritos?"

"Yeah, it was a good thing we weren't in court yet. The prosecutor would have been all over our ass." Leira settled back into her seat, trying to stay calm and looking around at the scenery. *Damn, why didn't I listen to Correk and leave the troll alone? This being calm shit is going to kill me.*

Hagan turned the corner and glanced at Leira. "What's up over there? You take up yoga, or some other kind of shit? No offense, but all of that seems outside of a comfort zone you don't really have. This have something to do with why you brought me doughnuts? You aren't sick or anything, are you?" Hagan started to look genuinely concerned.

Leira blurted out, not sure where to start. "My mother's not crazy!" *Damn, that probably wasn't it.*

"Okay," said Hagan, slowly, pulling up to a red light. "Not crazy at all or not crazy anymore? Spill it. You're a good detective. Cool under fire and you stick to the facts, so what

86

happened? It's been, what, over fifteen years since they carted her off. Sorry, locked her up for her own protection." He was getting himself worked up.

"Not crazy at all." The full weight of what he said—fifteen years—washed over her. All those missed years. A lot has gone wrong here.

The light turned green, but Hagan didn't move and it wasn't long before someone started honking.

"Damn tourists. Yeah, yeah." He waved at them in the rearview mirror but didn't budge. In Austin, locals still waved at strangers, even if it was a couple of fingers peeled off the steering wheel. No one jumped on their horn right away. The driver behind him started gesturing, encouraging him to go.

He leaned over and ran the siren for a moment, sticking his arm out the window and waving everyone around him.

"We have a lead to follow, Hagan. It's okay, and by that, I mean I'm okay. If you're thinking I'm finally following my mother's path, that's not it...exactly."

"Very comforting, Berens." He was still waving people around, giving the siren one more short blip and glaring at a driver who was yelling something from the safety of her car. "Look, I can handle the truth. I've seen a lot in my years on the force. You can't shock me, trust me."

"I'll lay it all out for you if you start driving. It's kind of a complicated situation and an intersection isn't the most conducive place to tell you. Go, I promise." She tried to reassure him with her usual cold stare.

"Only person I know that can make me feel better with a dead fish look." He finally moved through the intersection.

"You're the only one who can say that to me."

"Well aware, and if you don't start talking, I'm going to stop in traffic again."

"Not sure where to start..."

"Jump in the middle if you need to. The details will sort themselves out. What makes you think your mother is a normal kind of crazy?"

"I was asked to be a kind of consultant for a murder case. A prince was killed and..."

"A singer?"

"Not that Prince. A prince in a kind of... foreign land," Leira said haltingly. "He was knifed in a robbery. The suspect's name is Bill Somers. He's some kind of archaeologist and he made off with a rare necklace. Actually, I think the stone in the necklace is the rare part."

"I take it this has something to do with your PTO. So, you're answering one of my questions. How does this come around to your mother?"

Leira hesitated, just as the small troll turned over in her pocket. *I have to trust someone.*

"I know you read the reports about my mother. It's okay, I would have done the same thing. Get to know your partner, and all."

"You were a big unknown. You were only on the force a few years and you weren't good at sharing facts about yourself."

"Would you be?"

"No, maybe not." He moved through the light and turned a corner.

"My mother was always a little out there. She talked about faeries in the garden and two worlds that came together but only once in thousands of years. She told those same stories for as long as I can remember. She seemed like your average flaky mom who liked to wear flowy skirts and maybe was smoking a little weed when no one was looking. Don't give me the worried look, Hagan. It's okay, I'm grown now."

"That's the Leira I'm used to." He shifted in his seat as they turned onto Lakeline Boulevard near the Alamo Drafthouse. The latest Alien movie was the headliner on the marquee. Hagan drove past the movie theater and at the end of the block, he pulled into the parking lot of an old brick apartment complex and parked the car near the back. The Mustang tended to attract attention. Not always the best on stakeouts.

"Informant won't be showing up for a little while. Still at his job asking if people want fries or not. Best to be in position," he said. It was something Leira had heard him say a thousand times. Get there first, whenever you can. "We have a few minutes."

Leira thought about the situation. *My partner is asking for the facts and if I can take the crazy feeling out of it, that is more than doable.*

"My mother started talking more and more about elves, dwarves and magic bugs."

"I remember reading about that." Hagan scanned the area and sat back in his seat.

"She was even starting to give them all names. There were details that made no sense. Insects that could be controlled by magic or plants that moved when somebody sang to them. The worst was when she told the neighbors that she was visiting this world. This place that, according to her wasn't exactly Earth."

"Still not seeing the connection between you freelancing a murder case, which I have all kinds of questions about why you need the side work, and your mother's stories about flying things."

"That's right, she did talk about some kind of flying creatures, didn't she? Can't remember what she called those."

"Did your mom know this archaeologist?"

"No," said Leira, shaking her head. Best to get this part over with. "I've been there. It's called Oriceran. I've actually only seen a small part of the planet. The Light Elves, they're the ones who asked me to help with the investigation. Queen Saria's son was murdered because someone helped Bill Somers into what's usually an invisible castle and even worse, into a room that held some kind of relic. A very powerful relic."

Hagan's mouth was open slightly, as if he wanted to say something, but no sound was coming out. "This isn't funny, Berens," he said finally. "You're killing my sugar buzz, you know."

"Let me tell you the rest of it, first. Then you get to call me crazy."

"I don't need to hear the rest of it and in fact, it's better if I don't. I can't testify at your hearing that way. Uh, look at what you've gone and done." He rubbed his stomach with a sour expression. "Damn that acid reflux."

"The Light Elves needed me to find Somers because a human doesn't leave the same kind of trail. At least, not well enough. It gets worse."

"Of course it does."

"The clock is ticking. There are only a few more days before this thing will release its energy to whoever has it and go boom. Or Somers could get even more powerful than he already is just by having the thing."

"Great! Help, I'm trapped in a Marvel comic and can't get out," said Hagan, holding up his hands. He caught something out of the corner of his eye and started scrambling to get out of the car. "Perfect timing, as usual. There's our guy. Can you hold off on any more magic stories for the few minutes it'll take to grab this guy?"

Leira ignored the jab and opened her door, forgetting for the moment about the troll curled up in her pocket.

"Sam Thomas?" Hagan smiled, calling out in a friendly voice to the tall, lanky young man with long dark hair, as he walked quickly toward him. "Just wanted a word… damn!" Thomas took one long look, first at Hagan and then Leira and bolted, doing a nice one-handed vault over the railing between the apartment buildings to the parking lot on the far side. "Hate the rabbits!"

"Go around," Leira shouted to Hagan.

"Was there any doubt?" He headed around the tall, neatly trimmed shrubs, picking up speed despite his size.

Leira made the same easy vault over the railing, pushing off the flimsy, painted metal railing and hitting the ground running, easily closing the gap. Thomas took a couple of glances backward, his eyes growing wider with panic as Leira pulled up behind him.

"Stop or I tackle you!" she shouted. "You know it's coming. Only one of us will enjoy it."

Thomas seemed to be weighing his choices, slowing his pace. Leira matched it, keeping a short distance between them, waiting to see what he would do next.

She didn't feel the small troll drop out of her pocket, landing on one knee on the ground. He scampered for a nearby oak tree, scurrying up and into the branches where he could watch what was happening.

Thomas pulled up, breathing hard. "You're making the right decision, Thomas. You're not in any trouble. We just want to talk to you about the Leahy murder." Leira kept her hand near her gun, ready in case things went south.

Things went south way too often.

She saw where Thomas was looking, at a nearby metal pipe lying on the ground.

"Don't do it, Thomas. I'm faster than you, and I have a gun. Besides, right now, you're not in any trouble. My partner is coming around that corner and we're going to have a friendly chat. That's all. You didn't have anything to do with that murder, right? Oh shit!"

Thomas lunged for the pipe and Leira drew her gun.

A roar erupted out of the nearby tree just as Hagan rounded the corner, catching everyone off guard and for Leira, time seemed to slow down. The troll leaped from a high branch and as he fell toward the ground he was growing, stretching, reaching eight feet tall.

Thomas grabbed the pipe, raising it over his head, shaking it first at Leira and then at the giant troll.

Leira quickly patted down her pocket, wondering if it was

possible that a second troll had made its way to Earth, but no, her pocket was empty.

This was her troll. Pissed off and hopping mad.

The troll stomped first one foot and then the other, breaking off a large branch of the tree and beating the ground.

"Fuck! Yum! Fuck! Yum!" The words came out in a low, threatening rumble.

Leira shot a glance at the large troll. "We really need to work on your vocabulary," she yelled.

"Fuck! Yum! Fuck! Yum!" The troll covered the ground between them faster than Leira would have thought possible, grabbing the metal pipe with Thomas still hanging onto the other end. The ground shook as he stomped his feet.

The troll swung the pipe around, pulling Thomas like he was on a carnival ride, his legs flying out behind him, shrieking like a toddler.

Detective Hagan raised his gun, looking for a chance to shoot at the troll without hitting Thomas.

"Don't shoot! Don't shoot!" Leira waved her arms, getting between her partner and the troll.

Leira looked up at the troll and resisted the urge to yell at him. "That will not help." *He can grow Mothra big. I need to relax. Now.*

She stood still, watching Thomas swing around again and willed herself to be calm. The troll slowed down and looked at her, coming to a stop and finally dropping Thomas. He tilted his large head to the side and let out a sigh, never taking his eyes off Leira. She did her best to smile at him, neither one of them moving. The troll let go of the pipe and it clattered to the ground, rolling away. Thomas passed out cold with a wet stain spreading down his pant leg.

Hagan was still pointing his gun at the troll, his arm dropping as the troll began to shrink back to his normal size. Leira kept her eyes on the troll, trying to maintain a feeling of calm. The troll finished shrinking, then ran to her and neatly climbed up her pant leg, crawling up the outside of her jacket and ending up in her jacket pocket.

"You can put your gun down now, Felix." Leira said it soothingly. She rarely used his first name, but he was pointing his Glock right at her, his mouth agape and his face flushed with sweat.

"What the fuck was that thing?" he said hoarsely, finally put away his gun. "Is Thomas okay?" He went to Thomas, still glancing back at Leira's pocket while he knelt down and felt for a pulse. Thomas groaned and jerked as he slowly came to.

"I wouldn't mention what just happened to him," said Leira. "Let him think it was a hallucination. Give me a chance to tell you the whole story. Remember, you said you could handle the truth."

"Regular truth, Leira. Ordinary kinds of truth."

"So what? You'll have to change your definition of ordinary. Come on, let's get him up." She walked over and helped him get an unconscious Thomas to his feet, draping an arm over her shoulder.

"How were you able to get that thing to shrink back down? And why does it think you're home base?" Hagan adjusted the weight and they started to walk him toward their car, his feet dragging behind them.

"All good questions that I will answer."

He made a face. "Answer the first one, at least."

"Okay, okay." She tapped Thomas' face, hard, trying to get him to fully conscious. "As far as I can tell, it's tied to my emotions."

"You mean it responds to what we feel?" Hagan eyes were getting wider and he let out a grunt under the weight. "Why are all the skinny ones heavier than they look?"

"What I feel. It's tied to me. I can't say why until we get back to the car and I can tell you the whole story."

"Your... feelings?" Hagan drew out each word. "Then," he snorted, "we're all fucked!" He looked at her, a glint in his eye. "Unless anger comes in handy!"

"Very funny." She gave him the dead fish stare, ignoring that she'd had the same thought earlier that morning. "I can do feelings."

"Like I said, fucked. This story I cannot wait to hear. What the hell is happening?"

"My mother isn't crazy. That's what's happening. That and an entire Wikipedia of magical shit."

"That's deep," said Hagan, straining to adjust Thomas' arm across his shoulder. "We need to figure out a way to get her out."

"First things first. And first, I need to find Bill Somers and I only have a few days left to do it before something bad will happen."

"Bad like what, like large roaring monsters?" He wrinkled his nose, attempting to waggle his fingers while Thomas slipped off and started to slide toward the ground.

"I don't exactly know. Quit the magic hands." Leira jerked Thomas back up in time and rested the weight against her until Hagan could get the unconscious man's other arm back in place. They continued their steady march toward the car.

"What the hell?" Thomas' eyes were finally opening. There was a trail of spittle on the side of his face, running back into his thick hair and down his chin. His voice was whiny and sounded hoarse from screaming. "Did you see that?" He looked from Hagan to Leira, his shoes still trailing in the dirt.

"Use your feet, Thomas. This is not going to help his credibility as a witness," Leira observed.

"See what?" Hagan pulled him a little higher, waiting till he put his feet under him. "Stand up straighter, son."

"You must have hit your head when I tackled you. You shouldn't have gone for the pipe. I told you so." Leira grabbed a wrist and put the zip ties on him. "Love me some zip ties in the morning!"

She loaded Thomas into the back of the Mustang, still babbling about the monster with the bright green hair and drove him to the hospital to get checked out, just in case. When the attendants in the ER asked about the hallucinations, the officer watching him shrugged and repeated the theory that he must have hit his head.

"Buy you more coffee?" asked Leira, as they passed the cafeteria. "Still have a few doughnuts left in the car."

"It's hospital coffee, but I'll take it. Have to do in a pinch. You good with Mickey there, in your pocket?" He flapped a hand in the general direction of her jacket.

"Yeah, we're good, at least for now. I'm not really sure what the rules are for him. It's called a troll. Why Mickey?"

"That life-size mouse always scared the beejezus out of me. Frozen face, dancing around. Still, it's trying to be friendly at least to you. Seemed to fit."

They turned into the large open cafeteria with long tables and low, round seats that were permanently connected. Leira gave a shudder. "Reminds me of visits to my mom." She shook her head to clear the thought and made a beeline for the self-serve coffee.

"Reminds me of being in seventh grade," Hagan was making an attempt to lighten the mood. "Don't say it. Yes, I can remember back that far."

"I was going to say, yours is probably closer to PTSD."

"Definitely. Believe it or not, I was a small, nerdish version of myself. It did not go over big."

"Two large coffees." Leira handed over her debit card, leaning against the counter. "Come on, we should get going. I'll tell you what I can in the car on the way to the station. You still want to drive?"

"Nah, let's get the coffee and you drive. I've had enough

excitement for the next hour or two. Whew, should sip this slowly." He tried for another sip. "Ooh, hot stuff, hot stuff!"

She eyed him. "There's no rush, you know."

"Oh, but it's coffee, and time's flying by." They stepped out into the warm winter air that was typical for Austin. The temperature had dipped to just below seventy degrees.

Once they were settled in the front seat, Hagan took a large gulp of his coffee, swirling it in his mouth. "Hot, hot, hot... But good." Another thing he liked to say all the time.

Leira started up the car. The violet ball stirred in its hiding place, pulsing with yellow light in the very center.

"Tell me everything," said Hagan.

"You sure? Last chance," she asked as they pulled out into the street.

"If I can handle a giant Mickey jumping out of a tree and using a big-ass tree branch like a toothpick, I can handle whatever truth you got." He took another sip and smiled. "Bring it on."

She made it through a yellow light. "I was minding my own business when a hole opened up in the universe and these two Light Elves stepped through and asked me for help."

He turned to look at her, his coffee forgotten for a moment. "No shit!?"

"That's only the beginning of this story."

CHAPTER TEN

B ill Somers was pleading again. It was one of his worst traits, even he knew it. But he couldn't help himself. Everything he had been researching for years was real and soon he would have the proof.

"You don't understand." He was pacing back and forth, waving his hands around, wearing his usual uniform of a t-shirt and jeans and high-top sneakers. Today's t-shirt had the words 'Don't be a' with different elements of the periodic table below that were used to spell out 'HAtEr.'

"This isn't a simple necklace." He ran his hand nervously through his hair.

Dean Muston, the long-standing chair of the History Department at the University of Chicago, Illinois was bored and annoyed. He dangled the heavy gold necklace over two fingers as the lavender stone, carved into a diamond-shape with an 'O' inscribed in the center swung back and forth.

A younger professor, Richard Randolph, sat nearby at a long table cluttered with unfurled maps and research books. Only the wooden legs were visible underneath all of Somers' research.

Randolph was trying to give Somers encouraging looks, but he knew it wasn't going well and only managed to wince, alternating occasionally with a pained smile.

"Clearly," said Dean Muston. "The gold alone has to be worth something. I'm not so sure about this stone. It's far too gaudy for my taste but live and let live."

"No, no!" Somers said, a little too loudly. His usual bad start. "I'm sorry," he stuttered to his boss. "I get a little excited."

The dean glared at him, still dangling the necklace. "If I insulted a family heirloom," he said, sarcastically, "I apologize."

"I think what Professor Somers meant to say was there's more to this story. That's actually an ancient relic."

"Yes, exactly," said Somers, pacing again.

"You are quite good at burying the headline, Somers." Muston let the necklace fold gently into his palm. He pulled out a jeweler's loupe and looked at the thick, braided chain more closely. "Doesn't really look like gold but doesn't look man made either. Interesting. What's the backstory? Not you, Randolph. I want to hear it from Somers."

Randolph grimaced, trying to get Somers' attention.

Somers walked to the table and shuffled papers around, moving maps out of the way, looking for his notes.

"Don't do it. Don't say anything about magic," Randolph whispered, but Somers had waited for this moment for too long. It had been ten years since he was a graduate student and first discovered the evidence that told him there was more than one dimension. Earth was just one of them. Even better, the rules of science could be bent in a thousand different ways that no one on Earth could imagine.

Some might call it magic, but Somers refused to.

"There's no such thing as magic," he hissed. "Fools say that about things they can't explain."

"What's that about magic?"

"Nothing at all about magic." Somers found his notes. There was a coffee stain on the corner of the page. The stain had bled through, sticking several of the pages together.

"Magic is a distraction for children or ancient civilizations that needed a quick explanation for everything. We are scientists." He spit a little, shouting the last words. "We know better than that and we figure out how everything fits together organically. In ways that can be reproduced, proven, tested." He carefully peeled the pages apart, and jabbed a finger at a map,

"Here, see, the green shows places where people live longer with far fewer health issues. Santa Barbara is one of them. So is Austin, Texas, or here in the Mediterranean and in Sweden. This is where it all started. Where I first saw the connections." He was talking faster and faster.

He was cruelly aware how short Dean Muston's attention span was from past encounters. He was known to walk out mid-presentation without saying a word. His way of saying no to a project.

"You found the necklace in one of these places?" asked Muston.

"No, not exactly. That's where I started hearing stories about Earth's history, ancient stories. They talked about giants, and humans with wings and beings that used light to conjure up objects. String theory taken to a natural conclusion but used thousands of years ago."

"All of this from Santa Barbara?" Dean Muston stood up from where he had been leaning on the edge of a desk, straightening out his tie.

"Not giants, like different creatures, of course. There's a scientific explanation or an early confusion but that's not the important part anyway. It's the portals," Somers blurted out, desperate to keep Muston's attention.

There were too many years of being treated like a middling

archaeologist who was too unimaginative to come up with original ideas. Or worse, someone lost in their own fantasy who couldn't even make it in the middle of the pack. This was going to be his moment.

Randolph fidgeted with the maps on the table, refusing to make eye contact with anyone. He had known Somers since graduate school and wanted to be there for his friend without tanking his own career. Somers wasn't making it easy, or even doable.

"I really need to get back to work," said Randolph, standing up so abruptly he bumped the table, sending several of the maps to the floor. He knelt down trying to gather them, but Somers stopped him.

"You're tearing one of the maps. Stop!" He pushed Randolph's arm away. "I will get them. You don't understand, this is years of research," he said, carefully rebuilding the pile on the table.

"Portals?" Muston walked over to stand behind Somers, looking over his shoulder at one of the maps. "What is an Oriceran?"

"It's like it sounds, like a door but it's really more of a tear or an opening in the universe. Like a black hole but without the gravity. We believe in black holes, right? Not magic." He scooped up the rest of the papers, placing them gently on the table.

"But these doors, these portals work according to certain rules. They're not at all random and instead of being out there," he pointed toward the ceiling, "somewhere in space, they're here. Here on Earth."

"You're saying there's a door in Santa Barbara," said the dean, "that has managed to go unnoticed by all of California, and these phenomena gave you this necklace."

"Forget the necklace!" he shouted, grabbing it away from the dean. "The portals are what matter. The necklace is just a means to an end. The portals are these openings that are connections to a different dimension. Much like a black hole, right? That's the theory but this is real!" He jabbed a finger at the dean. "Right?" He looked back at Randolph for support, but he was carefully looking elsewhere.

"I've heard these stories in Wales, Egypt and even England. The same stories, the same details," he said, clapping his hands sharply. "There was a time, thirteen thousand, eight hundred years ago, give or take a decade, when these portals were open all the time and the laws of physics on Earth were entirely different."

"You mean magic," said Muston, pursing his lips with disdain.

"Yes, okay, some would call it magic but it's really just physics redefined, don't you see? And all of it operated on a set of very defined rules, still does."

"But the portals closed at some point," said Muston. "The only reason I'm still here and listening is because this is the most creative thing you've ever come up with, Somers, and I'm wondering what kind of favor you're going to ask to go along with it. Best excuse I've ever had to skip a board meeting."

"All the portals closed but before they did, great things were accomplished on Earth. Like building the pyramids of Egypt, or Stonehenge! We all know there's a commonly held theory that the pyramids were the work of the Old Kingdom society that rose to prominence in the Nile Valley between four and five thousand years ago. The same with the pyramids of Giza." Somers was talking faster and faster, sensing he was almost out of time. "But, you know, there's a lot of research that shows that can't be true. That they're a lot older, they have to be. Like nine or ten thousand years older than that. Same with Easter Island. When I was studying in Egypt, we did radiocarbon testing that called the earlier tests into question. I repeatedly tried to get the same conventional results, but the tests showed that the structures had to be older."

"I remember your testing, but no one else was able to reproduce your findings," said the dean.

"Not true! Several others got the same results, but no one

would listen! Even though the Turin Royal Canon that lists all of the pharaohs suggests I'm right." Somers held up his maps as if there was proof printed on them.

"Most well-established archaeologists do not believe in the Turin King list. Besides, more than fifty percent of that list is lost and what we were able to reconstruct was from well over a hundred different pieces. Not entirely reliable."

"That list was deciphered by Frances Champollion, the modern father of Egyptology. You know it talks about an Egypt that's thousands of years older, ruled by half human, half god creatures who were called Shems Hor, companions of Horus. What if they weren't gods," he implored, "but different species who travelled through a portal? Then, there's…"

"Please don't bring up the Manetheo texts," said the dean. "They've been debunked." He glanced back toward the door.

Somers felt a panic rising in his chest and tried taking a deep breath to fight it back. "No, they've been ignored when they didn't fit neatly into the established timeline. It doesn't mean they're wrong. The Manetheo texts were written in Greece. They called them demi-gods. The coincidence is amazing. The same details."

"Then there's the ostrich egg," said Randolph timidly from the background. He was still trying to help his friend.

"Yes, yes!" said Somers, shaking Randolph by the arm. "The ostrich egg that everyone agrees predates the pyramids of Giza by over three thousand years, found in an ordinary tomb that has a depiction of the pyramids painted on one side. How is that possible if some of this, I tell you, all of this, isn't true?" He paced in front of Muston. "Look, the human beings back then seem to have known about these rigid rules surrounding the portals. That as the portals closed, they would have the ability to use physics to their advantage…"

"Magic." The dean nodded his head, his voice heavy with sarcasm.

Somers plowed ahead, determined to lay out the rest of his story. "...but it would lessen with each passing year till it reached a valley when this energy was at its lowest before it started climbing again. Some referred to them as seasons, and the portals being wide open was called summer." His hands waved through the air in his excitement. "Others named the time periods after precious metals, like a golden age. They knew the fall season of their age, or a silver age was coming and while they could still use magic, they built the pyramids. Not as burial grounds but as focal points to gather energy and hold it, like a giant battery, for as long as possible."

"This is all very old, tired ground, Somers." Muston rose wearily. "I'm afraid it's even failed as a good distraction." He turned to go.

"The pyramids have something in common with that necklace, that relic that you saw. The portals still exist but they're smaller, weaker and occur only in a handful of places around the world. But they're there."

"You can show me one of these portals with this necklace. This is some kind of divining rod for the door." Muston shook his head but paused, waiting.

"It's more like a key to open the door. It stores this ancient energy like a battery that can be recharged. Didn't everyone think that electricity was bunk when Franklin said it could be harnessed? Or how about planes? All crazy science. Magic, the devil, or something that just wasn't discovered yet."

"You seem very sure of yourself. Okay, I'll play along." The dean looked down at his phone, checking the time. "I have a few minutes left. What's on the other side of a portal? You're talking like there's something specific."

"Another world, similar to ours but where the levels of energy have remained high. They call it Oriceran," whispered Somers, his face flushed.

"They, who is they? One bit of information from you only

leads to ten more questions. Now, we're talking about aliens all of a sudden. You should have been a writer, Somers. Maybe you too, Randolph."

Randolph squeaked and sat down hard in his chair.

"I have proof." Somers took a deep breath. "I can show you a portal."

"Great," said the dean, standing up straighter. "Okay, I'm ready, show me one, but be quick."

"It doesn't work like that." Somers' voice had taken on a slight whine.

"Of course it doesn't." The dean turned to go. Randolph fidgeted noisily in his chair, motioning to Somers to say something, twisting his mouth left and right, clearing his throat.

"But it will," Somers said abruptly. "In just a few days the necklace, the relic, will release its energy and then another portal can be opened. Opened right here!" He was trying to regain confidence he felt just moments earlier.

The dean turned back for a moment.

"You're talking about the department's centennial celebration, aren't you?" Dean Muston paused, eyeing the nervous Randolph who was still pretending he was elsewhere, and Somers who was trying to look calm, his left eye twitching.

"No," he said firmly. He turned and moved swiftly toward the door, and said over his shoulder, "Be glad you got invitations that I can't take back." He was out the door before Somers could get in another word. Somers stood frozen to his spot, looking at the empty doorway.

"Why didn't you tell him about going over there?" asked Randolph. "Why didn't you show him the pictures on your phone? That's what sold me."

Somers sat down behind his desk, his hands between his knees. "These days, anything could be explained away as a trick. He would think it was clever, but he wouldn't believe me," he said, dejected. "Why would he believe that I was minding my own business, grading papers when a hole opened up and the bar scene from Star Wars was recreated in my office? Different creatures in hoods asking for my help. Even I thought I was crazy at first, having a stroke."

"What changed your mind?" Randolph ran a finger over the map, trying to sound out the words.

"On my first visit when they just wanted to talk, I managed to take this." He opened a cabinet to show a tall white flower growing out of reeds in a small clay pot. "It was just a seedling when I took it and it did this in just days."

"I've never seen anything like it. It's beautiful." Randolph stood there in awe, staring at the flower.

"The petals follow the golden ratio, like a rose, but there's more petals and they can close individually and reopen in sections." He ticked off things on his fingers. "Doesn't need sunlight or water. I tried giving it a little water at first and the plant shook it off. Literally shook the water off! I half expected it to spit it back at me."

Randolph leaned in to inspect the flower more closely and it bent away from him every time he drew too close.

"Not too fond of you," said Somers. "It just wants music. Like it's fed by sound. I discovered that by accident."

"Like penicillin. A happy accident." Randolph leaned toward the flower from a different angle, watching in amazement as it drew away. "I'm even getting rejected by flowers now."

"Hates Beethoven, loves Mozart and the Beatles. Played a little Smashing Pumpkins and almost killed it. Since I got the playlist right, I've had to repot it several times. It keeps on growing. The dirt is more for show. I don't think it needs it but I'm not sure. I'm not even sure if Earth dirt would be the same as Oriceran."

"I get why you didn't show the dean your pictures, but this would be hard for anyone to deny."

Somers slapped Randolph's hand hard before he could pluck one of the petals. "Owwwww, fuck you Somers!" Randolph rubbed his smarting hand. "What could it hurt? You can't think it's got some kind of intelligence!"

"Randolph, you cannot believe what I saw in Oriceran," Somers said in a hushed voice. "There was a palace that seemed to hang in the sky and one moment it was there and the next, poof! There was nothing. I swear to you, I thought I saw a tree with eyes watching everything. But then, for a second..." he snapped his fingers, "the tree moved, and I realized it was a kind of man with bark for skin standing at the edge of a dense forest."

"What did the hooded guys want with you?" Randolph, finally let go of his other hand, shaking it a little, not quite willing to let his hurt feelings go.

"They wanted my help." Somers stood up straight, thrusting his chin out. "My help," he said, sounding proud and even a little surprised. "Saw my papers on ancient Egypt and the age of the pyramids and the testing I did and for once, someone knew I was right."

"That's creepy. They can watch us from over there. Like an alien NSA." Randolph crossed his legs tightly and shivered.

"I don't think they're bothering to watch us now," said Somers, irritated. He was tired, so tired. Ever since he had to kill that prince he hadn't slept well.

I just wanted the necklace. I needed proof. It was an accident, he thought for the thousandth time. I'm not a killer.

He squeezed his eyes shut, trying to forget the look in the prince's eyes as he died. Somers had never so much as balled up his fist before that moment.

"I am not some kind of crackpot!"

"Nobody said you were," said Randolph, startled. "At least nobody here."

He wanted to tell Randolph everything. The hooded creatures ambushed him just outside the relic room, waving their hands around, shooting out sparks and fireballs that pulled Somers across the floor, back into their clutches.

He still wasn't sure why they hadn't killed him right where he stood. They seemed to be panicking more than he was. No one even noticed that he had pocketed the necklace. He even managed a picture or two with his phone as they dragged him along, capturing their faces twisted in grimaces.

"Waste of time," one of them had said.

That's when he saw the man that looked like a tree watching them as the creatures dragged him down a different path to a clearing, opened up a hole in the world and tossed him through it, right back into his office.

He was free with no one following him. Those creatures had made it clear they just wanted him gone.

So be it. I'm sorry it happened but there are bigger things to think about. The portals will be opening again. I could lead the way. The thought exhilarated him. Maybe things were finally changing for him. It was an accident. He shook his head as the image of the dying prince crept into his thoughts again. No one can find you. There were no other witnesses.

He had been giving himself the same speech over and over again for days.

Somers went to the small fridge near his desk and took out two Half Acre Lead Feather beers, handing one to Randolph who'd finally lost interest in the plant.

He found the Beatles on his phone, sliding it into a speaker so that 'Hey Jude' filled the room. The plant bobbed to the melody and even stretched its reeds toward the speaker like it was the sun.

"They talked about some kind of Armageddon that's going to happen on their side of things and everyone from their side will have to come over here. Like a prophesy."

"Mass immigration? We don't like it when the people we've

already got here change locations from one place to another. Where would we put them all?"

"Not my problem." Somers took a gulp of his beer. "Right now, I just have to prove to everyone that something is coming, like a motherfucking asteroid, and I knew about it all along."

"Dude, you could benefit from smoking a little weed."

CHAPTER ELEVEN

The king held up a violet ball of light in his hand and sang into it. Fiery symbols crept up his arm. His eyes glowed a bright, deep blue. Images appeared inside the sphere of light. It showed Leira and Hagan driving back to the precinct.

"She's sharing her secrets about us with someone else. Her partner... another detective," said Correk.

"Good. We can use all the help that's available to us, Correk. Why does this detective call you Bert? Is this a human trait, to rename things?" King Oriceran stood with his back to Correk. He was staring out at the expansive view from the third floor of the invisible light castle. His view was slightly obstructed by the clouds just outside the window.

Down below, he could see several teenage Elves were tossing around a gold ball of light that was hard to detect, it was moving so fast, and small enough to duck into pockets or hide in the palm of a hand. A player made contact with the ball, giving it a good, swift kick and setting off a sharp noise, changing colors from white to blue to yellow and back to white.

"Two points, well done," called an umpire standing on the sidelines. "No hands, Sigland. Your side loses a point."

"It flew into my hands," the young elf protested.

"Tricky little bastard, isn't it," said the umpire. "Feet only, no spells. I see your eyes glowing over there," he said to another player, spraying sparks from his wide sleeve. The umpire caught the offending player off guard and swept him off his feet, leaving his hair smoking. The other children hooted with laughter until the ball zipped between them, darting off toward the woods.

"Oh great," an Elf yelled. "We lost another ball in the woods."

"Well, go retrieve it," said the umpire. "I've gotten the last few. Surely, some of you remember the spell."

The king smiled sadly, remembering Prince Rolim playing in the same fields. "It's almost too much to bear," he said quietly.

Correk came close enough to see what the king was looking at. "They call them nicknames. Bert, it's one of those, a nickname. That's the Earth name she's chosen for me." Correk shook his head, trying to distract the king from the window. "Something to do with my forehead. The detective said I had more of a nine-head. I have no idea what it means. There was some mention of my eyebrows and a doll she loved as a child." He scowled. "Ridiculous."

"A term of affection. She's bonded with you. I wasn't sure she was capable of that. She carries anger with her, always. I wonder if I might join her in that dark place," he said, glancing back at the window. "You trust her, don't you?"

"Yes, your majesty, as much as I would trust anyone from their planet. There are limitations, of course, but my reservations are based on their limited view of magic, not her integrity. They see magic as something only a fool or a child would believe in."

"Fair enough. It may become necessary to send you into her world to guide her."

Correk startled, shaking his hand as the ball of light faded along with the images.

The king noticed but ignored the reaction. "You've been by

my side for well over a hundred years now. Things have been peaceful here for as long as I can remember. The worst we've had to deal with is a dispute over land. The one thing we can't grow more of in Oriceran."

"Even that has been dealt with by decreeing the larger estates lift their castles up into the clouds. It was a wise decision, your majesty."

The king turned to face Correk. He was wearing plain green robes in keeping with the customs when grieving the loss of a loved one. On his head was a simple crown of Oriceran silver that had sprouted small leaves. When the leaves flowered it was time to let go of old pain and move back into society.

"Nothing seems to get easier. There were hundreds of years left of Prince Rolim's life. No one in the royal family has died at the hands of someone else since before the Great Treaty. The wars that raged over this planet killed thousands, including my grandfather and most of his kin. The dwarves were constantly at our throats and the Wood Elves took every opportunity to help turn the tide for whatever side was losing. They are very clever creatures—helping us to annihilate each other. Do you think the Wood Elves could have helped this human kill my son?"

"No, I don't. They would never go this far. Not now. We've been at peace for so long. The treaty was signed thousands of years ago and for the most part everyone has kept it," said Correk.

"Yes, for the most part. Only one being tried to change all of that."

"Rhazdon," said Correk.

"Yes, Rhazdon, that half-Atlantean who was more than half mad. He was defeated over six hundred years ago. Since then, peace has reigned. Untill now." The king waved his arms making the walls appear.

The details of a painting were moving around inside the

ornate frame. A tree troll with the familiar green tufts of hair, rolled out of its small wooden home nestled on a tree branch. It scampered off into the woods, into the depths of the painting.

"Nothing relieves this ache. There is nowhere I can go where I don't find a thousand memories of my son. Even some of these damn paintings remember him and he will appear for just a moment, walking through them." His voice was sharp. "Enough," he said, singing another note, and with a wave of his arm, the walls were invisible again.

Correk let the king speak. He knew that there was nothing he could say that would alleviate any of the misery. Only time, or vengeance or at least answers was going to do that.

The sound of crashing and glass breaking interrupted them. Correk and the king raised their hands, twisting their fingers, fiery symbols twining up their arms, their eyes aglow.

"Someone is attacking the castle!" the king shouted.

He spread his hands apart and half of the castle floors appeared below them like an oversized dollhouse open on one side. Several floors down, Queen Saria was suspended in air in the middle of a room that was still invisible. She was glowing from head to toe, an ancient language scrolling across her skin in dark red letters.

There were no assailants except her own agonizing grief. She screamed in pain, her arms outstretched. Everything that became visible around her was exploding into a fine dust that rained back down on her, melting as it touched her, falling to the ground as large droplets that came back together in a glittering, metallic puddle.

She sank to the floor, beating her hands against the stone.

The king sang, "Altrea Extendia," sending out a wave of bronze sparks that melded into cascading stairs.

He flew down the stairs, Correk following him as the steps disappeared just as rapidly behind him. They got to the vast library, still mostly invisible, where the Queen continued to yell, shattering the furniture and turning more than a few books into a rain of ash.

"Leave me to my grief," she screamed, her long brown hair fluttering around her, as a painting exploded, the image of two tiny elves with silver hair, their arms flailing, tumbling through the air until they dissolved into ash.

On her head was a crown similar to the king's, made of silver but the green sprouts barely showed through the thin metal.

Correk stretched out his arms at the books leaping off the invisible shelves. "Reflectus Moranus," he shouted.

The shelves appeared, a row at a time, stretching back for over a mile where they ended at a large vault with 'Nevermore' etched on its face.

"Hoomanna protector," he said, a shimmer appearing in front of the shelves. The books that were flying at the queen's head hit the shimmer and dropped to the floor just behind it.

Gnomes looked out from between the stacks, peering around the fallen books to see if it was safe to come out again. The poppies on their hats baring their sharp teeth and growling or hissing.

"This room is sacred," said the king. "Even we cannot break that bond."

The queen's screams grew even harsher, bouncing off the shimmering wall Correk had conjured, echoing in the room and out into the hall.

An invisible piece of masonry tore away from the outside of the castle, crashing into the grounds. Correk ran to the window to see if any of the children playing below were hurt. Someone was helping a tall elven teenager with a broken arm.

"A simple fix," said Correk quietly, watching them lead him away to the nurse.

Queen Saria screamed again, shaking the room, causing dust to rain down.

"Saria, enough." The king took both of her hands firmly in his.

She tried to twist away but he refused to let go. "I won't let you give in to this despair," he said, softly.

"Despair…" Her lip curled in disgust. "This isn't despair, it's anger in my very soul. I want revenge! I want to crush the killer's bones with my bare hands. I want to see the light in his eyes go out."

The king hesitated, unsure what to say.

"Then you shall have it, my queen." Correk bowed before her. "As payment for the hundreds of years you will live without your son. Will that ease your pain, your highness?"

The king let go of his wife's hands and drew back.

"You always were the clever one, Correk," said the queen. "I know that if I said yes, you would even bring me this human, this Bill Somers and break every law in Oriceran to do it. No, it will not, except for the moments I can hear each bone break. Perhaps that will be enough." She squeezed her hands together as if she could already hear the snapping.

A tear slid down her cheek and sought out the pool of liquid still on the floor, adding to it. The symbols on her face and arms began to fade and the fire in her eyes cooled to their normal luminescent green.

"I want my son back," she said, looking into the king's eyes. "Even if for just a moment."

"In all the world, this is one thing I cannot do. I'm so sorry. I have failed you."

"There is one place," said Correk.

"No!" the king cut him off. "No one knows how to find it and even if you look for it, no one has ever come back."

"The world in between." The queen took in a deep breath, rising to her feet. "All things are possible. Isn't that what you're always saying? All things are possible!"

"Not this. Not to the place where souls are caught between Oriceran and Earth. Not without the Gnomes' help and they will never give it. You know the stories. During the wars with Rhazdon, my own father begged them to let him speak to his father. He tried every kind of bribe, every kind of trick. He rightfully pointed out that one conversation could shorten the uprising."

"But they refused," said the queen in an icy tone. She looked over her shoulder at the Gnomes, still situated behind the shimmering wall. They were busy restoring order to the library shelves, darting about, their bowlers on straight and the flowers back to their more beautiful, and less dangerous resting state.

"We don't even know if our son is there. He may have passed on," said the king, giving Correk a menacing look.

"No, he's there. I can feel it," said Queen Saria. "The look on his face when he died. He was so surprised and confused. I know he's there."

"Entire races have tried to find the world in between, combining their powers and some have died trying, or worse," he argued. "Do not go down this road."

"You mean trapped. Some are trapped in the world in between and they're still alive. Never aging, seeing everything, mixing with the dead. That's what you mean."

The king's face clouded, and he chose his words carefully.

"You know what happened the last time someone tried."

"But if I could just talk to him. One last time," the queen pleaded.

"No! My only hope is, if he is trapped there, we never know." The king was aghast. "To be nowhere, trapped forever and worse yet, watching others enjoying life but unable to show yourself. The worst kind of prison."

"He wouldn't be alone," said the queen, in a hushed tone, refusing to look at the king.

"You would dare to bring that up? You would carve out a piece of that pain?" he shouted. "No one mentions my father. He is lost to us!" He stormed out of the room, slamming doors no one could see.

The room was silent for a moment. The queen held out her

hand, a ball of fire blossoming in her palm. She sang, "Immortus," into it and the shiny, metallic drops of water on the floor bubbled and streamed to her hand. They passed through the flame, the objects she had destroyed emerging restored and finding their places. Her tears fell once again to the floor, this time sliding away on their own.

"Even these things I can bring back from nothing," she said sadly. "So simple. A child's trick, really." She flicked her hand in the direction of the Gnomes. "You can release the spell. I'm done yelling to the heavens."

"Hoomanna erasa," Correk's eyes glowed and the fiery symbols necessary to complete the spell flowed up his arms and back again like a breaking wave.

The shimmering wall broke into crystal flakes that rained down on the floor. Several of the flowers on nearby bowlers hissed at the queen, baring their teeth. The queen hissed back, curling her lip. The seedlings atop her crown reappeared, but as a pale blue.

"You're planning something," said Correk.

"No, no more than we're already doing. I swear it on my life." But she said it with a cold, icy tone that made Correk shiver despite the warmth of the room.

"Then what has changed?"

"An opportunity is coming, whether my dear husband likes it or not. The portals are starting to open. There will be a way to more easily cross over to the world in between and I will find it. The veil between the two worlds will grow thinner." She slowly paced the room, her long dress sweeping behind her. "I know the king sees no hope for anyone trapped in there, living or dead. But I have seen strange things in my lifetime. Undiscovered creatures from the bottom of the sea, and great feats performed that older, wiser elves said were impossible. This world of ours still holds a few secrets," she said, opening her hand to reveal a blood red beetle.

Correk shivered again. The beetle beat its wings and took its place on the queen's crown.

"Bring me the rock digger," she said, as she swept out of the room.

CHAPTER TWELVE ·

Willen - Artist John-Paul Balmet

A Gnome from the nearby bookshelves waddled to Correk faster than his short, stout legs should have been able to carry him. He was using an old magic spell that Gnomes kept for themselves. Perks of the library.

"Take this," the Gnome said in a baritone voice that managed to sound like he was holding his nose. "You're going to need it." The flower on his bowler puckered its petals and gave a low whistle.

"Doesn't think you can do it," he grimaced, glancing up at the flower. "You're going to try anyway. This may help you stay alive."

Correk took the small book with a dusty green cover and pages with gold leaf edges. How to Pass for Human by Sydria Ganfried. Correk recognized the name. She was an elderly teacher when he was in school hundreds of years ago. One of the last remaining elves that remembered the Great War.

Correk flipped it open and as he did the words appeared. A familiar sweeping cursive that was written by Sydria, herself, and then magically reprinted. The words First Edition sparkled on the page.

He turned to a blank page and the words rolled across the first page of chapter one. It was an old elven spell that protected the books from being stolen.

Unless they were properly checked out by a Gnome and a record kept, the pages remained blank. Once the niceties were handled, the words and images would appear, but only on the page someone was reading.

"Be sure to bring it back on time," said the Gnome, tapping the book with a stubby finger.

"Or it'll come flying back on its own," said Correk, finishing the thought.

"And we'll revoke your privileges for a year!" the Gnome added, pointing for emphasis. The flower on his hat gathered its petals and did a raspberry, sticking out a pale green tongue.

"I remember."

"You were a troublemaker back in your day. We remember you still!" he warned, as he waddled back toward the shelves. "Two weeks," he shouted over his shoulder. The flower settled back into place as the Gnome magically zipped down an aisle, covering almost the entire mile before turning left.

"They never forget a damn thing," said Correk, watching him go. "Why humans worship them with those little garden statues I will never understand."

"They got the hat wrong, too." Correk startled and looked

down to see a silver Willen. No one's favorite creature. They were rodents the size of small dogs that could walk on two legs and were adept at taking things that didn't belong to them.

"Pretty bauble," said the Willen, balancing a ring between his paws. Correk looked down to see that the ring was missing from his hand and he snatched it back from the Willen before it was secreted somewhere in the folds of its silvery skin.

"Finders, keepers," snarled the Willen, reaching out with its long, thin claws fully extended.

"Not always," said Correk, slipping it on. "Slither off somewhere else." Correk got a tighter grip on the book, wondering if the Willen could steal it from his hand unnoticed.

"The ring for information," the Willen offered, his pupils spinning with excitement. Correk looked away. It was a way to hypnotize their prey long enough to strip them of their belongings.

"You mean gossip."

"Sometimes it's gossip, sometimes it's important. You decide. Do we have a deal?"

"No, not at all. I don't need to know about anyone's private life."

"Private life? Hardly worth a ring," said the Willen, drawing out the words. "No, this is about the human you secured for a task. You call her a detective, don't you?"

"Some do, and what could you know that would earn you a ring?"

"I'll tell you what," said the Willen, twitching its long, metallic tail. "I'll let you decide. The Light Elves are known for their honor. If my information is only gossip to you, I'll leave you be."

"But not the rest of the castle," Correk said.

The Willen shrugged. "Pointless, it's in our nature. Despite all your traps, and walls and shields, we have our ways. Besides, even if I didn't come back, we travel in packs." He smiled, his whiskers twitching. "I may exit the premises, but my cousins will bring back a little something for me. If it's valuable information, you give me the ring. As a gift, not theft. Deal?" The Willen smiled, his whiskers curling up on both sides and his pupils spinning again.

Correk looked up at the sky. "Agreed."

"She's not going to retrieve the necklace, the detective. Very powerful forces want her to fail," he squeaked then belched. "Some good, some not so good. Sorry, dined on a tasty plunkett fish this morning." He worked a fish skeleton slowly out of his mouth, still twitching. The Willen bit down, crunching the bones. "Satisfying." A little bit came back up again. "Tasty twice."

"What forces? Oriceran forces?"

"Of course. Most Willens don't care for Earth," he whined. "Our magic isn't strong enough there and the humans react so dramatically when they see us and that was thousands of years ago. Imagine what they'd do to us now. They have all those large machines. Run us right over," he squeaked, wringing his front paws. "Although some of our kind still live in the shadows down in the depths of the Earth. Many are in something called a subway. So many tunnels, I hear. Others are in underground cities."

"What forces?" Correk demanded.

"Right, right. Sure, sure. There are some who can sneak up on their prey even better than a Willen. Look for one among the prophets who is long extinct."

"A riddle?" Correk said angrily, his eyes starting to glow and his fingers twitching.

The Willen backed up on all four legs, ready to scurry away.

"Way more clues than a usual Willen riddle. I'm being generous. The ring?" He righted himself up on his back legs, holding out a paw.

"One added condition. You hear anything else about this extinct prophet and the detective, anything at all, you come and tell me. This ring," he said, sliding it off his finger as the Willen licked its lips, "is a down payment on that information. Deal?" Correk held the ring just out of the Willen's grasp.

"It's a dangerous thing you ask. The extinct one holds very dark magic, even more than the Gnomes." The Willen glanced nervously at the Gnomes, still scurrying around the shelves. A book flew through the air, its pages ruffling as a Gnome caught it, stamped it returned and replaced it on the shelf. The flower on his hat sneered at the Willen.

"It's an assignment that could kill even a Willen, if I'm caught. Small danger of that, though." The Willen pointed a claw at Correk. "Beware, you may find out more than you want to know," he squeaked, reaching for the ring.

"I will keep that in mind. Do we have a deal?"

"Of course, of course. A down payment on further information. As you wish."

Correk dropped the ring into his waiting paw. It disappeared into the folds of his skin with a 'plink' as the ring rolled against something metallic.

The Willen smiled up at Correk, one side of his whiskers curling tightly. "Enjoy your book. It's a fascinating read. Willens can only read books on the premises. None of the Gnomes trust us. Foolish. We could make some wonderful trades."

Correk's eyes glowed just enough to warn the Willen as it trotted upright out of the room, dropping to all four at the hallway and disappearing from sight.

Correk tucked the book into his cloak and hurried through the castle to the nearest outside wall. "Altrea Extendia," he said, sending out a shower of bronze sparks forming into a spiral staircase.

He hurried down the stairs, the steps disappearing behind him, and across the grounds, slipping into the deep woods. They were dense with tall canopies that towered far above the Oriceran ground below, cutting off most of the sunlight. Many of the trees were species brought from Earth, most of them transported over thirteen thousand years ago before the portals closed.

The forest was rumored to be tended to by a gardener who was rumored to be part human, part Wood Elf who still made the occasional trip to Earth to bring back different seedlings to plant in his garden. No one dared try and stop him. It was rumored he even collected rare species of animals and insects, many of them dangerous, and set them free in the darker parts of the vast forest where no one was allowed. Tales were told about his exploits to young elves and that no one had ever met him. A scary bedtime story.

Correk held out a fireball lighting his way and left another one behind him to mark where he had turned. He was veering off the path created by the Wood Elves and into the darker parts of the forest that stretched to the mountain range in the far distance. It was a shorter route over the mountains to Rodania, the lands of the Arpaks and Nychts, winged men and women.

No one was ever known to take the shortcut and venture into the darkest parts of the forest where the trees grew even closer together and the wilder beings lived. But Correk walked down the path, taking sudden turns and ducking under branches with ease.

The forest was suddenly alive with sounds he couldn't quite place.

Nuts and leaves crunched under his feet as he tore aside vines and stepped over old logs, keeping a sharp eye for anything that might leap out.

He knew there were beasts, big and small that could cause him harm. Bugs that crawled under the skin to lay eggs dipped in a kind of acid, and large flying creatures with armored tails. Still, he kept moving.

"Crawk, craaaawwwk." He heard the sound of wings flapping and the branches of the trees fluttering but he couldn't make out what had just taken flight. Its screeches faded away over the canopy.

His eyes glowed and a compass appeared on the fireball, the needle slowly turning till it pointed due north. Underneath were the longitude and latitude of Oriceran. He was in the right spot.

"Show yourself. I don't have much time." He scanned the perimeter looking for any movement.

An old oak started to shake as if to shed all its bark. It was in front of a thick stand of elder trees, many of them covered in vines.

Two eyes blinked open, looking around for signs of movement. Each eye had two round, green irises with a dark black pupil in the center and each one moved independently of the other, sliding around the eye, looking in every direction.

Correk smiled, relieved. "We're alone, at least from anything that isn't interested in us solely as dinner. Show yourself. Completely."

A Wood Elf stepped forward and small squares all over his body began to flutter and turn, flipping over and changing the surface of his entire body from the texture of the nearby oak tree to the smooth brown complexion. The irises all slid toward the center of the eye. The multiple irises helped him to take in information from a wide field of view, processing it into one complete picture. They were the great chameleons of the forest.

"Perrom, hold still!" warned Correk.

A yellow lizard the size of Correk's arm with bulging eyes that rotated independently, dangled from a nearby vine right by the Wood Elf's ear. The Elf's left irises moved to get a better look.

"It's merely a lizard," said Perrom. The scales along the elf's arms flipped over and over, blending in with the fauna and back to his natural state of honey brown.

"Move slowly. We're in the darker, uncharted parts of the forest. I have never believed any of the stories either, but now is not the time to find out I was wrong."

"I grew up in these woods, Correk. You know that."

"Doesn't mean you don't look like a snack."

The Wood Elf slowly turned his head to watch the lizard lazily open its mouth, unfurling its long, pointed tongue. At the end was a small green caterpillar with a large circle of red on its face surrounded by a black stripe. Two thin, red and white-striped antennas extended out the back, bobbing up and down. Two black eyes were fluttering, dazed.

The caterpillar turned over, curling into a tight ball and the lizard rolled its tongue back into its mouth. At the last moment, the caterpillar opened its mouth wide, revealing a pair of sharp incisors it used to rip off half of the lizard's face. The lizard let out a sharp squeal, opening its mouth again, trying to shake the caterpillar loose, but it was too late.

Perrom took a step back, the squares all over his body flipping over again, blending back into the surroundings. The irises of his eyes spread out, keeping watch.

The caterpillar opened wide and bit down again, tearing off another chunk. The lizard fell to the forest floor as the caterpillar chewed, dragging off the squealing lizard.

When it was over the Wood Elf stepped out again, his appearance returning to their resting shade.

"It's good to see you again, Perrom." Correk watched the caterpillar's retreat with a shake of his head.

"After that little display, I'm not so sure. Your insistence on meeting in the dark part of the forest is foolish. My kind live among the trees and even we never travel through these parts."

"That's why I chose it. It was the only place I could think of where we could be assured no one else would be watching." Correk shifted his position, moving his foot away from a sand pile filled with fire ants.

"I've known you most of your life. You aren't usually big on the drama. What's changed?"

"Too many things." Correk pulled out a small figure-eight

made of metal with a green scarab in the center. There were two figure eights intertwined on the back.

Perrom drew back, the skin along his arm and face fluttering as he tried to decide whether or not he should stay.

"Where did you get that?" he demanded, horror rising on his face. "Those were all destroyed over six hundred years ago. Do you know what you're holding?"

"I'm well aware that it's the amulet from a Rhazdon follower."

"Not just any follower. That's the scarab of an elder. If that's the familiar of an elder, it contains very powerful dark magic. Where did you get it? Surely the Gnomes didn't give you something like that? Dammit! They have Rhazdon's dark magic in that damnable vault too?"

Correk turned the amulet in different directions, looking at the details. "Slow down. It didn't come from the Gnomes. I believe it came from a Rhazdon follower. A current one."

The skin on Perrom's arms fluttered again and the irises in his eyes moved in different directions, looking for anyone or anything close enough to hear them.

"Not possible! They've been dead for over eight hundred years! Since the uprising! Our elders made sure to exterminate every last one of them. Every warring faction came together to make sure that happened. They worshipped darkness and drew it into their magic! They were the cause of the last wars!" Perrom was practically shouting.

The birds overhead took flight, squawking and tweeting and a large brown snake slithered through the branches overhead.

"Keep your voice down. I'm telling you it's from a follower. I found it in the village where the prophets stay when they gather to meet. I think it belongs to one of them."

Perrom put his hands on the top of his head, trying to take in what Correk was saying.

"Impossible. The prophets have one purpose. To talk endlessly about the seer, Tessa and interpret the quatrains! They care about nothing else, especially as we get closer to the opening of the portals. You and I have both stood before each of them. It's more likely one of them foolishly kept this as a souvenir. Rhazdon and his kind are gone from this world."

"What if they've learned to disguise themselves, like you but using dark magic?"

Perrom held up his hands. "No, no, impossible. If what you're saying is true, then some of the rules we live by, the treaty, would be lies."

"I was about to leave to meet you when a Willen tried to steal my ring. I gave it to him in exchange for one of his riddles. He said to look for one among the prophets who is long extinct. The Willen has seen the imposter."

"Two moons! May the forces help us. Rhazdon's followers were barely defeated and at the cost of hundreds of good magicals. To think that someone has been inspired to take up Rhazdon's twisted cause? There's no one left now who would even remember how his magic was defeated. Your father tried to use the same magic years later and look…"

"Don't bring my father into this," said Correk, between gritted teeth. "I need your help, and whether you like it or not, you owe me. The Willen claims there are forces, good and bad, who are out to stop the human detective, Leira Berens from finding the prince's killer so they can take the necklace for themselves. I need to make sure that doesn't happen."

Perrom focused all his irises on Correk. "The king wouldn't be happy if he knew you told me about his plans. What's my part in this?"

"I need you to watch over things here if I get sent through a portal. Don't act surprised. We both know that magicals have been taking chances and opening portals to Earth for a long time."

"I've never tried it. Wood Elves have died or worse, ended up in the world in between."

"Getting caught would be worse. Trevilsom Prison."

"Put that thing back in your pocket." Some of the scales along Perrom's face flipped over to match the vines behind him, making it appear that half of his head was gone. A nervous tic. "Be careful with it. Energy could be seeping out of it and poisoning you already. Never underestimate their magic or what a Rhazdon admirer would do to another living being just for fun." Perrom shuddered, remembering the stories from the wars.

"If I go through a portal, no matter what, keep watch on this side. You can transform into your surroundings. Tell no one unless you have to and be careful," said Correk. "When we know more, we will expose the imposter prophet together." He grabbed Perrom by the shoulders, ruffling the surface of his skin.

"First, we will have to figure out which one of the fifteen prophets is the liar."

Correk gripped the ring in his hand till his knuckles were white. "That's where this archaeologist will help us. Someone powerful helped him into the castle without being seen. We have to find him and bring him to justice if we're going to get the whole story."

CHAPTER THIRTEEN

"I'm supposed to be looking for a killer." Leira pulled the Mustang onto Parmer Lane heading back to the station.

Hagan took another large sip of his coffee and swallowed slowly. "First part of this whole story that makes sense. Go on."

"The killer was a human being who somehow made his way onto their turf and killed a prince. Stabbed him clean through and stole a kind of magical necklace. Not all of it makes sense to me, yet. There's a steep learning curve."

"No fucking kidding," said Hagan.

Leira glanced over at a man looking down every few seconds, driving with one hand. She blared the siren, glaring at him. He looked up startled and dropped the phone, putting both hands on the wheel. Hagan leaned forward and chuckled. "Nice catch. I know they're sure, but are you sure they're after the right guy?"

"As sure as I can be. I saw Bill Somers do it, well kind of saw him. On Oriceran dead bodies can do a kind of instant replay of the last hour but it only lasts for a few days."

"I know that this family of what, elves? Whatever. I can understand they want to see justice, whatever that adds up to on their side, which is another potential problem, Berens. But, why do you have such a hotfoot to solve it?"

"That magical necklace goes off like a timer in a little more than a week, maybe less and will transfer the energy to whoever is in possession of it. I don't have much time left to find him. When their two moons are full again the power is released."

"This is a lot to take in. Two moons, no less. A necklace that can transfer magical energy. This Somers is a magician too, I take it."

"Something like that, maybe not, but I think he has to know how to use it. Kind of fifty-fifty about whether he's got the skills. He's an archaeologist, I don't know much more but I need to find him, and I have to hurry."

"And you have to take your tiny friend with you."

"It's a duckling kind of thing. I saved his life and now he's imprinted on me. If I'm understanding the directions that came with him, where I go, he goes," Leira grimaced. The lump in her pocket stirred and the troll poked its head out.

"Smile at him, Hagan. Let him know you're friendly."

"How do you know it's a him? Did you check? They would have to be tiny." Hagan looked at the troll, doing his best version of a smile, resisting the urge to pull his weapon. The troll trilled and mirrored his smile at him.

Leira gave him the dead fish look and rolled her eyes. "I'm going with my gut. the troll is attached to my emotions and is not always good at reading the room. Geez, is that what I look like when I smile?"

The troll leaped out of Leira's pocket, grabbing Hagan's moustache, and started licking his face.

"Holy crap!" yelled Hagan, not sure how to get the troll to let go. "What the fuck is it doing?"

"Yum… fuck…" The troll dropped down on the seat, sitting between them, licking his paws. "Yum… fuck…"

"What you get for smashing doughnuts in your face. I think Mickey licked off the rest of the icing for you," Leira smiled.

"That's not his real name, you know."

"What, you have a better idea?" She merged the car into the next lane, speeding up.

"Yeah, it's obvious," he shrugged. "It's Yumfuck. Hey, look, he loves it!"

"He loves the doughnut." She couldn't help herself, smiling at the troll, who was crawling up her sleeve to sit on her shoulder.

"Yumfuck Tiberius Troll. That's his name," Hagan said, satisfied. "What? Gives it a little polish. Who doesn't love James T.?"

"You are too much." Leira gripped the steering wheel a little tighter. "I need to research Somers without getting caught before I go on leave. Any thoughts on that?"

Hagan reached out his hand to try and pet the troll's head, but the troll threw back his head and howled and Hagan pulled back. "When are you taking off? You don't have a lot of time and you don't know where he is right now. He's in this world, right?"

"Yeah, that's why they needed me. Non-magical detective for hire. Apparently, their magic doesn't translate very well here. Go figure. They needed a professional who knows how to detect the non-magical way."

"There's the whole getting caught and not being human part too," said Hagan. "That has to have crossed their minds."

"You're not quite buying all of this, are you?" asked Leira, glancing at him as she pulled into the precinct's parking lot.

"Hard to completely deny with the small green-haired friend here. But, not entirely wrapping my arms around the idea that there's a whole other world and my kids' movies with flying carpets are real. Was there a little mermaid too?"

"I didn't see a carpet or a mermaid but I'm not the expert on Oriceran. Frankly, they got tired of my questions pretty quickly."

"When you ask the Captain tell him it's a family thing. You need some time off. Be vague," he said, waving his hand.

"Vague," squeaked the troll, waving arms in the air.

"I think Yumfuck likes you." Leira scooped up the troll, wrapping him back in her underwear, and sliding him into her jacket.

"Oh joy, my usual level of fandom. Come on, why underwear?" He looked up at her. "I have to ask." He slid out of the car, remembering at the last moment to grab the pink box. He looked inside and saw small bite marks in the Grape Ape. "Not cool, Yumfuck! Not cool," he said, and slammed the door.

A muffled, "Vague… yum… fuck…," came from Leira's pocket and she took a slow, even breath.

"Sounds like a rock band my son would like," Hagan told her.

"What kind of family thing could I bring up with the Captain?" Leira got out of the car and walked across the hot parking lot. "Austin in winter messes with my head sometimes," she said, trying to change the subject.

"It's a warm spell. You grew up here, you know this. We dress in layers year-round except for summer when we wear as little as possible." Hagan startled, and his face grew warm. "Shit, sorry about that, kid. Right, what family? You claim that bar owner who leases you the guesthouse out there as some kind of relative, and there's all the regulars. Think about them when you're saying it. Then, not so much of a lie. Will come off more believable."

"You don't think the Captain will remember I don't have any family?"

"Aw, come on. Lots of people have some distant cousins tucked away somewhere that they'd show up for their wedding or a funeral or something." Hagan stopped and shook his head. "He's not gonna ask you a lot of questions. It's the Captain. Details of our private lives are not his thing. How it affects the job is his only concern. It's one of his finer attributes."

"Completely agree." Leira looked back to see if there was anything unusual around the Mustang. The fireball was already well hidden in the engine, waiting for her return.

"Geez, I'm still hungry." Hagan patted his belly, adjusting his pants higher. "Maybe I need some protein or something. Think I still have that jerky in my desk Rollins gave me for my birthday."

"I think Rollins meant that as a joke and that's faux food, Hagan. Worse than a doughnut."

"Meh, before it was processed it started as real meat. That'll do. Lasts forever. Oh, hey, wait a minute."

The older detective fished around in his coat pocket and pulled out a short strip of jerky, brushing off the lint and a few crumbs, turning it over to inspect it for anything else that might be clinging to it.

"Huh," he said, satisfied, tearing off a piece with his back teeth.

"You think food is supposed to be that hard to chew?" asked Leira, trying to look away.

She felt the troll move around and poke his head out of her pocket, sniffing the air.

Her partner looked down. "Look at that! Little fellow has a pretty good sense of smell. Here, you want a piece?" asked Hagan, holding out the jerky. The troll lunged forward, sinking its claws into the jerky, snatching the whole piece and dragging it back into the pocket.

They could both hear the gnashing and tearing followed by more than one long slurp.

He shook his head in wonder. "You should just burn that underwear at some point, Berens. Lost cause."

"Good tip, Detective. Do me a favor. Try not to engage in conversation with Yumfuck while we're in there. And no food references either. None," she said firmly, as they got to the door.

He smiled. "Anything to avoid bringing down the Feds over something smaller than my..."

"Don't go there," said Leira, screwing up her face.

Hagan scowled, pulling open the door. "Not in front of you. I was gonna say my hand. All this time we've been driving together, and you haven't noticed that I keep it pretty Mr. Clean, for the most part. I know I swear less than you. Fuck this, fuck that. You have a potty mouth, Detective."

Her pocket squeaked, "Fuck yum!"

"Don't say that word either," Leira whispered, as they headed down the hallway.

"We're going to get caught and interrogated in some subterranean site where everyone wears black and has no sense of humor," muttered Hagan. "Hey, how's it going?" He nodded to an officer passing them in the hall.

"Stop watching TV late at night after a lot of pizza." Leira turned around long enough to give him the dead fish look.

"That look is still oddly comforting," he said and glanced up the hallway, "Eyes front, Captain incoming."

"Berens, you wanted to see me. Now's a good time," he said gruffly, turning for his office without waiting for an answer. She was used to his style of leadership. Assume everyone already agrees with you. At least it was efficient. Leira liked that much about him, anyway.

He never asked her how she was feeling or wanted anything resembling a conversation. Just the facts, in and out, and on your way. Leira was counting on that today to get her out before anything jumped out of her pocket.

"Shut the door," he said, as he took a seat behind his desk, checking his phone for messages. He looked up when Leira didn't move to sit down but stayed by the door.

"It's really not that big of a thing." Leira kept her pocket turned away from him, her hand on the outside.

"Okay, well, you rarely ask for anything so it's some kind of deal. Take a load off, act like you're in the room."

Leira took in a deep breath and let it out slowly, picturing the sweet tackle of a suspect from last week when she had to keep pace with him for well over a mile, waiting for him to get tired. It made her relax, even almost smile, to think about the nervous glances he kept throwing over his shoulder, checking to see if she was still at his heels.

She thought he was going to just give up and stop at one point, but he got a second wind and kept going just as Leira closed the gap and caught him round the waist, knocking him to the ground. Yeah, that was a good one.

She heard soft purring from her pocket. That's new.

The hum of the air-conditioning masked the sound from traveling very far in the room.

"I uh, I have a family kind of thing. I need a few days off, maybe a week, starting tomorrow so I can travel to... uh, where they are, and handle it," she said, haltingly. Lying was never her strong suit, at least outside of an interrogation room. There it was a necessary tool.

Breathe, Berens.

The Captain looked away from his computer and held her gaze. Leira kept talking, hoping there were no questions coming her way.

"I checked with Hagan, and he's fine with it. We have no major cases right now and nothing headed to court for at least a couple of weeks."

"You never take any time off," he said, still looking directly at her.

"No, that's true." She admitted. "Not very good at down time, I suppose."

"Geez, it's about time. Take an extra day. Go to a movie or something."

"Great, okay, well, great," she said, slowly rising from the chair. "So, good talk. Okay, well, you have my contact info if you need me."

"Leira, these days we can track you no matter where you go or what you do. You'd have to leave the planet," he snorted.

Leira almost tripped over her own feet. "Right, leave the planet, sure."

Her pocket squawked. The Captain arched an eyebrow but Leira wasn't sure what he'd noticed.

He pointed a finger at her, pursing his lips for a moment. "And even then, you'd need to get out of the range of the satellites flying over our heads before we couldn't pinpoint your location. Once you log into the internet and get yourself a smart phone, your chances of being a no-name hermit are over." He went back to looking at his computer. A sign he was done talking.

Leira gave him a curt nod and stepped through the door, ready to escape. The Captain was being chattier than his normal five words that equaled an entire conversation.

Bad timing.

"Good to hear you've got some family," he muttered, typing with two fingers.

It caught Leira off guard and for a moment she froze, remembering again she was only twenty-five but had no real tribe to celebrate with or complain about to friends.

Enough, she thought, as she left the Captain's office. "Not even true. I have a tribe, of sorts."

CHAPTER FOURTEEN

"What's the word from the Captain?" asked Hagan, as she sat down at her desk.

"I got the time. Was easier than I expected." She reached for a pen and flipped open a folder.

"I was beginning to wonder. You were in there a little while."

"Yeah, he was saying something weird about how easy it is to track anybody. You know, he's right. A possibly dangerous wizard-to-be terrorist is a good reason to use Travis County resources to track down a suspect, right? The more detailed the background, the better."

"How will you know when you've found the right Bill Somers, archaeologist? It's not like you brought back fingerprints or background on him." Hagan opened a drawer, rattling loose pens, an old pager, and some paper clips till he found the post-it notes.

"Remember, I saw him do it. That virtual world in the here-after. I know what he looks like."

"What are you going to do once you have him? They give you some kind of magical saying to yell or a magical burner phone to get in touch?"

"All good and also weird questions. They said they'd know.

They're very big on tracking things in this world or the other," she said, typing in the physical description, approximate age, profession and the name, Bill Somers. It didn't take long for his driver's license photo from Chicago to appear on the screen.

"Got him! He's a professor at a university in Chicago. Look, easiest thing I've done all day. There's his address." Leira swung her screen around for Hagan to see.

"Found him on Facebook." said Hagan, slipping on his reading glasses to get a better look. "He posts a lot about Egypt and something he calls green sectors, or something. No pictures of his food, I like that about him."

"Too bad about the killer thing."

"Yeah, that's a major strike against him." Hagan leaned closer, nodding. "Look, be careful. This guy looks as nervous as a virgin at a prison rodeo, but he managed to get the drop on a magical elf. No elf on the shelf either, from your description. Don't drop your guard, don't take too many chances, and don't do anything that will end up getting you arrested. It'd be a tough one to explain. Just find the necklace and click your heels together three times or blink really hard and hand it over, so you can come home."

"You know, Hagan, the easy part is going to be finding him. It's everything after that will be a bitch to pull off."

"It's just a couple of days, a week at most. You're good at what you do, you'll find him." Hagan leaned back in his chair, taking of his glasses. "I'll hold down the place while you're gone but if things go south, I'll be on the next plane north. Don't let me find out you didn't know how to ask for help," Hagan said sternly.

Leira thought about giving him a hug but rejected the idea as a little too dramatic and instead ended up patting him on the shoulder.

"I'm touched," he said. "Oh yeah, if that troll operates off your feelings, you're screwed. You have basically one channel. Hunker down and get it done."

"Not a bad channel."

"Does make me feel better that you'll be taking an insta-grow guard dog with you in your underwear pocket, there. At least I know if some weird shit breaks out and weapons from one world or another are drawn, you have some firepower on your side."

"Thanks, Hagan. I'll call you after I hand the necklace over."

"Let me know how you contact them. Maybe it's some magic word shit."

"Fireballs, glowing fireballs. I'm pretty sure that's how they do it."

"Like an iPhone one thousand."

"Something like that, yeah. I'm going to go home and pack and hit the road. I'm pretty sure I don't want to chance flying with a magic troll in my pocket who doesn't do well in angry situations. There are no friendly skies these days. Cover for me, okay?"

"Let me know you got there safely. No phone blackouts."

"Sure," she said, as she waved goodbye and headed down the hall. She managed to get out to her car and on her way with no more troll incidents.

Leira found a spot on Rainey Street just a house down from Estelle's and walked through the side gate to the guest house. The lunch crowd was just finishing up and the regulars weren't there yet, leaving the streets fairly empty right by the bar.

At the other end of Rainey, the food trucks were still going strong, serving the tourists plenty of brisket and barbeque, tacos of every kind, Thai or Indian food, alongside oversized cupcakes with cream fillings, or shaved ice. There was even a vegan truck doing a steady business selling raw smoothies.

Leira thought of the parking lot as her grocery store.

She came through the gate lost in thought and looked up at the sound of a greeting.

"Hey honey!"

Leira would know that raspy voice anywhere. Estelle was sitting at the outdoor bar that stretched across the back of the patio, smoking a cigarette. The smoke swirled around her teased red bouffant giving her a few more inches of height.

"What are you doing home so early? Shift's not over yet."

"You keep track of my work schedule?" Leira dug for her key in her oversized purse. She balanced it on one knee, tilting it toward the sunlight.

"Somebody has to. You don't look sick. You forget something?"

"Taking a few days off. Driving up to Chicago. You watch the place for me?"

"Well, it's about damn time." Estelle took a long drag on the cigarette, squinting up at her. "Though why you have to go so far away to have a little fun is beyond me. Chicago. I suppose that's a certain kind of fun. I'd say I'd water your plants but we both know you're not into roommates of any kind."

Leira tried to smile, fidgeting with the key in the door.

"You locked the door? That's not your usual." Estelle gave her a longer look but Leira ignored the question. Estelle arched an eyebrow and blew out a steady stream of smoke. "Bring somebody home from Chicago. Let us vet him, if that's what you're worried about. We're like family. We'll give him the stink eye and ask all the wrong questions. It'll feel more like home," Estelle called after her. Leira waved and shut the door.

She dropped her purse on the red velvet chair by the door. She went to the bedroom and dug out her old blue suitcase with a faded sticker from Schlitterbahn amusement park from the closet, hoisting it onto the bed. She gently worked her way under the underwear in her pocket, scooping out the troll, and set both on the bed next to the suitcase where she could keep an eye on him.

"Yumfuck. The name suits you somehow."

He opened one eye and stared at her.

"I'm going to ignore the side eye and get packing. We have a long, strange trip ahead of us, straight up the middle of the country."

It was going to be a seventeen-hour hard drive from here to there and the sooner she got started, the better.

She hunted through her small, narrow closet for every sweater she'd ever owned, and anything else that looked like it could add warmth. Leira had spent her entire life in Austin and wasn't even sure what a Chicago winter would feel like, other than bone-chilling cold.

"I remember these," she said, pulling out a handful of tights in every color that she got years ago when she was going through a phase. "Ugh," she said, throwing them into her suitcase. "Not sure what I'm going to do about a real winter coat. Never needed one before. Where's that ugly scarf Estelle's niece made me?"

She went to the living room closet and dragged out the milk crate shoved to the back. "Here it is, oh yeah, a hat. Score." She tried on a grey knit hat with a large red pom-pom on the top.

"This I can do something about." She pulled off the hat and bit the yarn that held the pom-pom fast, grinding the stitches between her teeth till it fell off. "Much better."

She dug further and found an old pair of dark brown leather gloves that Craig and Scott, two regulars from the bar, had given to her a couple of Christmases ago.

"Done. Here's hoping a t-shirt, sweater, and a Texas-style winter coat will work long enough to grab Bill Somers and beam him up, Light Elf."

She went back to the bedroom to check on the troll. He was digging down into her suitcase, about to bite down on a shoe. His mouth was wide open, an even row of sharp little teeth poised over the toe. She quickly pulled him away and dropped him on the bed, shaking a finger at him. He shook one back at her, smiling.

"It's going to be really hard to figure out how to discipline you if I can't get even a little angry. You'd just blow up like a Macy's parade balloon," she said, zipping up the suitcase.

She held up the pair of blue cotton underwear Yumfuck had been using for a nest and the distinctive odor of beef jerky wafted to her nose. "Oh no," she said, tossing them toward a trash can. "We're starting over. She dug for the back of the drawer where the old underwear was stashed and pulled out a green pair with yellow polka dots that came in an eight-pack from Target. "Never knew what to do with these, didn't want to throw them away. I sure didn't think this would be the reason I'd need them," she said, scooping up the troll and sliding him back into her pocket. "I'm gonna have to buy more underwear if this keeps up."

She pulled the suitcase off the bed and headed for the door. "Okay, we're off to see the fucking wizard. Hopefully, before he actually becomes one."

Out on the patio Craig and another of the regulars, Paul, were eating nachos and drinking beer. There was no sign of Estelle.

"Leira!" they called in unison, laughing. "Come join us! We're starting a new tradition. Happy hour starts right after lunch."

"Hey, what's with the suitcase?" asked Paul, glancing up from the guacamole he was loading on a tortilla chip. The chip broke under the weight.

"It's not a spoon, dude," said Craig. "Show a little restraint."

"Pay attention. Leira's got a suitcase. We've been parking ourselves here for a few years. This is a new behavior in the wild. You okay?"

"Taking a road trip to Chicago. Nothing's wrong, it's all good." If you can call chasing the killer of an elven prince, all good.

"Road trip!" Craig pumped his fist in the air.

"How are you two planning to get this new happy hour off the ground and keep your jobs?" asked Leira, trying to steer the conversation in another direction.

"Joy of being a pharmaceutical salesman," Craig replied. "It's Thursday, which all of my customers, the good doctors, call Friday Eve. They're already on the golf courses by now. Might as well come see Estelle."

"I took a half day," said Paul, smiling. "Marketing musicians in Austin is a tough gig, trust me. Live music capital of the world means there's a lot of competition. Needed a break. He's only planning to tap into the new happy hour every once in a while. Don't worry, others will come." He patted the seat next to him. "Come on, join us for a minute."

"You hear Diana got that gig at Banger's just down the street from here? She's playing with her new band this weekend," said Paul.

"'Fraid I'll have to miss that. Take some video and send it to me." Leira stopped for a moment near the gate.

"I can bring Peanuts with me," said Craig.

"I know dogs are welcome there but wasn't Peanuts banned for nipping at someone?" asked Leira.

"On probation and it was more of an enthusiastic bite of their hotdog. If he hadn't knocked over their beer no one would have mentioned it." Craig shrugged. "I bought a round for the table." He took a big gulp from a Shiner Bock. "Almost drove me nuts waiting for them to figure out what they wanted."

"Over a hundred beers on tap will do that to some. Amateurs. Stick with the proven," Paul chased a hot pepper around the nearly-empty plate with a chip, finally popping it in his mouth.

Leira managed a crooked smile. "I have to go but take it easy on the nachos. It's still early. You guys need to pace yourselves. Everybody else won't be here for hours."

"Hey, you gonna be back in time for bowling night?" Craig swiveled around and got up off his stool.

"I know you're not about to try and carry my suitcase for me," Leira said, staring him down. "I'm a detective, Craig. I got this."

"Hey, I was born and raised in Texas. Have to offer, every time. My momma would roll over in her kitchen, if she knew."

"Just feel it, sitting in her kitchen, huh?" laughed Paul.

"Be there for the bowling!" said Craig, as Leira picked up her suitcase.

"Can't make tonight. Will do my best for next week. I told you, with my schedule I can only be a floater."

"Playoffs start tonight! Semi-finals next week. Still good timing," he said. "Can we hug you?" he asked, getting back off his barstool.

Leira smiled and opened the gate.

"Like a creepy uncle hug," said Paul, slapping Craig on the back. "Come on, you can buy the next round. I'll let you."

Leira could hear their laughter as she worked her way around the side of the house. "Ladies and gentlemen, my family." She smiled again and threw the suitcase on the backseat, shutting the door. She got down on her hands and knees to look under the car. "I know you're under there. Let's not start this relationship on a dishonest note. Come on, Correk, show yourself."

A violet fireball the size of a softball slipped from between the engine parts, squeezing itself into a teardrop shape as it squeezed out, then rolled back into a perfect ball and bobbed just at the top of the front tires.

She peered under the car and glanced to her right and left. No one was nearby. "So, this is direct dial, and you can hear me in real time. I suppose magic is like that."

She looked at the ball, the light turning over and over inside the pulsing violet sphere, and she slowly reached out to touch it, to see if it was warm. Curiosity was always leading her down some strange and dangerous alleys.

As her fingers got close, she braced herself for scalding heat or a zap of electricity.

The pulsing light was warm on her skin and her fingers easily pushed past the membrane of the fireball. A cool, thin violet line shot up her arm, through her shoulder and out her eyes, making them glow. She opened her mouth and a puff of cold air emerged in the heat, quickly disappearing.

It all felt vaguely familiar, like a memory from a long time ago.

She wanted to leave her hand there and see what else might happen, but the light pulled back, staying just an inch or two away from her fingertips.

Her eyes glowed again, the light flickering in them, and she distinctly heard a voice say, "Get out of here." She rocked back on her heels, shaking violently, gripping the side of the car. It was a voice she hadn't heard in years and barely recognized. Her mother, Eireka Berens was telling her to run.

She took a deep breath. The troll screamed from inside of her pocket. "How did you do that from inside of a psych ward?" She looked back under the car and saw the fireball fade and disappear.

She got in the car fast before anyone came to see if there was a problem. How the hell would I explain any of this?

"You may not know this about me, but I don't run from a goddamn thing, Mom," she said as she drove off, the tires squealing. She made a point of keeping her eyes off the rearview mirror. The tips of her fingers still hummed, and her nails had turned violet.

CHAPTER FIFTEEN

Correk was sitting in his chambers at the top of the castle. A small room with just a bed and a nightstand but it served its purpose. He chose the smaller quarters mostly because of the glass cupola that stood in as its ceiling, giving Correk a panoramic view for miles, even when the castle could be seen hanging in the sky.

He was trying to decide if he should tell anyone else what had just happened. He saw the icy fire that had spread up Leira Berens' arm. Her eyes were glowing. Something had changed.

"That is impossible," he said, trying to make sense of it. "She can't be...We would have known."

A passenger pigeon fluttered outside the window at a small pane at the bottom, waiting for it to be cranked open. Even though the window was at present invisible, birds in Oriceran could still navigate the castle with ease.

"Hello Palmer." Correk held out his arm for the bird to land and the Light Elf pulled him inside. The iridescent brown feathers around its neck sparkled in the sunlight.

"You have some mail for me?"

The bird dropped the postcard in Correk's other hand. The

card was trimmed in silver and had the crimson stamp of the prophets. It was embossed with the word, Post Office in the center. It morphed into a ball of wiggling worms. He held it out to Palmer who made a quick meal of them, cooing as he slurped up the last one.

Correk eased Palmer back out the window and watched until the bird flew away. He strode out of his room and made his way down the hall to the side of the building where a door appeared to lead to just a long drop to the ground. He held out an arm and fiery symbols appeared on his hand.

"Altrea Extendia," he said, and a bronze staircase appeared heading down the side of the building. He took the steps two at a time, used to the long trek, descending past several others on shorter suspended staircases that only went from one floor to the next.

Druina, the teacher who had the unfortunate task of trying to educate young Eltor, was on a silver staircase carrying her marking book. Correk could see that it was locked with a thorny vine wrapped around it.

"Correk, rushing off? Don't forget you promised to come and speak to the class next week." She swirled her hand in the air, releasing a silver bird made of light that gradually grew feathers, disappearing into the clouds.

Correk waved and kept hurrying downward. A postcard invitation from the prophets could not be ignored or even put off till later.

Correk looked up and saw several other passenger pigeons leaving different windows of the castle, finishing up the afternoon mail drop, and flying back to the post office. The birds were kept by the gargoyles who operated a mail system out of an old apothecary that had once been the sanctuary of the Atlanteans who had emigrated to Oriceran thousands of years ago.

Correk made his way across the open pasture and past the

royal gardens and headed down the mossy path toward the post office on the far side of the Light Elves kingdom. Giant oaks hundreds of years old hung their heavy, leafy branches over the path, dappling the sunlight. Trolls jumped in and out of the large twisted roots where they were known to build nests, and a cloud of red and orange pinching bees swirled around a branch high over his head, building a hive.

He crested a hill and saw the post office in the distance. The imposing building rose high out of the mist. The gargoyles had never seen the need to hide the building. It was one of the oldest landmarks on Oriceran.

It was built out of pale yellow stone from a nearby quarry that was now a fresh water swimming hole used by elven children and stocked with fish, including one mislabeled tadpole that had grown into a hundred-foot lizard that kept mostly to itself at the very bottom, hundreds of feet below.

Correk liked to go there and sit under the ancient elms when he needed a quiet place to think.

It had been easy to convert the building into a post office once the potion books were transferred to the Gnomes' vault at the back of the library and the medicinal herbs were carefully moved to a secret location.

The one-room building stretched upward for a thousand feet and was a perfect square, each wall was five thousand, two hundred and eighty feet. One mile exactly.

Correk entered the vast building and took a moment to look up at the crested gargoyles carrying out their duties, sorting thousands of pieces of mail in a moment. There were hundreds of them flying around in the center of the building without ever colliding. The nimble workers opened and shut thousands of drawers that stretched from floor to ceiling.

The walls of the post office were covered with wooden boxes of every size that were created from the enchanted part of the forest, each with a narrow brass handle. They were a remnant from the days of the Atlanteans.

Every box had once held one of the thousands of ingredients the ancient tribe had used for their magic. Many of them were now forgotten or kept secret by the Gnomes in the library.

The crested gargoyles were highly prized for their work ethic and their ability to focus on a task. No bigger than a Gnome, their bodies were covered in oversized gold scales that rippled as they moved, claws on their back legs that ended in a tail with a razor-sharp point. Their heads flaunted a deep black crest that ran to the base of their tails.

The bottom boxes were rented out to different elven societies and some dwarves, while the vast array of boxes that hovered higher up were used by the prophets for official business. They never clarified what that meant and weren't about to start.

Correk passed the large bronze plaque that read, Dedicated to the memory of Tessa, the mother of the Word. Etched in the bronze was an elderly blind woman with children gathered around her.

He glanced at the plaque as the figure of the bronze woman moved around in her seat and the children at her feet squirmed. A small girl looked directly at him, holding his gaze for a moment. The art enchantment spell was one of his least favorite. Too lifelike, he thought as he shuddered and hurried through the building.

A group of schoolchildren were gathered near the entrance with their teacher, listening to a Wood Elf explain the history of the post office and the seer, Tessa, depicted in the plaque. Every elven child was taught in school about the seer, Tessa who spoke in quatrains, predicting the future. Four-line riddles that were scribbled down by the Gnomes and then left to the interpretation of the prophets. Her predictions talked about every aspect of Oriceran life for thousands of years to come and underlined the foundation that kept everything running smoothly. So many of them had already turned out to be true.

The bronze memorial was created upon her death, well over a century ago. Her death was also shrouded in secrecy.

One of the boys was sticking out his tongue at the plaque, trying to make someone in the magical depiction grimace back at him.

Correk smiled, waiting for the trick that someone had cast over the plaque.

A small bronze boy turned and looked at the child standing in front of the plaque, his tongue still sticking out, crossing his eyes. He laughed when he saw someone looking back at him.

The figure in bronze hooked his finger and beckoned at the child to come closer. He leaned in and the head of the boy in the plaque turned into a timber howler, the hairy apes that lived in the trees. The head grew in size until it was larger than the child in front of him and stuck out of the plaque, opening its wide mouth, jagged teeth shining in the light, giving its signature howl.

The elven school boy fainted dead away, hitting the marble floor with a loud thud.

"That should cure him of any more pranks," said Correk.

"I remember when you had the very same trick played on you, Correk." It was his old teacher of basic elven magic, Lucenda. It was the custom for elves to not take a last name and were known by their tribe.

"I had a headache for a week."

"Nonsense," said Lucenda, waiting for the boy to get back on his feet. She adjusted the voluminous blue robes around her short, stout body. Her long silver hair was tied back in a neat braid rolled into a bun.

"Sorry," the boy said when he came to, rubbing the back of his head.

Lucenda gave a satisfied, "Hmph," and waved her hand over his head, her eyes glowing, turning a brighter blue. "Portasus," she said, and the top of the boy's head glowed briefly. It was a basic healing spell.

"I hope you've learned something about respect for your elders," she said. He nodded earnestly at her. "I don't mean me. For Tessa, or her formal name, Teressa Doe. Go on, go back to the group."

The Wood Elf waited till the child was back with the group before going on with the tour. All the while, the two irises of each eye were scanning the room, keeping track of everyone.

"They really make the best teachers," said Lucenda. "Never miss a thing."

"I don't remember you healing my head. You made me wait it out."

"You had a harder head." She gave a wink. "What brings you to the post office?"

"I got a postcard. The prophets want to see me."

"A silver postcard?" Her eyes widened and she bit her bottom lip. "Official business, very important. Then I won't keep you." She turned and patted the plaque. "Such a wonderful role model for everyone. So selfless."

The same small bronze boy turned and gave her a raspberry, sticking out his tongue.

"Cheeky!" said Lucenda, annoyed, marched back to the school group. "Should really get someone to remove that spell. It's just magical graffiti, I tell you."

No one asked much when it came to the inner workings of Oriceran. So much of it was hidden and dealt with by the prophets. After enough time passed, everyone took the system for granted.

Correk hurried to the rail system just past the mailboxes that would take him to the prophets meeting room.

The prophets were from every society on Oriceran. One per magical tribe. Their group was founded even before the death of the seer, interpreting the quatrains as she produced them. After her death it was discovered that she had hidden the last of the quatrains. Without her, these interpretations only became more complicated. Some thought convoluted.

The very last quatrain spoke of the next opening of the gates far in the future. Her words convinced the group that once the gates began to reopen the magic energy, the very life force of Oriceran would drain away to Earth, eventually ending in a cataclysmic explosion. Oriceran would cease to be.

"All aboard!" A crested gargoyle called out, folding in its wings.

The two-seat trolley that ran on the tracks that wove through the building, arrived with just one metal car. The gargoyle opened the gate and beckoned to Correk to take a seat.

"Hurry it up," it squawked. "Make sure all hands and feet stay inside of the car. We won't go back for missing parts."

The gargoyle rang a bell and gave the car a push as it took off. The steel tires squealed against the rails unrolling in front of the car and rolling up behind it. Seconds later, Correk found himself at the back of the building.

He got out just as another gargoyle gave the empty seat a push, sending the trolley speeding up the wall off to another destination. Correk looked up, wondering who could be up at the top of the building that would need a ride back down.

CHAPTER SIXTEEN

"Correk! Correk, you're late!" Ossonia, a tall Light Elf who worked closely with the prophets had a ledger under her arm and was tapping her foot. Correk tried not to smile when he was around her.

He didn't want her knowing his crush dated a hundred years ago, back when they were in school together.

He followed behind her quickly moving feet, trying not to notice her long brown tresses bouncing from side to side as she walked.

She raised her right hand, making signs with her fingers as fiery symbols flared. The mailboxes in front of them flipped over and over, revealing a door.

"What's a back door doing here?"

"Not a back door," Ossonia replied. "Just a door."

It slid open, disappearing into a pocket, revealing a large chamber with four levels of gallery seats ringing the room. This was where they spent their days getting ready for the golden year, issuing warnings, and working on ways to save as many of the living things on Oriceran as possible with a planned move to Earth.

Correk recognized some of the prophets, giving a slight nod.

Down in the center of the room, beneath where the prophets sat, was a large, worn leather-bound ledger under a tall, glass dome. Correk knew from all the stories he was told as a child it was the book that contained all the ancient quatrains. The original notebook of the elder Gnome who recorded the blind seer's quatrains.

The sight of the prophets gathered together in the deep recesses of the post office, away from prying eyes, instantly darkened his mood. He scanned the room, wondering who could be a new follower of Rhazdon's methods, posing as a friend and an ally.

It wasn't going to be easy to ferret out someone powerful enough to remain undetected by the other prophets. After all, they were a suspicious lot by nature.

He needed to be calm and gather information. Take his time. Surely, there was time if the game had been going on for hundreds of years already. It had to be a slow-moving plot.

"Correk, please step into the center of the room," said an Arpak, a winged man, sitting on the second tier.

Correk complied, his face a mask. Twinkling lights descended, bobbing in the air. He looked up and was startled to see it was dark.

"It's just an illusion," Ossonia whispered from her nearby post. "The prophets find it calming."

"Do you know why we asked you here?" asked the Dwarf. He was dressed in an ill-fitting suit, a size too small. Dwarves were loath to wear anything but worn-out pants. The formality was not a good sign. They're worried about something. Correk took a look around the room until the Dwarf cleared his throat, drawing his attention back.

Over the Dwarf's suit was the customary blue robe with the two moons on the pocket inside of a large O. On the back, twinkling star systems radiated and changed position as the prophet moved around, staying aligned with the sky directly above them.

All the prophets wore the robe over their customary attire.

He took a deep breath before he answered, sensing what he said next would matter more than he realized. "The truth is, I do not."

He stole another look around the room, but no one looked uncomfortable or warier than usual. Of course, if it was true and there was an imposter in the room, whoever it was may have had hundreds of years to perfect their lie. There was no way of knowing when it all started.

A Light Elf named Kyomi stood up. "Correk is a Light Elf and therefore a Cousin. I will direct the remaining questions, as is customary. First, let me start by saying for the entire council, we are sorry for the loss of Prince Rolim. A great tragedy made more so by the usual peace that we now enjoy on Oriceran," said the older Light Elf. He had been serving on the council for over a hundred years.

"Thank you. I will see that the king and queen hear your condolences," Correk said, trying not to sound annoyed.

"That peace is a result of all parties, over thirty different intelligent species, agreeing to abide by the treaty. How much do you know of the Great Treaty?"

"I've learned the basic outline that the prophets require."

"Tell us—"

"Then, you know about the ban on opening portals between Oriceran and Earth?" asked the frowning Wood Elf prophet, cutting the Light Elf off.

Correk watched how the relationships connected, looking for clues. *Who is the traitor? The Wood Elf is a distant cousin of Perrom's. There are so many here I've never met.*

"Do not flaunt the rules!" Kyomi jumped to his feet, slamming his hand on the curving wood table in front of him. "You will

155

direct your answers only to me," he said to Correk and glared to the side at the Wood Elf. "Tell us, what are the three most important points of the treaty?"

Everyone is more short-tempered than usual. Even though Correk was only appearing as a courtesy to the council, he wasn't interested in insulting them. They held sway with too many people who believed in their readings of the quatrains. Besides, someone among them is an imposter. Don't let them know you're on to them.

"The sectioning of the lands between the different kingdoms. The respect for life and property, equally for everyone."

"And?" asked the elder Light Elf, before anyone could interrupt.

"The ban on opening portals between Oriceran and Earth before the next Gold Age."

"They were all put into place for the security and well-being of everyone on Oriceran. Would you agree?" asked the Crystal prophet, who had travelled from the most northern reaches of Oriceran for the gathering. His entire body was made up of solid icicles that protruded everywhere, and his presence was causing a chill in the air.

Correk slowly nodded his head. All the Wood Elf's irises were pointed at him. Their version of a cold stare-down.

"I'll need you to verbalize all of your answers, please," said Kyomi.

"Yes," Correk sang, his eyes glowing for a moment. He had let his anger get the better of him.

He knew where this was going. Leira Berens.

"Then can you explain why a portal was opened to Earth and a human who was unaware of our existence was brought to Oriceran?"

"We were in need of her help," he said, quickly deciding honesty was the best play to calm the council's fears. "It was a human that killed the Prince."

The prophets started to whisper among themselves.

"She could threaten our plans," blurted a wizard. "What if too many on Earth learn of our existence?"

"They could plan against us," said the Crystal prophet.

"Correk, you know this for certain?" demanded the Light Elf loudly, silencing the others. "Was it this detective?"

"No..., no, but we are certain it was a human. We saw the death revenant. The killer was a man who came here to steal from us. He took a very powerful amulet and escaped back to Earth. Out of respect for the treaty..."

"Stole an amulet?" the Wood Elf shouted. Correk noticed several of the prophets looked genuinely surprised. No one was giving themselves away.

"And because your magic wouldn't help you on Earth," Kyomi said flatly.

"Yes, that's true. That played a part as well. However, we demand justice for the death of the Prince as well as not wanting that artifact to give its power to the wrong person. For that to happen, we needed help. We chose the woman, Leira Berens, from a place called Austin, Texas."

"Why this woman? Isn't she a fairly new detective? New at the job of finding out who did something wrong?"

Correk realized they must have been watching Leira. As usual, overly vigilant when it comes to anything to do with Earth.

"Her skills are already proven in her world and her circumstances fit our needs. She has no one who would need a long explanation about where she was going and when she would be back."

"Or if things went wrong, would miss her," added Kyomi, looking down his long nose at Correk.

"Yes," he said, quietly. "That is also true."

"Did you know she took a magical creature with her when she left Oriceran?" Now it was Correk's turn to be startled as he let the surprise wash over his face before he could compose himself.

157

"Good. You are surprised. That's the problem with bringing a human into our world. They know nothing about the dangers of Oriceran. She must have rescued a troll while she was here. They are very determined pests. It went back with her," Kyomi said, his mouth a thin, annoyed line. "Damn troll," he muttered under his breath.

"There's a risk of exposure. Word of the troll has already spread," the Dwarf added, looking nervously around.

"Tell us about the stolen artifact. Convince us that the detective is not being used solely for revenge," said Kyomi.

Correk looked up at the sky. Orion was overhead with the Cassandra belt of stars. The same formation as the last Great Year. The prophets are nostalgic, he thought. Use it.

"The artifact was one of two pieces of lavender stone brought from Earth during the last Great Year. It held special powers to begin with but over the millennia, has been endowed with magic energy from every king of Oriceran. It rightfully belongs to the next heir to the throne when they become an adult."

"Why is this the first we're hearing of it?" asked a clearly angry Wood Elf.

Reminding them of the past had failed miserably.

"It is not my place to speculate."

"So, the necklace is familiar to the royal family and is not only a rite of passage, but a sign of their nobility," said Kyomi. "The energy that runs through it must feel so comforting, and now it's gone."

"Along with the prince's life," added Correk. "It could cause great harm in the wrong hands. It has to be returned and I ask you to understand that Queen Saria needs the man brought back to justice."

"Not revenge."

"No," said Correk, "Trevilsom Prison will satisfy." Trevilsom Prison was carved into rock on an island in the middle of the ocean. Correk had seen the effects of the prison on a dwarf who was caught trying to steal from the library. A rare book on forbidden magic that was promptly returned to the vault.

The dwarf came out of the prison unable to think straight long enough to cast a spell or sing a line of magic and was reduced to begging and taking odd jobs. It would be enough justice for the prince's killer.

The Light Elf prophet looked relieved at his answers. "Thank you for your rigorous honesty. We needed to be sure of your character because we have a favor to ask of you. We will need a moment to confer."

"Of course," said Correk, and stepped back to stand next to Ossonia. The prophets got up and gathered in a huddle on the third level, whispering to each other. It didn't take long before there was an agreement and they went and took their seats.

"Let us be clear. Your help is vital to us," said an Ogre that towered over the other beings sitting on the council. The robe was draped around his shoulders taking up yards and yards of material and was large enough for the entire constellation of Canis Major, the Great Dog. Other robes had only a few stars.

"Of course," said Correk, stepping back to the center, steeling himself for the request.

"We need you to go to Earth and assist Leira Berens in retrieving the necklace, the troll and the killer, without detection."

"You want me to go to Earth?" asked Correk, confused. "But the treaty?"

"We feel it's necessary to make an exception. You see, we are the ones who brought over Bill Somers in order to trade information. We will need to be the ones who apply justice."

"What?" Correk stumbled backwards, steadying himself by touching the glass dome.

"No," Ossonia gasped, when Correk made contact with the

159

MARTHA CARR & MICHAEL ANDERLE

glass. A sharp pain stabbed through his head and he recoiled, pulling back his hand. The pain lingered and he squeezed his eyes shut until someone muttered, "Portasus."

The top of his head cooled and the pain lifted.

"Why would you do this to us?" he asked, his voice rising. He was looking directly at Kyomi.

"We did nothing to you. We are only responsible for choosing poorly. We have our reasons and they're more important than everything that's happened. You will have to trust that the eventual safety of everyone on this planet was a worthwhile sacrifice," said Kyomi, holding up his hand to stop Correk from speaking.

"There is so much you don't know. Give it perspective."

"Do not ask me to understand any of this," Correk said angrily, his eyes glowing.

"Be assured," said the Wood Elf rising, his eyes aglow. "We are not."

The tension in the room rose as Correk felt the words of a spell cross his lips. A flame rolled out in front of him, licking at the robes of the Wood Elf. He waved his hand over the flame, putting it out before it could do any real harm, glowering at Correk. Ossonia stepped forward and stood by Correk's side. He could see that her ledger was trembling in her hands.

"This is not productive," Kyomi said. "Unless someone is considering breaking the treaty altogether, I suggest everyone calm down."

Correk flexed his hands, willing the symbols to fade back under his skin. "When do you need my voluntary help?" he asked. He wondered how he would face the king and queen and not tell them.

"Now," said Kyomi, and he opened a portal. "You are to stay for as long as it takes. Keep the detective safe and bring Bill Somers to us, along with the necklace. No one on Earth can know you are there. We have learned the hard way that human beings don't always do well with the truth."

On the other side of the portal was the interior of the green Mustang and Leira driving down the highway.

"What the fuck?" she blurted, hitting the brakes. "Yum fuck!" came from somewhere deep inside the car.

CHAPTER SEVENTEEN

"Of all the stupid shit!" Leira yelled, pressing herself against the driver's side door, yanking the steering wheel to the right, and veering off the road. The Mustang mowed down a green highway sign that snapped neatly in two. There was a loud hiss from the front of the car, and steam and smoke rose up over the hood.

The troll, sensing danger, sprung out of her pocket, growing larger and filling the car, making it even harder for Leira to keep it under control.

A man in a minivan looked over and saw her struggling to get away from a large, hairy creature baring its teeth and swerved across two lanes of traffic, barely missing a bus full of seniors on their way to a casino.

Leira was in no mood to try deep breathing and help the troll shrink to its normal size. She looked up to see Correk peering through the portal, a pretty female Light Elf by his side, both looking very worried.

A voice from somewhere on the other side boomed, "Jump!" and an enormous, hairy hand appeared, shoving Correk and sending him tumbling into the back seat of the car, headfirst. The female came through briefly, reaching toward Correk but she was just as unceremoniously yanked back into Oriceran then the portal sizzled and the image faded.

"This isn't a fucking bus stop, Bert!" yelled Leira, starting to see the wisdom in getting her heart rate under control. Yumfuck was still growing and was pushing against the roof. He had already put a long scratch in the seat from one of his claws.

"Not the leather, Yumfuck!" she ordered, making him growl and press his face up against the window. A driver sipping coffee did a double take, his eyes locked on Yumfuck. The troll opened its mouth to roar, baring its teeth.

They were in danger of getting found out before she'd even made it out of Austin.

Leira shifted into detective mode and calmly assessed the situation. She watched the driver stare at Yumfuck, shaking all over, spilling the coffee on his hand.

"Must be hot coffee," she said, as he moved his hand too quickly, spilling more. Leira made herself take a deep breath and even reached out to pet Yumfuck who was leaning against her, anyway. Correk would have to wait a minute.

He was swearing in the back of the car, pushing against the troll, who was practically sitting on his back. At least, Leira assumed that loud singing was swearing on Oriceran. It didn't take long before he let loose with a few he had picked up on Earth.

"Twinkle, twinkle, little star," she sang. It was the only song she knew all the words to.

"What the hell are you doing?" yelled Correk from the back seat.

"Singing. You should recognize it. You do it all the time. This was a favorite of mine when I was little. How I wonder where you are," she continued, rubbing Yumfuck's arm. The troll trilled and started shrinking.

The highway was starting to get backed up. Everyone in the

lanes closest to the Mustang was craning to get a better look. One driver had even lowered his window and was holding up a cell phone. Leira turned her head away, hoping he didn't get a shot of an oversized troll, a frustrated detective and an elf, rolling around in a Mustang. "It's like the start of a fucking joke," she muttered. There was no chance that wouldn't go viral.

Yumfuck shrunk until he was back to five inches and without Leira saying a word, he crawled into her pocket and curled up inside the pair of underwear waiting for him. She sighed with relief and took a moment before trying to talk to Correk.

"Ohm, Leira, stay calm," she said, shaking out her arms. She turned around slowly and found an angry Light Elf on her back seat, his hair mussed and his robe hanging off to one side.

"What the fuck are you laughing at?" Correk snapped. He caught a glimpse of himself in the rearview mirror and patted his hair down.

"So, you know a few of Earth's finer swear words as well. Very useful stuff. It'll help you blend in," she said. "Uh oh, this isn't good. Don't say anything."

The red and blue flashing lights on top of the Travis County police car could be seen from a distance, weaving in and out of the heavy traffic. Leira knew they were searching for the green Mustang. She pulled out her badge while there was still time and waited, holding it and resting her hands on the wheel.

"Way too many opportunities for me to keep getting pissed off," said Leira. "But, no, not with my feel-ometer right next to me, alerting the world with a growth spurt."

"I believe I warned you not to rescue a troll in the first place," Correk said, turning around to watch the approaching lights.

"No one likes somebody who has to be right, Bert."

"Correk."

"What?"

"Correk, my name is Correk," he said, doing his best to control his own anger and not sing the words.

"Well, then, Correk, it sounds like your voice is breaking and you finally hit puberty. How about if we leave all the talking to me and you sit way back in the seat and say nothing at all," Leira said.

The black and white police cruiser pulled up neatly behind the Mustang, the lights still spinning. The traffic slowed even more. She did her best not to look in their direction.

She kept an eye on the rearview mirror and watched as the officer called in her plates. "Good," she mumbled, "he'll find out this is a slick top."

She watched him get out slowly and walk over to her window where he could see the badge she was clutching between her fingers. He signaled to her to lower the window and she removed one hand to push the button. He glanced back at the lines of traffic and then at Leira, a look of confusion on his face.

"He's wondering where the monster is," whispered Correk.

"Not now," hissed Leira. "Shut Up."

"Aren't you Detective Leira Berens? I've seen you at the precinct" he said, bending down to get a better look at Correk in the backseat. He stifled a smile.

Leira refused to acknowledge that there was anything strange about having a grown man in what looked like a costume in the back of a police cruiser.

"Sir," he said, nodding at Correk. "Detective, are you okay? We got a report of a large wild animal, maybe a lion, loose in someone's car."

"Nothing like that here. We're in one piece with no animals on board. Just about to call a tow truck."

"You see anything? We got more than one call. They said a green Mustang. Any chance you saw another car like yours pass through here?" he asked, puzzled, peering into the distance as if the car would appear.

"Haven't seen another Mustang but I haven't been looking. No large wild animals of any kind either."

Correk cleared his throat and gave the cop a cross between a grimace and a tight smile. Leira saw the look in the rearview mirror.

"Yes, we're fine," she said, trying to distract the officer. "Headed out of town and thought I heard something rattling. Something must be up with the steering," she said, hoping her lie would pass muster. "I took out an innocent highway sign." She smiled, hoping the questions would stop.

"Sure it wasn't a lion?" asked the officer, smiling back. "Tear off a hose or something?"

Leira slid her right leg over just enough to cover the rip in the seat. It looked too new and she couldn't easily explain where it came from. He laughed like they were all in on a joke and leaned down to get a better look at Correk. She watched his face as he took in what Correk was wearing, and the pointed ears.

"Can you tell me where you're headed?" he asked, his smile growing wider.

"Chicago Comicon," said Leira, wondering how that idea came to her. "Big fans. Bert back there couldn't wait. He's Lord of the Rings. You know the story."

"That's a long drive to wear your costume the entire way. I admire your dedication. What's your costume going to be?" he asked Leira, bending down again to get another view of Correk who was rolling his eyes.

"A hobbit," she said, doing her best to own the statement. It was the first thing that popped into her mind. She could hear a snort from the backseat but kept looking at the officer.

"That's an interesting choice," he said. "You're from Region Two, right? Make sure you get a lot of pictures. There'll be a lot of interest."

Leira did her best dead fish look and added a hint of menacing. "You work in traffic, right?" she asked in an even tone. She was trying to push just enough to slow him down on sharing some of the details when he got back to the station, without annoying him to the point where he asked everyone to get out of the car.

The expression on his face changed and he stood up a little straighter, hooking his thumbs in his belt. Message received.

"Well, you get a tow truck here as soon as you can, Detective, and make sure they check out the steering," he said, giving her a sharp nod, and knocking the roof with his fist.

Leira instantly regretted being such a dick and started to say she heard there were openings in the CRASH unit when a high-pitched whine came out of her pocket.

"That's what regret sounds like from a troll," Correk whispered, leaning forward. "They're emotional truth-sayers, hobbit." He drew the last word out into two long syllables.

"You were going to say something, Detective Berens?" asked the officer.

"No, we're good. Thank you, Officer." She watched him walk back to his patrol car, glancing over his shoulder twice before finally getting in his car and speeding off, sending a little dust in their direction.

"Someone is going to get a helluva ticket off that guy today," she said.

"What's a ticket?" Correk asked.

"Yeah, that's the biggest question on my mind, too," said Leira sarcastically, twisting in her seat. The troll squeaked. "What if we start with, why the hell are you dropping in unannounced while I'm speeding down the highway, instead? Was it that big of an emergency?"

Yumfuck slipped out of her pocket and scrambled up to the top of the front seat, shaking his fist at Correk.

"Trolls are annoying in general," he remarked, plucking the troll off the seat and depositing him next to Leira. "To answer your question, yes, it was an emergency but not for the reasons I was sent here. There are now two groups that seems to want Bill Somers and the necklace back, but for different reasons."

"Can you get up here in the front seat, so I don't look like a glorified Uber driver? You just squeeze the handle right there."

"We may not have the same level of technology," Correk said, climbing into the front seat, "but I've used a handle or two in Oriceran."

"I thought maybe with magic you didn't bother."

"Lazier than I aspire to."

"Going to have to get a tow truck out here. It's going to delay things for at least a day."

"Good, then we can talk about what you may find in Chicago."

"Good? I would think you'd be antsy to get moving. That makes no sense. You dragged me to your world, just one day ago, and told me to hotfoot it because this rock Bill Somers stole has a timer on it. I found him, and by the way, he's halfway across the country. A very long drive."

"You have planes. I've seen them. Yes, we can see you."

"Creepy and we'll talk about that later. But, I'm absolutely certain trolls aren't allowed on planes. TSA would have a field day."

"Go back to Austin," he said seriously. "There's a lot to explain and things have gotten a lot more complicated."

"Is that why you were sent here? I saw that big helping hand you got."

"That was the Ogre prophet. They felt you needed some assistance in order to get the job done in the time that's left."

"If that's true, why aren't they opening up a hole from Austin to Chicago and just shoving me through it?" she asked steering back onto the road.

"Portals between two places on Earth are even more dangerous for both the conjurer and the traveler. That's a last resort option."

"Good news. We're not at last resorts but it's more complicated. How complicated?" She looked over at Correk, settling himself on the seat and adjusting his tunic.

"Oriceran was not always a peaceful planet," he started.

"You're going back to the beginning of time? Fuck me."

"It's necessary if you're to understand all of the pieces of this puzzle."

"All of that magic literally crawling under your skin and you can't make people tell you the truth."

"Even magic has its rules and its limits. Breaking those rules or testing those limits has very real consequences."

"Here we call that prison," said Leira.

"We do as well. Trevilsom Prison in the middle of the largest ocean."

"How do you keep a magic creature in a cell? We have a hard-enough time with human beings. Can't figure out how to just hold down a regular job but they can make a knife out of almost anything."

"Trevilsom is cursed. Magic turns in on itself there and the mind follows. The entire island gives off a gas that only the jailers who are from the island can tolerate and remain sane. No one comes out of Trevilsom unchanged."

"That's not justice," Leira said.

"I've seen your justice system. I've been particularly interested in watching how you enforce laws. Your system has just as many problems and breaks just as many people."

"We're really going to have to talk about the watching thing," said Leira, her voice growing cold. She was learning how to get her point across without getting angry and growing a bigger troll.

Enough with the deep breathing, she thought. She called an old friend of her mother's who owned a repair shop. He came out with an old Toyota with one of his young employees following behind in a tow truck.

"Nice to see you again, Leira. Seems like the only time I hear from you is when a car breaks down."

"Sorry about that, Ralph," said Leira. "I meant to call you…"

"It's okay," he said, patting her shoulder with a leathery hand. "I expect it's tough to run into your mother's old friends. I get it."

"Same deal?" she asked.

"Same deal. You pay me cash, and no one has to know you bent up the police cruiser. Looks like your radiator. You're in luck. I think I have one that'll fit back at the shop. This really important?"

Leira nodded her head.

"Then, I suppose it'll be ready by morning. Promised your mother I'd look out for you, when you'd let me. You should let me more often," he said with a smile.

Leira didn't even wait for the Mustang to get on the bed of the tow truck. She gave Ralph a hug and drove off in the Toyota, looking at him in the rearview mirror. He gave her a wave and watched her drive off.

She took the Cesar Chavez exit and turned on to 5th Street, headed for home. Traffic was heavy along the popular route. It was the time of year when tourists from the north flooded Austin for the warm air and cold margaritas. Austin was never meant to be more than a sleepy capital of Texas. The roads were always clogged with cars and bikes.

It was all Leira had ever known and she was used to the slow crawl.

"You say this puzzle is key to this case. All you're talking about are some leads that look connected. Fine, tell me the whole story. If I can't get on the road, I'd like to know why," Leira looked over at Correk.

"And what might be hunting me," she asked him.

CHAPTER EIGHTEEN

"Thousands of years ago, all the different kingdoms of Oriceran were at each other's throat over as many different disputes, some of them even forgotten. Still, the fighting continued, and everyone lost people they loved."

"Including your family?"

"Everyone. Light Elves see everyone who is a Light Elf as family. We don't break into smaller clans like the Dwarves. The war raged on for hundreds of years, across generations and over many lands. It's a long story, and it's worth the telling but we don't have time for all of it now. Someday, I hope to tell you more."

"What finally ended the conflict?"

"A treaty was proposed. Not the first time that had happened, but this one came from the prophets. Like your Supreme Court. A ruling body that serves for life with a member chosen from every society. They oversee everything on Oriceran, across our entire world. Everyone was weary of hating their neighbor by then, and there was almost unanimous acceptance."

"I suppose the key word there is almost."

"Yes, it is. One tribe, the Atlanteans, refused to even listen.

They were a privileged race who did their best to forestall the treaty."

"Atlanteans like Atlantis, like underwater lost city?" asked Leira.

"There are connections. The Atlanteans are distant cousins of the race from Earth. Originally, they came from the sea and looked just like humans except for their hair, which were actually very clever tentacles."

"Here on Earth we don't normally refer to hair as clever."

"These tentacles are detachable and can be used to track others. It's racial memory from when they had to hunt for their food."

"You were going to say prey," said Leira. "That's what one of these Atlanteans would see me as, prey. I can assure you that's not the case."

"I agree or I would have already moved you somewhere safer. The Atlanteans managed to stay out of most of the fighting and were quite happy to let the rest of us wipe each other out. In the end, they were the ones wiped out."

"Sounds brutal," Leira said.

"It was complicated," Correk replied. "They had managed to stay out of much of the fighting by using dark magic. A kind of magic no one else was willing to practice."

"Even to stop a war?"

"They saw it as an outside issue for hundreds of years until there was talk of a real treaty. My father told me stories when I was a boy about the Atlanteans and how they were suspected of using their dark magic to plant seeds of jealousy and hatred in the different kingdoms. There were stories that the Atlanteans' dark magic was responsible for hardening hearts against each other and that's what had taken down earlier treaties."

"Like an epic tale of Dungeons and Dragons."

"That game was started by a Light Elf who lives among your people."

"So many questions I want to ask right now. Like a hundred different rabbit holes I could get lost in," said Leira, as she turned the car onto Rainey Street. The lunch crowd was in full swing with lines in front of all the food trucks. As usual, Carra's Taco Truck, painted a bright red with the lettering in yellow and blue had the longest line.

"But I'm more interested in how this all pertains to you showing up out of nowhere in my car," she said.

"The Atlanteans saw that the treaty was gaining ground and they did the unthinkable. They used a kind of dark magic that has only been used once before and was forbidden, even during the wars. They tried to send the prophets to the world in between. A nether world that is full of the living and the dead where nothing ever happens and no one ages. I think your people call them ghosts."

"That's really a thing?" she asked, a chill running down her back.

"The kings from all the realms, all across Oriceran, finally came together and in a battle that raged for days, weeks even, they managed to kill the Atlanteans. The ground was soaked with the blood of both sides, but the wars were over. Somehow, that tragedy from thousands of years ago reared up again, six hundred years ago to poison the mind of a half-Atlantean named Rhazdon who turned Oricerans from everywhere into his own apostles."

"A resentment that spanned across millennia is impressive," said Leira.

"He was seeking revenge and probably enjoyed the irony of using the different races to avenge his forgotten race. To join his movement every follower had to swear to purity of mind and embrace Rhazdon's philosophies."

"We'd call that a cult on Earth. I'm familiar with what it can do to human beings when they drink the poisoned Kool-Aid."

"Rhazdon didn't care about anyone or anything else.

Vengeance was his only motivation. To prove the Atlanteans, this part of himself he had embraced, were superior. He used his followers to cause dissent, eventually leading them into small battles that were only growing worse. The kings stepped in and there was one enormous battle that wiped out most of Rhazdon's followers. A great painting to commemorate the worst and best day on Oriceran hangs in our post office."

"So many things I want to ask. The only things in our post offices are wanted posters and ads for stamps."

"After that, lasting peace came to Oriceran," he said.

"An entire group of people had to be wiped out, twice. That is intense. What about their leader, this Rhazdon. What became of him?"

"The king of the Light Elves chased him into the castle. He was cornered in the tower when it began to burn in a fire set by magic, engulfing everything. Rhazdon was trapped inside. The tower collapsed. He couldn't have survived in the burning rubble. Their magic, their books, their potions, all of it was taken and locked away by the prophets. Gnomes protect it to this day."

"Sounds like a happy ending," she said. There was no place to park right in front of Estelle's, which was unusual for Leira. She even circled the block once, she was so sure that something would open up.

Instead, a Chevy truck backed out of a space in front of the food court and Leira gave in, sliding into the spot.

"I suppose my luck had to run out sometime," she said. She started to open her door but Correk grabbed her arm.

"There's something more to the murder of the prince. The pieces all fit into something. The Prince's murder by a human being, the Willen warning me of something not extinct. Then, there's the scarab," said Correk, pulling a small drawstring pouch out of his pocket. He reached into the pouch and pulled out the green stone set into a scarab. He turned it over to show Leira the figure eight, the sign of infinity.

"This is a symbol of Rhazdon's old dark magic."

"You think one of his followers survived the last battle," said Leira in a hushed voice, her eyes growing wider.

"If one did and passed this down through their family then Rhazdon's dark magic may still be out there where it can be used. Magic most of us have never heard of and do not know how to combat."

"What does all of this have to do with the sudden urgency from all sides to get Bill Somers and return the necklace?"

"You're a good detective, Leira Berens. I don't have all the answers yet. I wonder if you're also somehow the key to solving this mystery. I saw what happened when you reached out to the fireball."

"Nothing happened," she said abruptly, changing the subject. "We need to come up with a plan. Are you here for the duration or was this a drive-by?"

"I was given a directive to stay for as long as it takes. To keep you safe and to return Bill Somers."

"I can keep myself safe. Don't use that as an excuse to get in my way. I'm the lead detective," she said fiercely. Leira got out of the car, leaving the luggage behind. "We need to get on the road, sooner than later. What are you doing?"

"What is that wonderful smell?" he asked, turning around in a circle, smelling the air.

"You're easily distracted like a dog and a squirrel. It's got to be the Bangers truck in the food court. They sell all kinds of hot dogs. It's like a tube of hot meat. Delicious. Yes, I'll get you one," she said, nodding.

She stepped into the line behind two men talking about a bet.

"We only bet a dollar and he argued about losing. A dollar!" The two men were laughing, betting another dollar on whether their friend would ever pay up. Leira watched them, wondering what it would be like to have friendships like that. Losing her mother and then her grandmother had set her on a course that

175

didn't leave a lot of time or desire, until now, to just hang out, cracking jokes. Her pocket uttered a muffled, high-pitched whine, causing the men to turn around and look at her.

Leira tried a half-smile on them, acting like she was just waiting to order.

"How fortunate you found a place right in front of this truck to put your car," said Correk, nodding to the person next to him. "Hello."

Leira turned around and looked at the car and back at Correk, puzzled. "Yeah, kind of lucky," she said.

"Nice costume, dude," said the young man in cargo shorts standing behind Leira. "You doing some kind of medieval gig?"

"This isn't medieval. Entirely different era. This is one of my favorite capes," Correk replied.

"I get it," the man said, nodding his head and smiling. "You got your own thing going on. Keeping it real. Should monetize that feel and get a booth at the Sherwood Forest Faire. People would eat that up. Look, you even have the ears!"

"Two bratwursts with everything," said Leira. She handed over a twenty and took the two sausages piled high with mustard, peppers and onions, passing one of them to Correk. "Here," she said. "Stop playing with the locals."

She waited for the change and threw a dollar into the tip jar, taking a big bite of her bratwurst before heading back toward the house.

"Yummmm, fuuuuuck," drifted from her pocket before Leira could clamp a hand down over the opening.

"Should have known." She rolled her eyes.

"Should be their new slogan," the young man laughed. "Yum fuck!"

Correk was already halfway through his sausage when Leira caught up to him and they walked down the block together, weaving through the crowd. A few people took a second look at Correk but no one said anything else.

"Do I stand out that much?" he asked, taking another large bite.

"You're good. This is Austin. We keep it weird."

"What was that language that man was speaking back there? How do I monetize that feel?"

"It's Austin English used mostly by street performers," she replied. "Means you don't have a regular job. You might want to slow down a little. A bratwurst can talk back to you if you eat it too fast. Could find yourself face down on the floor. Do you even eat normal things over there on Oriceran?"

"It's very similar to Earth but nothing like this. You don't take advantage of the nutrition in insects."

"We eat Doritos in eight flavors. That should count for something."

Correk groaned softly as they neared Estelle's, pounding on his chest with his fist. "Ooof," he said and belched, the smell of bratwurst lingering in the air. "That's better."

"Told you. You could have left that cape in the car."

"I have too many valuable things in it."

Leira held the side gate open for him. "I get it. Like a man purse."

He glared at her but walked through the gate.

The regular crowd was already filling seats near the bar. Craig and Paul were still there listening to Janice tell what looked like a long, involved story. Most of them were dressed in blue bowling shirts with their names embroidered on the pockets and the team name, Pin Pushers, embroidered in navy blue on the back.

Leira thought about trying to slide by them, hanging back behind the crowd at the edges. There was a table of women, some of them with a dog sitting at their feet, all talking at once.

Fat chance of that with a giant elf in a cape, she thought.

"Leira!" several of them called out.

"Hey, I thought you would be passing Dallas by now. Who's your tall friend?" shouted Paul.

Mitzi's schnauzer, Lemon let out a sharp bark.

"Ooh, good, does this mean you're not going?" Craig asked.

"Don't say that!" said Margaret, swatting Craig on the arm. "She was going to take an actual vacation! And from the looks of things, a really good one."

"What's your friend's name, honey?" Estelle was tending bar on the patio, standing on a metal box behind the bar so she could reach all the taps and get the beer across to the customer. She was wearing a similar bowling shirt but her participation on the team was limited mostly to cheering them on and a free round back at her place after games.

A cigarette was dangling from her mouth and one eye was closed as smoke spiraled above her bouffant. No one who came to Estelle's would rat her out for any health violations.

Estelle inspired that kind of loyalty in her customers by treating them all like family. She showed up at bedsides in hospitals, fed hungry musicians, and gave unasked for advice that turned out to be right.

"This is Bert," she said, not looking at Correk. It was bad enough she was going to have to explain the outfit. A long conversation about his name and where was it from was not on Leira's agenda.

"This a regular getup or for something special hon?" Estelle asked, looking Correk up and down. She opened two Shiner Bocks and put them down near Correk and Leira. Estelle claimed she knew best what people needed to drink or eat and often ordered for someone before they had a chance to say anything different. Leira found it easier to go along with it, and besides, there was something oddly comforting about her confidence.

Leira handed Correk the beer, whispering, "This won't send you over some magical edge, will it? We don't need to see your skin suddenly light up with some ancient language or sparks shoot out of your hands."

"The next time you're on Oriceran I'm going to give you a

longer tour. Somehow, you've gotten the idea that we're fragile creatures wandering around, barely getting by. Who do you think taught your ancestors how to grow good hops?" He took a large gulp of the beer. "Perfect thing after that sausage."

"You went to Bangers?" Mike asked. He glanced sideways at Estelle.

"As long as you don't bring it back in here," she growled, as she poured a shot for someone at the other end of the bar.

"Be right back," he said, sliding off his stool.

"Not the side gate. We're not that close," said Estelle, pointing over her shoulder at the bungalow she had turned into the bar.

"Bring me back one," yelled Craig.

"Yeah, with everything," said Margaret.

"Me too!" said Mitzi. "Don't worry, I'll share pumpkin," she said, looking down at Lemon.

Mike looked back at Estelle, waiting to see if she objected.

"Bring me one too," she said, sucking on the cigarette. "Just this once." A cloud of smoke hid her face for a moment. Correk coughed and tried to blow the smoke away from his face.

"Okay, sucking on burning sticks is one thing we don't have," Correk whispered at Leira, coughing again.

"Craig, come help me carry," Mike yelled. They could see him scooting around the tables inside, making for the front door.

"You have a friend for your road trip," Margaret said cheerfully. "Good for you!"

"It's not like that," Leira insisted. "Bert needed a ride at the last minute."

"Honey, a fine-looking man like that suddenly shows up wanting a ride with me somewhere and I promise you, I'll become wittier, prettier and tittier, like that," Estelle quipped, snapping her fingers.

Even Leira couldn't help laughing at that, even in the middle of all the chaos.

CHAPTER NINETEEN

The black bespoke tuxedo was costing Bill Somers a month's salary, but it would be worth it. All the local press would be at the university's centennial celebration and stories would be posted online.

When everyone saw what he could do, there would be pictures. He wanted to look good.

"You only need a deposit today, right?" he asked nervously, running his hand down the expensive wool, smudging a chalk mark. The tailor gently pulled his hand away.

Never bat at a paying customer.

"Professor Flanagan sent me," he said, remembering what his friend Professor Randolph had told him to say. The tailor owed Flanagan a favor and was known to give discounts to friends of friends.

"You'll have this ready by the weekend? Seems like a lot of work," he said, admiring himself in the mirror. He couldn't remember ever looking this good.

The tailor was deftly pinning the hems of the pants and nodded his head without looking up at Somers.

"This will change everything," Somers said in a hushed voice. "No one will ever doubt me again."

"The single-breast gives a man some authority," said the elderly tailor, in heavily accented English. Somers was sure it was German, or maybe Viennese. It added to the experience.

"Slims you down," the tailor smiled. He was pulling pins from a black pincushion attached to his wrist, steadily moving around the suit and adjusting the fit. "No bow tie. Go with a nice silk tie. Let's them know you're not a child and you're not retiring. Old men and little boys. They should wear bow ties."

"And a good white shirt," said Somers, smiling nervously at his reflection.

"Perfect," said the tailor. "You will get all of the attention."

"You have no idea," he replied. "Are you done yet? I have to be somewhere."

"Done," the tailor said with finality, smiling and holding out his arms as if he was conducting an orchestra. Somers liked being treated as if he was worth all this trouble.

It had never happened to him before despite his best efforts.

"Let me help you out of the jacket," said the tailor, easing the jacket off Somers' shoulders. "Wouldn't want the pins to shift."

Somers went back to the small changing room and pulled the heavy blue velvet curtain shut. He looked down at his jeans and t-shirt and felt embarrassed to put them back on and march past everyone. Today's t-shirt had a picture of a wanted poster featuring a cat that read, 'Wanted Dead and Alive, Schrodinger's Cat.' A puffy green coat completed the ensemble.

He was sorry he didn't think about what he was wearing a little longer this morning.

"You have the pants off?" asked the assistant who had shown him to the dressing room. A hand appeared through the curtain, hand open, waiting to receive the pants.

"One, one second," he stuttered, sliding the pants off. One of the pins in the hem caught on his sock and he found himself

MARTHA CARR & MICHAEL ANDERLE

hopping over to the bench and plopping down next to his clothes. The wooden bench felt cold against the back of his legs.

There was a chilled glass of champagne waiting for him next to his pile of clothes. He jostled it as he sat down and lunged for it, sloshing some of the champagne on his hand.

"Everything all right?" the assistant inquired, pulling his hand out

Somers licked his hand and looked around for something else, settling on wiping the rest on his faded white underwear, gulping down some of the champagne. The bubbles tickled his throat and made him want to sneeze.

"Not now," he muttered, not wanting to look like he was at a complete loss in such a nice place. The truth was the shop was small and worn. It was the customers who were important, for the most part.

Somers felt a sharp pang in his chest, wondering what the person who delivered the glass must have thought.

"I'm no better than him," Somers said quietly. "A glorified academic errand boy for Dean Muston." The spark he felt seeing himself in the handmade suit was fading. He opened his leather satchel and dug around inside, panic rising in his throat when he had to dig deeper.

"There it is," he said, grasping the stained leather pouch. He pulled the drawstrings and looked inside at the necklace. "You are my ticket to something better," he whispered.

"The pants?" came the voice of the assistant again, the hand poking back through the curtains. Somers handed over the pants, still holding the pouch. He dressed quickly and went to the front, putting down the necessary deposit.

"I'll pick it up on Saturday morning?" he asked nervously.

"Yes, it will be ready for you when we open," the tailor replied, the same gracious smile on his face. It was only making Somers feel worse.

He left without another word and stopped on the sidewalk for a moment, getting his bearings. He lacked the ability to know instinctively where he was standing and was terrible at maps too. His mother called that ironic.

He learned to take note of certain landmarks when he got off the subway. Visual cues usually did the trick.

"Walgreens," he said, doubting himself already, even though he was crossing the street and hiking up the long flight of stairs to the train platform. He was resigned to the idea that he could be wrong and might end up having to come right back down again, crossing the street and up the other stairs. It happened all the time.

"Today, it's a character flaw," he said. "After Saturday, it'll be a quirky habit."

He had picked right the first time, bolstering his confidence. He went and stood in one of the warming booths Chicago turned on during the winter. He hit the button and the red lights came on overhead. Across the platform a flock of pigeons were standing around doing the same in another booth. He wondered how they figured out how to press the button.

"Anything is possible," he reminded himself. He wanted to wave at the birds to see if they waved back. A sign from Oriceran.

A man in a suit and a black wool overcoat joined him in the booth, standing on the other side, his eyes glued to his phone. Somers made a mental note to get himself a better coat when the money started rolling in. "Saturday," he said quietly.

He could see the Brown Line in the distance, the silver cars rattling on the curve around the Loop. When it arrived, the doors slid open and people streamed out, brushing past the small crowd waiting to get on the train.

Somers pushed his way on, getting the last seat. A man with a cane got on and stood in front of Somers, looking down at him, raising an eyebrow. Several others on the car were watching, wondering what he'd do, but no one was offering their seat instead.

Somers got up slowly and made his way to the pole near the door, not looking back. The man with the cane muttered a thank you, and sat down, letting out an "Oof," as he landed.

Somers was stuck on the pole by the door and at every stop he had to adjust his position, depending on the stream of people pushing on or off the car. The doors opened at Fullerton and a large group of college-age kids got off, headed to the nearby campus. He slid into one of the seats by a window and looked out at the people anxious to get on before the doors closed.

"Doors closing. Do not hold the doors," said the conductor over the loudspeakers.

No one ever listened to that admonition. The doors made feeble attempts to slide shut and someone shoved them back.

Somers reached inside his backpack and slid his fingertips into the pouch, checking it was still there. He felt a small buzz that crept up his arm and filled his entire body, lifting his mood. He saw a glow from inside the pouch when he looked in the backpack.

A woman carrying a large Marshall's bag slid into the seat next to him. She held the bag on her lap, glancing at Somers and looking away. He pulled his hand out of the satchel and felt the friendly hum drain out of him.

I'm special, he thought, reminding himself that the hooded creatures that found him, picked him out of all the archaeologists they could have chosen. Intelligent life from another planet wanted him.

The murder was an accident, he thought. An accident. Not a chance I could have seen that coming.

The dark mood was returning. He slid his hand back inside, feeling around for the pouch. He found it and pushed his fingers inside, opening it wider so he could hold the stone in his hand. He squeezed hard, feeling the edges digging into his skin.

The buzz was stronger, pulsing through him. He felt relief as the energy flooded his brain. "It worked again," he said.

The woman next to him gave him the side eye. He smiled at her saying, "Looks like you found some things," indicating her bag.

The train stopped at Wellington and the woman shut her eyes, saying loudly enough for everyone to hear her, "God grant me the serenity not to knock this fool out. The courage to let him live and the wisdom to do it anyway if he's stupid enough to bother me again."

A couple sitting in another row started snickering.

Somers squeezed the rock harder, feeling the pulse strengthen. It was responding to his touch. He found himself enjoying the attention.

"Next stop, Paulina," the loudspeaker squawked and Somers got up, pushing past the woman and her large bag as she rolled her eyes, letting out a loud 'tsk'. People looked up as if they expected something to happen.

Somers felt emboldened by the energy coursing through his veins and paused at the doors. "Have a fucking miserable day. Or in other words, an average day for you," he said in a cheerful voice. He stepped out of the car as the woman scrambled to her feet, spilling out a stream of mumbled expletives. Her shopping bag was banging against people who were trying to get out of her way.

"Doors closing," the loudspeaker said, and Somers waited patiently on the platform to see if she was going to make it off the train. He didn't care. He even wondered if he could take her.

The doors closed on her as she pressed her hands against the glass, yelling, "I'm gonna find you and kick your skinny little ass!"

He smiled and gave her the finger as the train slid away, picking up speed. A man in the back of the train gave him a thumbs up. He returned the gesture with a sharp salute. His other hand was still clutching the stone.

"I am somebody," he said, grinning widely, and he set off for his apartment on Leavitt Street. "I just needed a little juice."

He stepped out of the station, a cold wind hitting him in the face. He took the necklace out and put it on over his head, quickly tucking it under his t-shirt not wanting to attract any attention. He could feel the metal against his skin start to warm and the buzz grew inside of him. A train rumbled over his head, adding to the dizzy feeling.

He staggered to one side, and stopped, trying to will himself into walking a straight line.

"It's not even happy hour, dude," said a man walking toward the train. "Get help," he sneered.

Somers didn't care. A wave of nausea came over him and bile rose in his throat. He swallowed hard and marched toward home. He still didn't care. He navigated down the wide sidewalk, drifting back and forth, swimming in the feeling that he didn't have a care in the world.

It seemed to take forever to make his way into the middle of Roscoe Village and turn down his street. The recent snow had turned into ice and he was having to pick his way down the sidewalk.

"Whooooop!" he yelled as his left foot went forward and his right leg went back. His bag twisted behind him, slapping against his back. He braced himself for the fall, putting out his arms, then his legs found the strength to come back together, leaving him upright.

He knew it had to be the necklace. "Hot damn!" he whispered, still wobbling, his arms outstretched. "Hot damn!" he yelled again, raising his arms higher.

The few people on the sidewalk made a point of giving him a wider berth. He watched them pick their way carefully between the icy patches, their shoulders hunched against the cold.

He took a step forward and felt his foot slide and magically come back just in time. He did it again, taking two steps, then three. He strolled, gaining speed, first jogging, falling into a run. He wasn't even sure if his feet were always hitting the ground.

The nausea rolled over him in waves, reminding him of riding a roller coaster.

He stopped at a corner to catch his breath, doubled over with his hands on his knees.

"Oh man," he said, and he puked on a pile of snow that already had a frozen mound of dog poop. He shook his head, clearing his mind, and laughed out loud.

"Small price," he muttered, and took off running again.

He got to his front stoop and kicked his neighbor's neglected wet newspapers to the side. Every other day they were another reminder to Somers of how inconsiderate the world could be to him. Today, he got a charge out of watching them slide off the step and into the bushes.

Problem solved.

He put his key in the lock and jiggled it hard to the left while pulling back on the handle. The finicky door unlocked and opened.

"First try!" he exclaimed. He stepped into his studio apartment. The beige couch in the front doubled as a bed. Professor Randolph had given it to him when he bought a new one. There was an old pizza box shoved under the coffee table and dishes scattered everywhere.

His laptop and research papers were on the coffee table. A nearby bulletin board was covered with articles about unexplained phenomena around the world. He had circled important parts with a yellow highlighter.

The galley kitchen was tucked into a back corner and consisted of a short refrigerator, a sink and a gas range that had seen better days. Two of the burners had never worked.

A plastic basket of clean clothes sat next to his empty dresser that doubled as a TV stand.

He usually hated being at home. Everywhere he looked reminded him of how far he hadn't made it in life.

Today was different. Nothing seemed impossible.

He took off his coat and stuffed it into the only closet, setting it on top of a hamper full of dirty clothes. He went searching under the sink for the plastic grocery bags he was always cramming under there. He pulled a few out, shaking off the water that leaked from the pipes, and started piling trash into them, tying them off when they were full.

He folded the clean clothes neatly and put them away in the dresser. The dishes took him longer but eventually the small place was neat as a pin. He wondered why he'd waited so long.

He stood still in the middle of the small apartment, sweat beading on his forehead and his chest felt like it was burning. He stripped off the two layers of shirts he always wore in the winter and looked in the bathroom mirror.

The necklace was glowing, and the skin underneath it looked like it was sunburned. He gingerly lifted the chain and felt his skin. It was tender to the touch.

He took the necklace off for a moment and set it on the back of the toilet, waiting to see what might happen.

It didn't take long for the energy to start draining out of him and the self-recriminations to start. What if I can't make it work on Saturday? And in front of all those people. I'd be finished. What if this is the way my life will always be? What if this is the best I can ever do?

All he wanted to do was sleep.

He snatched the necklace off the top of the toilet tank, scraping the gold against the ceramic and put it back around his neck. The energy started flowing through him again.

He looked at himself in the mirror and noticed his eyes looked shinier than he remembered. He really wasn't such a bad looking fellow after all.

He winced as the necklace warmed against his skin.

"Totally worth it." He put his shirt back on. "Ack, ow," he said, moving the necklace around under his shirt. "The skin will get tougher, like a tan," he told himself. "I just have to make it to Saturday." He felt his newfound courage return.

He stood in front of the small mirror over the sink and flexed his muscles, admiring the way he looked. He felt good. He relaxed and let the energy fill him.

Images of Oriceran ran through his mind and he imagined the night he would tell his world, or at least a large academic celebration, about this magical place.

As the feeling grew inside of him, his reflection in the mirror blurred in wavy lines. Somers blinked hard over and over again, trying to get it to stop.

He turned around and leaned on the sink for support, wondering if he had gone too far. He fell back into the space where the sink should have been, where it just was, and landed on the ground.

He felt the dirt under his hands and looked up at the trees. There was a hole hovering above him, ripped through a large oak tree. His bathroom was on the other side of the hole. He could see the faded yellow ducks on his shower curtain.

The air around him was warm and humid and he was surrounded by dark, dense forest on every side. Ancient American elm trees that Somers knew were largely gone on Earth, stretched upwards, blocking out most of the light. The ground all around him was mossy, making the forest floor look like a deep, green, fertile ocean.

Something clattered over his head and he looked up and saw crab beetles, a large claw for a head, scampering across the front of the tree trunk. They were making their way toward a nest tucked in a crook where several branches met.

Somers watched in fascination, frozen to the spot.

A small fuzzy head resembling a vulture peeked out of the nest, prompting a chorus of squawking. The line of beetles reached the nest, pincers clicking and clattering, making their way over the edge of the nest.

Somers braced himself for the carnage, unable to look away as he waited for the first baby bird to lose its head. At the last moment, up out of the nest the mother appeared, her iridescent feathers rippling, neatly picked off the beetles, crushing them in her beak and feeding them to her babies to loud squawks.

Somers got up slowly, keeping a wary eye on the bird, and brushed off his pants, He noticed the red glow from the relic was showing through his shirt.

"Oriceran," he whispered. "I've opened a portal." he said awed. "I can do it. If I did it once I can do it again. Best day ever!" he said. He looked at his bathroom through the portal, waiting a few moments to see if the portal closed.

Nothing happened.

"Stable, good," he said. He took a look around at his surroundings. "Samples," he muttered. They'd be perfect for the university celebration on Saturday. "More proof." he said and gingerly stepped off the path and looked for something to take back with him.

"Nothing to fear while I'm wearing this," he grinned.

He noticed the tall grasses near where he was standing gently swaying every time he spoke. "Well, hello there," he said, watching the grass undulate back and forth. "Red dog, blue dog." He marched back and forth in front of the plant to see if movement affected it at all.

"It does," he said in a hushed tone. "Perfect! Boom, shakalakalaka, boom, shakalakalaka!" He danced around, shaking his hips, watching the plant dance along with him. "Woot! Woot!" He knelt down by the plant and started digging around the roots. The plant quivered and let out a deep moan.

"Sound, no less!" Somers was getting more excited. He was picturing his big night and every night after that as the start to the life he had always deserved. The plant moaned again as he uncovered the roots.

A great roar went up from the dense forest, making the ground rumble. The plant shivered and drew back.

Somers startled and tried to steady himself. He could feel the ground shake under his hands as the forest roared again, closer this time.

He looked at the portal, still hanging over the path behind him, his bathroom just on the other side. "I can still do this" He gritted his teeth and turned back to pull out a handful of the plant. The plant moaned piteously, screamed and went limp in his hands.

"Got it," he said, hoping the grasses could be revived. He got up to make a run for it.

He had only taken a few steps before something in the forest roared again, shaking the ground so hard he fell to his knees.

A large male lion with a full rack of antlers leaped into the clearing. It was carrying a tall, muscular elf with dark brown skin and thick brown hair. Plants and bugs wove in and out of his long hair.

"Thief!" the Wood Elf shouted. "No one steals from the Gardener!"

Somers scrambled back to his feet and dashed for the portal, still clutching the plant. He threw himself through the opening just ahead of the lion's snapping jaws. He tumbled in head first, crashing over the sink and landing in the tub.

The lion's head burst through the portal, roaring loud enough to rattle the ducks on the shower curtain.

Somers tore off the necklace, dropping it by his side. The lion fell back to the other side, back to Oriceran as the portal closed.

Somers smiled despite almost getting mauled. The energy was draining rapidly, but he clung to the feeling that everything was good in his world. "Things are working out for me," he muttered. Another thought fought for his attention. "It was an accident," he whispered.

CHAPTER TWENTY

"You sure you'll be okay?" asked Leira, eyeing Correk suspiciously. "Aaaaa!" She held her breath trying to hold back another sneeze. "Cold came on pretty fast. I don't usually get sick." She sneezed hard, holding the crook of her arm over her mouth.

A tiny, "Yum fuck," could be heard from the other room where the troll was nestled in a shoebox with a pair of fresh underwear.

"Aw, that was like a little bless you." Leira blew her nose. "Make sure to watch for cars. They're pretty wild around here, driving on the side of the road and trying to beat red lights."

"I've consulted with kings and prophets. I think I can handle walking to a merchant. We have roads and shops on Oriceran," he said, an edge to his voice. He eyed her warily.

"What?"

"Nothing," he said. "The trip to Oriceran. It may have over-charged the energy in your body. It'll pass."

"Is that your way of saying I got a magic cleanse? How is that even possible? A little heads up next time, that Oriceran has that effect on humans."

Correk looked like he wanted to say something but thought better of it. Instead he said, "You stayed at the bar too long."

"That's what you do with family. Yes, that's my family of choice. That's a thing here. You pick your own and they can be all kinds of creatures."

"Is that why you agreed to this bowling? Never mind. It's a necessary distraction, I understand. I can handle going to a shop. I'll be back."

"But do you have CVS Pharmacies? Whole other animal. Don't get lost in the, as seen on TV aisle. You could be there all day," she said, pulling out her phone. "Turn left out of here and look for a sign that looks like this," she said, holding up an image on her phone. "And they're going to hand you a long piece of thin paper at the end that's proof you paid for your things. It'll go on forever and have a coupon on the end. It's their thing. We call it a receipt. Don't let that throw you."

"You're using a lot of strange words. This is still English? What's a coupon? You're not a very trusting lot. You make a deal with someone on Oriceran and that's the end of it."

"That's a lot in one burst. First, you don't need receipts on Oriceran because you can zap them with a fireball. It's a fiery receipt and second, a coupon is a piece of paper that says you can have something and give them less."

"Bartering with a note, interesting."

"Never thought of it that way, but sure. Here, you'll need this," she said, handing him her credit card. "There'll be a little machine by the cash register. You swipe it," she said, making the motion with the card. "I'm beginning to think this is not going to go well. Don't tell them you borrowed the card. No one will believe you. Make sure you get Doritos, the cool ranch flavor."

"What am I getting?"

"I told you to write it down. Do you know how to write? That's insulting you too, isn't it," she said, shrugging a shoulder. "Okay, from now on I'll assume you have the basics. Hang on."

She dropped the blanket and went to the kitchen and pulled out a plastic bag.

"In here somewhere," she said, digging through the trash. "Nectar of the Gods!" she announced, pulling out the crumpled blue Doritos bag. "Take this with you. Anything that comes in a bag like this and is in the same aisle will be suitable," she said, handing him the bag.

"I'm taking a bag of trash with me to the shop?"

"We call these snacks."

"Are they even food?"

"Depends on who you ask. They're good and they take years to kill you. I know, sounds stupid when I say it out loud. I hear it. But if we're going to go on a road trip together, then we have to have them. Got it? Toilet paper and snacks for the road, when we eventually get on it. We don't have much time left."

"Fully aware," said Correk. "We have to be sure we're not walking into some kind of trap."

"I want to ask you if you use toilet paper on Oriceran but I'm sensing that's out of bounds too." Leira looked up and saw that Correk wasn't moving.

"Yes, I know something's wrong," Leira said, annoyed. "I'm still a damn fine detective and this is my town. Hell, this is my country, my world. I don't run from anything. If there's a monster out there, we'll find it, tag it and bring it in. Go to the store. I've been taking care of myself for years. I'll survive another hour on my own."

"I'm not worried about that. I want your word you won't decide to leave without me."

"That's sweet, you do get me," she snapped. "Don't make me say this to you again, Bert, I'm a fucking good detective. I don't run into situations without knowing as much as possible, first. You say there's more to the story, then there's more to the story. I'm beginning to think there's an entire fucking anthology."

The troll, the size of an overgrown house cat bounded into the room growling at Correk.

"See? Nothing to worry about. I have an attack troll, a gun and a pretty good right hook. Wait, you can't go out there like that unless you want to keep telling people you're heading to work at Sherwood Forest. Not sure they even have elves."

Leira dug around in the bottom of her closet and found an old red knit hat from the milk crate in the back. She pulled a large green windbreaker off a hangar and handed them to Correk.

"Put these on. The jacket should fit you."

"I assure you, my cape has seen me through many Oriceran winters."

"I'm not doubting the cape, just the look. Take the coat. I borrowed it from Hagan when we were on a long stakeout. The rest just looks like a typical day in Austin," she said, looking at the brown suede pants that laced up the sides. "Very typical Austin, where hippies go to retire."

"That is the second time someone has suggested this forest."

"Let it go. Earth humor," said Leira, sneezing again. "If I tell you to get Dayquil, do I have a shot at seeing it?"

"Can you add some remnant of it to my trash bag?"

"Can you conjure up an image of it with one of your magic fireballs? By the way, I know you've been following me from the moment I got back from Oriceran."

"Yes, you yelled at me underneath your car. That clued me in." He pulled the hat on over pointed ears. "Something you should know about magic on Earth. It can be limited. I have to conserve my energy for times when a fireball or an incantation is really needed. Making sure I get the right snacks for you doesn't count."

"It's medicine. You're never going to remember all of this. Here, let me write it on your hand," said Leira grabbing a pen from a nearby drawer. She wrote Dayquil, toilet paper, snacks in the palm of his hand. "Wait, get Coke too. Not Pepsi, very important," she said, adding to the list on his hand.

"I appreciate that you assumed I could read English."

"It's become apparent that Light Elves are giant peepers and you've been watching humans on Earth for a long time. Go, so you can get back and we can figure out who the hell else is after that necklace."

Correk shut the door behind him as quietly as he could and tried to stay to the shadows as he made his way around the patio to the side gate. Everyone was still at the bar, laughing at Paul's stories.

"Bert!" Paul called to him, waving him over. "Happy hour's almost over!"

Correk waved but kept moving. There was too much to do already.

"See you in a couple hours," Estelle said from behind the bar. She was standing on her box pouring peanuts into bowls. "We'll loan you a bowling shirt. Hey, you fools quit your drinking. I don't plan on losing tonight to those less thans, the E-bowlas," she said, sliding a bowl of peanuts in their direction. "What'll you have, honey?" she asked in her deep-throated croak to a young woman with long blonde hair. Estelle was already pouring her a glass of wine.

Correk went out the gate and around the house, keeping his head down, trying to blend in with the crowd moving up and down the sidewalk in front of the bars.

He looked to the left and saw the red and white sign in the distance. He weaved through the crowd, not looking at anyone, making his way to the store.

A black tentacle slithered through the grass next to the street, gleaming in the street light, following just a few feet behind him. A drunk woman in high heels holding a red plastic cup staggered onto the grass, her heel grazing the tentacle.

"Oh my God, Darlene!" her friend shrieked, backing away and pointing. The tentacle melted into the street, turning into liquid as it ran down the gutter, still headed in the same direction as Correk.

"What? What?" the woman yelled, looking at her feet.

"Shit, I could have sworn I saw a snake right by your shoes, Darlene!" They both peered at the grass.

"Those dirty martinis always mess you up, Jasmine," she snorted. They held on to each other laughing, the plastic cups in their hands spilling onto the sidewalk.

Correk glanced back but didn't see anything and quickly turned away, not wanting to draw any attention to himself.

The black liquid in the gutter reformed into a tentacle, and slithered after Correk, keeping to the grass.

"Hey, look out," yelled a man on a bike as Correk darted across the street. A truck leaned on the horn. Correk leaned back, whispering "Decantata," his eyes glowing, and the truck swerved enough to avoid grazing him. The driver shook his fist out the window. Correk looked around to see if anyone had noticed.

A few people had turned to see why someone was honking but quickly went back to what they were doing. No one had seen him cast the spell except the tentacle that curled up by the lamp post, waiting, as Correk went into the drugstore.

He stood dazed in the front of the aisles looking out over the rows of things to buy. Directly in front of him were square fuzzy pillows that could vibrate. Each one had a large, 'try me' sticker on the front. Correk pressed gently and felt a tingle go through his hand as the pillow hummed. "Hmm," he said, tucking one under his arm. He wandered down the makeup aisle passing by the large Revlon and L'Oréal signs, smelling a lotion scented with peppermint. He put a little on his hand and rubbed it in.

"We don't do samples here, mister," said a short, stocky woman in a bright red vest.

"Of course," said Correk, taking the lotion.

He moved further down the aisle and turned the corner,

amazed at the rows upon rows of products meant to hold something, cure something, or dress something up.

The same clerk came up behind him as he was looking at athletic socks and handed him a shopping basket. "Looks like you're gonna need this," she said. She wandered off before he could answer.

He threw two pairs into the basket along with the other things.

"Can you point me in the direction of the Doritos?" he called to her.

"Aisle two," she yelled back, bored. "Right across from the milk in the refrigerated section." He looked over the aisles, hesitating. She sighed and pointed. "That way. You'd think he'd never seen a CVS before," she muttered, wandering off toward the photo counter.

"Ice Cream Magic: Personal Ice Cream Maker," Correk read. "That's not magic," he said, reading the directions on the back. "That's poor science." He worked his way down the shelf picking up the ultralight, slim book light and magnifier, tossing it into the basket. "Cat's Meow Motorized Wand," he mumbled. "What do they need with all of this?" he wondered and tossed it in the basket. At the end of the aisle was a red oval sign that read, 'As Seen on TV!'

"She did warn me about this." He reluctantly pulled himself away from a Hurricane Spin Scrubber. He went in the direction the clerk had pointed, pulling out the empty Doritos bag, looking for a match.

"Damn," he said in awe, as he stood in front of the rows of different flavored Doritos. "This is incredible." He pulled out the cool ranch and dropped it in the basket. Then he paused, glancing up and down the rows and shrugged. "Why not?" He filled the basket with bags of Cheetos and corn nuts, sea salt potato chips and honey roasted peanuts.

At the end of the aisle he found the different flavors of beef jerky and threw in one of each, along with a Whitman's Sampler and a box of mini-Charleston Chews.

He got in line behind a man just buying diapers and glanced down at the smeared words still visible on his hand. "Dammit. She was right."

"Problem?" asked the clerk.

"Toilet paper and Dayquil? I'll need the Coke, not the Pepsi," he added, showing the clerk his hand.

"Let me guess. Wife is sick, it's coming out both ends and you're having to take over. I'd guess for the first time in a very long time. Never mind. Coke's right there. You want the regular, the cherry, the lime or the diet? Take the regular, can't go wrong with that. Right this way. Let me walk you to the other things on your list. Can I help you carry any of that? The pillow, sure."

She kept up the running commentary as she walked him to the toilet paper. "You care about softness or thickness? You don't know, do you? Okay, let's go for on sale. Come on, this way," she said, holding on to the pillow and the toilet paper for him. "Dayquil. I imagine whoever's waiting for you at home didn't want the stuff that would knock her out. Probably needs to keep one eye on you, huh?" she laughed. Correk raised an eyebrow and reached for the Dayquil.

"Listen, don't feel bad. We get guys like you in here all the time. On Mother's Day, Valentine's Day and Christmas Eve this place is packed with you guys, buying all kinds of weird shit and asking if we'll wrap it. Guy talked me into wrapping a skillet and a spatula once. Said his wife needed a new one. Bet she hit him with it."

"Thank you for your assistance," Correk said stiffly, standing up straighter to make himself look more dignified. He set the basket on the counter as the clerk added the other things and went around to ring him up.

"You have a discount card? What about a phone number? It's like you just got here or something. You must be from another country. Don't have much of an accent, though. Should get to know the area while you're here."

The clerk bagged everything in large shopping bags, pushing them over the counter to Correk.

"That's a hundred and fifty-six dollars and ninety-seven cents. Just slide your card," she said, pointing at the small black machine partially hidden by one of the bags. "Dear Lord, honey, you need to get out more. You one of those fellas that just uses cash most of the time? Dollar, dollar bill! That's what my Sam is always saying. Don't know where he got that from. There you go. You need cash back? Press no. Sign there. All done!" she chirped, clapping like he had achieved something remarkable.

"Thank you," he said, as she held the door for him. The line waiting behind him glowered as he grabbed his bags and headed for the door.

CHAPTER TWENTY-ONE

Out on the street the sun had set and the moon was out.
Correk looked up at the lone moon, missing his own
planet's two silvery orbs. It wasn't like him to be homesick. He
remembered the look on Ossonia's face when he tumbled
through the portal.

The black tentacle unwound itself from the shadows and
slithered into the gutter again, following just close enough to see
where Correk was going and waited patiently just inside of the
gate, watching him walk back to the cottage on the far side of the
patio.

"Estelle, you got a damn snake in here," yelled a woman who
was trying to bash the tentacle with a deck chair. The tentacle
slithered under the gate and out into the darkness, back to where
it had come from.

Correk looked back from the cottage door, catching a glimpse
of the tentacle before it disappeared.

"No," he whispered, a cold chill passing through him.

"Damn snakes!" said Estelle. "You'll get it next time, honey,"
she said, and coughed.

"Hey, there's Bert!" Mike exclaimed from the bar. He had

changed into his blue bowling shirt. "We found you a shirt!" he yelled, waving a large blue shirt, 'Pin Pushers' clearly visible.

"We gave it to Leira," said Janice.

"Keep your shirt on," said Craig.

"So funny," said Mike. "Keep drinking. It helps your game."

Correk tried to shake off an eerie feeling and went into the cottage.

"Did you get everything?" Leira asked, still wrapped in a blanket on the couch.

"You're not well enough to go anywhere tonight," Correk, said grimly.

"Not true," she replied, shaking off the blanket. She was already dressed in her bowling shirt. "I already feel better. Something weird must be going around but I never stay sick for long. Good DNA."

"Look, I think whoever wants that necklace too has put a tail on us," Correk said hesitantly. "I can't be sure of what I saw. There was hardly any light and it was only for a second..."

"But..." said Leira, rising off the couch. "What do you think you saw?"

"A black tentacle. Something I've only ever heard of from stories in the past."

"You mean like an Atlantean. That's not necessarily bad news," said Leira before she looked at him a second time. "Or is it?"

"If it's an Atlantean who wants the necklace, it's for a spell. Dark magic of some sort."

"It doesn't have to be a dark plot. It could just be good old fashioned greed, which is a very popular motive," Leira said. "Let's not get ahead of ourselves here. Don't worry," she patted his arm. "We got this."

She noticed all the bags he'd dropped on the red velvet chair. "Whoa, what happened here? You went down that aisle, didn't you? Rookie mistake. Hey, this pillow is pretty sweet." She held it against her chest as it vibrated.

"I don't think I've seen a Whitman's box of candy since..." Leira stopped herself. She was about to say, since her grandmother was here. She put the pillow down and took the bags from Correk. "We should get going."

He followed her into the kitchen. "I got your Doritos and something called a Cheeto."

"I can see that. You got a nice mashup of junk food. Will make for a great road trip even if we're hunting for a killer and a suspect to be named later." She could feel her mood growing darker.

The troll moaned from the other room.

"Yumfuck's going to be a problem at the bowling alley," Leira said, as she put the Coke in the refrigerator.

"You can tell him to stay in his nest. He'll listen to you."

"What? That would have been very useful to know yesterday."

"I didn't know you were taking a troll home with you."

"Just tell him to stay, like a pet?"

"It's a little more than that. Say Nesturnium to him," Correk instructed. "Stand right in front of him and wave your hand over him."

"Next thing you're going to tell me to wave a dead chicken over my head under a full moon."

"Live chicken, and takes two full moons, like on Oriceran." Correk moved to the opposite side of the bedroom where he could face Leira.

"So, you do know sarcasm." Leira arched an eyebrow but Correk ignored her. "Okay, here goes. Nesturnium," she said, waving her hand over the troll. Her hand tingled and she felt her face warm. The troll trilled and settled down in its nest.

Correk saw her eyes starting to glow. Not human, he thought. Not entirely at least.

"That's a relief," she said, watching the troll's tiny chest move up and down as it slept. "Come on, let's get our bowl on."

"How do you put on a bowl?"

"So much slang, so little time," said Leira. "Keep that hat on. I can explain away everything else because, well… this is Austin. Keep it weird, dude. But your ears would cause some questions. Here, change into this." She tossed him a blue bowling shirt. "Estelle brought it over while you were gone. It'll help normalize the Robin Hood pants." She grabbed two pairs of socks, glancing at Correk's feet in the large boots. "These will never fit you," she said, waving the socks, "but they'll have to do."

"Not to worry. I picked up some more while I was out," he said, digging them out of the bag.

"How much did you put on my card? Never mind. Good call. But you are to stay out of Target."

"This is a lot of trouble in order to be with friends. It's an odd thing with humans. Great tragedies can occur, and you seek each other out to do mundane things like this bowling. It serves no purpose."

"I suppose that's the point. Change in there," she said, pointing to the bedroom. "And make it snappy."

Correk shut the bedroom door holding up the shirt to smell it. Leira yelled from the living room, "I want to win a trophy!"

"I can fashion you a trophy in a matter of moments," he yelled back, buttoning up the shirt. The troll was snoring happily in its nest.

"Trophies are just useless junk unless you earn them by beating the bejeezus out of somebody. It's even better if it's someone you know."

Correk came out of the bedroom and reached for the knit hat. He noticed the look Leira was giving him.

"What?" he asked, holding out his arms like he was ready to be inspected. "Do I not look human enough?"

"Fortunately, in these parts, humans come in every shape, size and description. Very fortunately… Come on."

Correk pulled the hat down over his ears as Leira grabbed her leather jacket and purse sitting on the chair by the door.

"What? It's convenient to leave my stuff right there," she said, waiting for him to follow.

"I have no comment on how you choose to live."

"No, just plenty of elven looks."

The bar was full of patrons but everyone from the bowling team was already gone, including Estelle. Though her cigarette smoke still hung in the air.

A few college students from University of Texas were playing cornhole, tossing large bean bags toward the raised wooden board with a hole in the center.

One of the bean bags landed at Correk's feet.

"Hey, dude, can you toss it back?" asked one of the young men.

Correk hesitated and Leira was about to step in when he flicked the bean bag up in the air with his foot, caught it and threw it all in one fluid motion. The bean bag dropped through the hole.

"Nice!" the man said, smiling broadly. "Whoa, that was down-right evil. You gotta show me how to do that."

Correk headed for the gate and Leira let him pass, a crooked smile on her face.

"This trophy is in the bag," she announced.

"I'll have you know, Light Elves are known for their athletic ability."

"Without…"

"Yes, even without magic," Correk cut her off. "It's not really a test of athletic skills if you bring magic into it."

"Good to know."

Correk let Leira get in the car while he took a long look, scanning the street, paying careful attention to the ground around him. It was too dark to see any further. He couldn't shake the feeling someone, or something, was watching them.

"I haven't been around Light Elves long, but I'm picking up on a few things," Leira said, as Correk slid into his seat. "What? Did you see anything out there? Hello? When you don't answer me that usually means there's more to the story than you've told me. I don't play well with people who keep things from me. So, start talking."

Correk considered how much to share with her, including his suspicion that she wasn't entirely human.

"Our two worlds connect more than either side would like. It's just a feeling," he said finally, not willing to say anything more.

Leira stopped at the red light and turned to look at Correk, her face set in a determined look.

"It looks like you and I are partners on this job, at least for now. Whatever sent you through that portal gave you a pretty good shove. They seemed pretty determined. Partners don't keep shit from each other. That's how someone ends up dead. I'm the non-magical one in this equation and even though I have a gun, I don't like the odds. So, you're going to need to be more forth-coming. You may have been under the impression earlier that I was asking. I wasn't. Tell me what the fuck is going on or I quit right now. You can be the one to explain it to the grieving queen." Her voice was hard.

"All I can give you are pieces that add up to nothing at the moment," Correk said.

"That's how a detective works. We take all those pieces and look for the ones that fit in with them. But, when you don't give me what you have I have to bust my ass to find out shit you already knew. And now, apparently, with magical shit chasing after the same prize. Gives everything a whole new stink to it."

"Remember what I told you about the Atlantean, Rhazdon?

"The one who has some follower that might still be alive. Yeah, I remember. Hard to forget a maniacal six-hundred-year-old."

The light turned green and Leira turned, heading for the

bowling alley. The tall pink and orange letters, Highland Lanes was visible in the distance.

"Rhazdon was no ordinary being, even by Oriceran standards," said Correk. "He matched his arrogance and need to be something with an innate talent for magic. He was considered gifted from the very start."

"Probably attributed that to his Atlantean blood."

"He attributed everything to that. The stories that are told usually leave out that he was only half Atlantean, from Earth, because after a while Rhazdon forgot. He researched the Atlanteans thoroughly, retracing their steps from thousands of years ago, resurrecting their magic. Dark magic."

"How dark are we talking? Gargamel with some cute smurfs or did he go all Lord Voldemort and build a following?"

"He took what he learned and went from town to town, recruiting other lost souls from all the different kingdoms and lands of Oriceran, building his own following."

"You'd have thought that someone from such an aristocratic background wouldn't like mingling with just anybody."

"He was after purity of thought," said Correk. "In the end, what bothered him wasn't what you were made from but how you thought, how you believed."

"Fuck, that's deep." She pulled into the parking lot and found a space right by the door.

"Pull around to the back of the building," Correk said, looking around. He saw Leira hesitate. "Humor me," he said.

She started the car and gently eased out of the space, turning down the strip of narrow blacktop alongside the long building.

"Park over near the back door."

"You're anticipating trouble at bowling? Low score or magical shootout?" She parked the car and turned off the engine.

"You may be right, and we're being followed by a clever thief. But if someone is trying to mimic Rhazdon, they are not to be taken lightly. If they have managed to gain even a tenth of his power, then darkness approaches. At his height, he had thousands of followers and had built his own kingdom, complete with a well-fortified castle. From there, he began his revenge, attempting to destroy those who he saw as responsible for the end of the Atlanteans."

"So, basically everyone else."

"Yes, and eventually we were at war. I believe here on Earth you would call it a world war. So many died enforcing the treaty, pushing back Rhazdon's followers."

"Didn't all of the other kingdoms combined outnumber his followers? And it sounds like they were chosen for their weakness of mind and heart, not some kind of fighting machine. Not exactly the recruitment poster for a strong army."

"We should go in," said Correk. "Your friends will be wondering where you are. There will be plenty of time on the road trip to tell you the rest of the story."

They got out of the car and were headed for the door when Leira grabbed Correk's arm, pulling him back a step.

"The dark magic. It's that powerful?" she asked in a hushed tone. "He was able to threaten the very existence of everyone else on Oriceran by using the dark magic."

Correk nodded his head solemnly and his expression was grave. "Every bloodline, every kingdom felt the losses. For some, their name was ended for all time. He would tell captured soldiers, and women and children to follow his path or die. Most chose death."

"Where is this story going?" she asked.

"It took all the kingdoms of Oriceran working together to defeat Rhazdon. He died in the final battle, burned alive in his own tower. Those who survived were sentenced to Trevilsom Prison. All the evidence of his existence, every relic, every artifact, every book of spells was hidden away in a vault that is guarded at all times by very vigilant Gnomes."

"But…" Leira sensed this was all adding up to a lot more trouble. It wasn't just about finding Bill Somers anymore. The necklace was just as important.

"But I came across a Rhazdon artifact in Oriceran. That shouldn't be possible. It means some of his magic is still out there in the world."

"And there's no way of knowing how much or what kind," said Leira.

"Precisely. And a Willen traded a trinket for a riddle whose only answer is that there's someone new who could be picking up where Rhazdon left off."

"A Willen," said Leira.

"A giant silver talking rat. Unlike Earth, Oriceran is full of different creatures with varying amounts of intelligence and we all exist together."

"Nice dig at us ordinary humans," Leira said, pulling open the large door.

"You have only one intelligent species that is native to Earth and regularly shoot each other. Finding out who did it is a large part of your job description."

"Unless you come up with anything concrete that says we shouldn't head to Chicago then we're out of here at first light, no arguments," she said. "If you don't agree, you don't have to come." She strode into the bowling alley without looking back. Her mind was made up and she would leave it to Correk to decide for himself if he was on board.

I didn't ask him to come.

"I realize I was not part of your plan," Correk said, catching up with her. "But we need to work together to ensure the right outcome."

"The one where we get the killer and the necklace back and everyone is still in one piece," Leira replied. "Then you tell me the truth about everything from now on and we'll work the case together. That's not a request."

"Leira! You brought Bert! Perfect," Craig, yelled waving from the top of the seventh lane. "Get your shoes, we're just about to start."

Leira waved back and pointed Correk toward the shoe counter.

"You totally got that smurf reference. You've been spending way too much time watching us so-called common humans."

"Only for cultural context," he replied tersely, making sure his hat was still pulled down far enough.

"I don't judge. Everyone needs a little Papa Smurf sometimes," she said, trying to lighten the mood. "The end of this story is that someone is trying to rally the thought police again and this time may be traveling over to Earth, too."

"That last part is only a feeling. I have no proof. But we use feelings to guide magic and take them very seriously. I think the saying on Earth is, we will have to watch our back."

"Oh, you've been watching cop shows too. Respect," Leira smiled, pulling off her blue and orange Merrell running shoes. "Size eight," she said to the girl behind the shoe counter. "He'll try a twelve."

CHAPTER TWENTY-TWO

"Okay, Bert, you're up!" said Mike, taking a large sip of his beer. "Perfect sport. Roll a ball, drink a beer. Roll a ball, eat some fries. At the end of it all you might even get a trophy."

Correk leaned in and whispered to Leira, "I blame you for this Bert thing."

"It's a beloved Muppet," said Leira. "Go, take your turn. You think you got this?"

"Get the heavy ball down the middle of the lane and hit the pins at the end."

"Without using magic or stepping over that painted yellow line."

"I'm not useless without magic just like you're hopefully not useless without your coffee machines and smartphones," Correk retorted. He looked down at the red, black and white shoes on his feet. "These things are ridiculous."

"And have been worn by hundreds of strangers, some with questionable hygiene," said Leira. "You don't want to know." She laughed when he grimaced. "That would be like getting a good look at who used the restroom stall before you and had their naked ass right where you're about to put your naked ass. You don't even exchange a nod. Better to look away."

"Go get 'em, honey!" yelled Estelle. "Beat those fuckers! Sorry, yes, I know," she said, waving at the people in the official Highland Lanes shirts. "No more swearing. Won't happen again," she promised, making an X over her heart.

"That's got to be getting close to a hundred times just this week," said Scott, laughing.

Correk glanced back at Leira who gave him a thumbs up. Leira was anxious to get on the road and work on the case but if she had to be in a bowling tournament, she wanted to win.

Correk picked up a blue ball and tested the weight in his hands. Too light, he thought, putting it back. He tried a black bowling ball, fitting his fingers in the holes like he'd seen the other players doing and held it up to his chest. Still too light.

He put his hand on each ball, feeling their weight, connecting with the energy of the ball.

"This one," he said, picking up the gold ball.

"My man is going for the King Kong of balls," said Paul, smiling. "I like it! Confidence! You hear that E-Bowlas? We got this!"

Correk stepped up a few feet from the yellow line and held the ball up against his chest. He stood there for a moment, calculating the friction of the ball against the wood in the lane, combined with the pitch of the floor and the distance to the pins. He took a deep satisfied breath and strode up to the line, swinging the ball back, letting its weight carry it forward, and releasing mid-stride, right at the line.

The ball was already rolling as it hit the ground and swerved momentarily to the right.

"Ooooooooh." An anxious murmur rose from the crowd behind him.

Just as the ball neared the gutter, still going at a fast clip, it curved back to the center of the lane, barreling down the middle, smashing into the center pin, toppling everything around it.

"You got a strike!" Leira yelled, forgetting everything else for just a moment. "You did it!" she exclaimed, jumping to her feet.

Mike pumped his fist in the air and Estelle pounded Correk's back when he came back to take his seat. "Good job, Bert! Your next beer is on me," she said.

"Beer's free to tournament players tonight, Estelle," said Janice.

"Which she knows," added Mitzi with a smile.

"Well, then I'll pour it for you," said Estelle. "Keep throwing like that and I may even buy you a beer back at my place."

"Now, that's saying something!" said Scott.

"Leira, we like your new friend," Craig said, holding out his fist to Correk who stared at the fist, confused. Leira leaned over and quickly fist bumped Craig.

"You have a few things left to learn about us," Leira said to him when he sat down next to her. "That was a perfect roll. No magic, right? I want to win but not by cheating."

"Simple mathematics and a strong arm. No magic," he replied. "Not necessary. It's an interesting pastime but does not require magic. Now Lutea ball, that's a game that requires magic if you hope to win. Dragons have been known to get involved in the longer matches and incinerate your roffle."

"You can tell me on the long ride to Chicago tomorrow what a roffle is," said Leira. "Big believer in singleness of purpose and right now, we have a match to win. I'm up!"

Leira grabbed a black bowling ball and went up and stood at the line. Out of the corner of her eye she noticed a young man with wavy brown hair from the other team smiling at her in a way she wasn't used to.

She did a double take to see if he was trying to throw her off her game.

"Not going to work," she yelled to him. "I am focused and ready to roll."

The man smiled harder, showing even, white teeth and Leira

felt her face flush. She wasn't used to men taking that much notice of her. Her hard edges were good at sending out a stay the fuck away signal.

What the hell is happening to me, she wondered, shaking her head to clear out any other stray thoughts. She took a deep breath and let it out slowly, stepping forward and swinging the ball, letting it go, willing it to stay true.

The tips of her fingers started to glow as she watched the ball take a similar path as Correk's roll. She quickly shoved her hands in her pockets and her heart beat faster in her chest.

The ball seemed to respond to her sudden panic and veered off course at the last second, hitting the pins to the right of center.

Leira plastered a blank look on her face before she turned around to face everyone. They were used to her dead fish look.

"You can still get a spare, honey," Estelle encouraged. "We can use one of those too."

Leira didn't look up to see if Correk had noticed what just happened. She went over to the balls and slowly pulled one hand out of her pocket, looking down to see if the fingertips were still glowing. Her hand was shaking slightly but back to normal. She felt her chest lighten as she pulled out her other hand and looked down. No glow.

Stay calm, Leira.

She stepped back up to the line and noticed the young man was still there, but he was no longer smiling. Instead, he was looking at her as if he was confused.

She looked away, knowing he must have seen it too, and focused on the pins.

Look where you want the ball to go. She took a step forward and threw the ball down the lane.

"Singleness of purpose," she whispered. She wished her grandmother was there. My mother, she thought, feeling a pang of guilt that she hadn't done more to get her out yet.

The ball rolled neatly down the left side of the lane, striking the rest of the pins, earning her the spare. Cheers went up behind her. She stood there for a moment, centering herself before she went back. This feelings thing is going to get me in trouble.

She glanced at the other team, but the young man was gone. Scared him off, she thought.

"Singleness of purpose," she said again, hardening her resolve. "First, we get the killer, then we get my mother out."

From across the room, the young man who had seen Leira performing magic was making his way through the crowd to the restrooms at the back. He was hurrying, going as fast as he could to find his friend Ernie, still in one of the two stalls.

"Ernie, Ernie, dude, you have to come out here." He banged on the stall door.

"Dude, not cool!" Ernie yelled. "Give me a second. The place isn't on fire, is it, Peter? It's not, right?"

Peter leaned down to make sure the other stall was empty. "Light Elves are here," he whispered urgently.

"What?" Ernie asked.

He came barreling out of the stall, still zipping his pants, already headed for the door. A strip of his belly showed between his black pants and the red E-bowla shirt. The tie under his bowling shirt was crooked. The fluorescent lights gleamed off his smooth, bald head.

Ernie grabbed Peter by the arm, dragging him out of the bathroom, down the hall and out the front door of the bowling alley. They stood in the parking lot in matching red, black and white bowling shoes. They both looked around to make sure no one was close.

"How can you be sure you saw a Light Elf? Was it the ears?" Ernie asked. "This is Austin. That could be like a man bun and somebody's idea of cool."

"I saw it. I saw her hands start to glow. Glow, Ernie! We have to tell someone."

MARTHA CARR & MICHAEL ANDERLE

"You sure we want to do that? You know what happens if we tell the Order. This gets moved up the chain of command, they do an investigation and if it's true…" He drew a line across his throat with his finger. "Order don't play."

"What if they find out we knew? If they can connect us to her at all and we didn't say anything…" Peter stammered.

"Good point. Did you get her name?"

"No, but she's the cute one on the Pin Pushers team."

"The one with the short dark hair. Yeah, noticed her too."

"Right? I was thinking about asking her out," Peter said.

"Bad idea for so many reasons." Ernie shook his head, crossing his arms over his chest.

"No kidding, asshole. She's some kind of Light Elf that can't control herself and we're both wizards."

"Too bad, too. You would have had a lot in common. Well, at least a whole other world."

"Yeah, I got that," said Peter, annoyed. "You go call it in and I'll see if I can scope out her name. See if she's the only Light Elf on the team or not."

"I knew there was a reason they were wiping the floor with us! Bunch of cheaters," Ernie grumbled.

"That's not our biggest problem right now. Do us both a favor and leave that out of the phone call to the Order. Stick to the facts, Ernie. I can trust you, right?"

The door swung open and the girl from behind the shoe counter leaned out. "You guys will need to return those shoes before you leave. You're not supposed to be outside with them on."

"Because a thousand sweaty feet is no problem, but some sidewalk dust will ruin the fine Corinthian leather." Ernie gestured with his hands and did a little dance, turning in a circle.

"Douchebags," the girl said, and went back inside, letting the door swing shut.

"Way to keep a low profile for us, Ernie," Peter snapped,

pulling open the door. "Make the phone call and keep it short and sweet."

"That was a little douchie of me, wasn't it? She was kind of cute."

"Oh my God, stay on point, Ernie or by the time this is over, we'll be in Trevilsom."

"How? The Order can't send us back from here."

"They have their ways."

Peter ran back inside as Ernie pulled out his phone. He stripped off the bowling shirt, straightening his tie. He wanted to look his best for his first official report.

He called the number he had memorized when he was inducted into the Order of the Silver Griffins. He had never had the chance to use it before and at first his voice came out in a squeak. He cleared his throat and started again.

"Hello? This is Silver Griffin two hundred and one. There's been a sighting in Austin. Magic was being used in the open. We believe it's a…"

"Hold please," the voice on the other end cut him off.

Light jazz played while Ernie waited, considering how he would tell this story later. It would be a lot more exciting and he'd play a bigger part. Maybe he'd say he saw the girl's hands light up. Peter wouldn't need to know.

"Hello?" The music stopped and there was a series of clicks on the phone.

"Your location has been recorded. Someone will be there shortly. Do not leave the premises. Get a picture of the offenders but do not approach."

"We, I mean, I, yeah, I," he said, wondering if this could get him a promotion. "I think it's just the one offender. A pretty cute girl."

"Get a picture. Don't leave the premises," the voice said firmly and then another click. They were gone.

"Rude." Ernie put the phone back in his pocket.

Peter barreled out, breathing hard.

"I can't find her," he said, panic rising in his voice.

"What? What do you mean? She was just there. The tournament just got started. Did you at least get a name?"

Peter shook his head hard. "No! The Pin Pushers clammed up. That little old lady kept poking me with her finger."

Ernie was disgusted. "Dude, you're a wizard. You know magic and you're afraid of a chain-smoking grandma?"

"That's no one's grandma," Peter said. "We can't use that magic any more than anyone else."

"Except to save our own lives." Ernie rolled his eyes and looked around for signs of the Silver Griffins.

"I'd like to see you explain to the Order how you were saving your life from a five-foot old lady. What's with the tie?" Peter asked him, flipping it up in the air with his hand.

"You know, Men in Black. We're the good guys keeping the world safe from magic and all things it doesn't need to know. I'm Will Smith. It's a vibe of coolness."

"It's a vibe of ridiculous. We're at a bowling alley. You already stick out like a sore thumb even when you're wearing the bowling shirt."

"Nah, chicks dig it. I look responsible, like I take things seriously. Check it out, I even have the sunglasses." He reached into his shirt pocket and slipped on a pair of black Raybans.

A blue minivan pulled in and parked in the back of the lot. Two couples got out dressed in jeans and t-shirts, headed for the bowling alley.

Ernie held the door nodding his head and saying, "Ma'am."

They stopped and looked at him sternly.

"Really?" asked Peter, exasperated. He leaned toward Ernie and said, "Those are the Silver Griffins that we're waiting for. They don't run around in black suits or battle gear."

"Except when necessary," said the taller wizard, winking at Ernie.

CHAPTER TWENTY-THREE

The woman pressed her mouth together. "Don't encourage them. They're new and they need to learn the right way to keep themselves out of trouble," said the witch, who was clearly in charge.

"Thirteen, fourteen, fifteen," whispered Peter.

"What are you doing?" asked the wizard. "Counting to yourself? I get it. Takes a few years to really fit into the Order of the Silver Griffins. The key is remembering you're part of a team. A healthy dose of courage doesn't hurt, either."

"In case someone tries to use magic on you?" Ernie asked. It was his greatest fear and his greatest wish, depending on how something like that turned out in the end.

"We see all kinds of things in our service," said the wizard.

"If you're done with trying to impress the novices," said the stern witch.

"I'm Ernie, I mean Silver Griffin two hundred and one." Ernie put out his hand to the friendlier wizard, who shook it back.

"We don't do a lot of chitchat in the field, Ernie. We like to stick to the mission. Things tend to turn out better that way."

The witch at the front of the group scowled at Ernie but he

didn't notice. He was too busy basking in the glow of being a part of a mission.

"Our first mission," he said in a reverent voice.

"Oh, for the love of…" the witch snapped.

"Ernie doesn't mean anything by it. We're both new. Recent recruits."

"You don't say," said the woman in the front of the group. She looked more like somebody's mom here to pick up her kid from a birthday party. She pulled a portable wand out of her pocket, letting it unfold and click in place.

"Oh man, she has the latest version!" exclaimed Ernie, reaching out to touch it. Peter batted his hand away.

"Keep watch," she said to the others. The other witch and wizard went just inside the building while the wizard who was being friendly with Ernie stood on the stairs, looking out toward the parking lot. He kept the same easygoing look on his face while he kept watch.

"Don't let his demeanor fool you. He's dispatched plenty of magical creatures who wanted to cause trouble here on Earth," said the witch, as she tucked a strand of blonde hair behind her ear. A charm bracelet dangled from her wrist.

Peter noticed the charm with the two interlocking circles that represented the Silver Griffins and the connection between Earth and Oriceran. It was swinging between a charm shaped like a soccer ball and a large dog.

Ernie swallowed hard, looking at the wizard. "Dispatched? You mean dead?"

"Of course I mean dead. Well, dead or Trevilsom Prison where you'll wish you had died. We have hard and fast rules. You wantonly display magic in front of the home team, the humans, and we take care of it. There are no second chances," she said. She had been with the Silver Griffins for well over a decade. "Now, which one of you saw the woman performing magic?" she asked.

"That was... well... that was," Ernie stuttered. He was afraid to move a muscle.

"You then," said the witch. She traced a small circle with her wand next to Peter's ear. A shimmering gold circle appeared, unwinding into a thin line, vanishing into the wand,

"Memorialum," she said quietly but firmly.

The wizard standing on the stairs joined them, pulling a device from his pocket no bigger than a smartphone and held it to the tip of the witch's wand. The phone sucked out the swirling gold lines with a soft whoosh, as the wizard tapped the small screen.

"So cool," said Ernie, trying to look over his shoulder. "Look at that, Peter! It's what you saw! Like we're looking through your eyeballs."

The images played on the screen, intently focused on Leira as she set up to throw the bowling ball. For a moment, the focus drew in on her ass. Everyone turned to look at a blushing Peter.

"It's my day off. I thought she was cute," he said sheepishly.

"There are no real days off," said the witch.

They turned back to the screen and watched as she seemed to be concentrating and then let the ball fly, her fingertips aglow. A look of panic came over Leira's face and she shoved her hands into her pockets.

"It's the detective," said the witch. "Just like the reports from the Order said."

"Reports? You know about her?"

"You might say she's a friendly. We're here to help if she runs into trouble."

"She's with us!" said Peter, brightening.

"That's Light Elf magic. She must be only half human. They left that out of our briefing," the wizard said.

"Doesn't look like she knew that was coming," the witch observed.

"That's good news, right?" asked Peter. "Intentions matter."

"We let the Order decide those things. Our job is to track magical objects that are loose in the wild, like the suburbs," the wizard smiled, "and take them into possession to be stored in our vault."

"And to hunt down and stop all magical creatures from wantonly displaying magic where humans could see it," the witch said pointedly. "It's fine," she said, looking at Peter's anxious face. "Leira Berens is a special case. We have orders to stay back and only step in if the detective or the elf traveling with her need assistance."

"Roger that." Ernie saluted. The witch stared at him for a moment mumbling something about thin pickings for new recruits.

"You do realize we're expected to blend in as well," she said, looking him up and down.

"Totally," said Peter, jumping in to try and protect his friend.

"How long you been a Silver Griffin?" Ernie asked the wizard.

"Going on my second decade. Third generation. My great grandfather was born on Oriceran."

"No kidding!"

The witch's phone started to vibrate and she pushed the button. The other witch's voice came over it, the urgency clear.

"We have a level one problem in here. Get in here immediately."

"Level one," said Peter, trying to remember his training. "Isn't that the worst level saved for some outdated Atlantean thing or something?"

The witch didn't answer his question or even look back. She ran into the bowling alley, not bothering to keep a low profile, drawing stares and looks of concern from other bowlers. Soon, someone was bound to ask if they could help.

Peter knew they were breaching protocol right and left, which meant whatever the other witch and wizard found, it was bad.

"Diggin' the Men in Black thing you've got going on here," the wizard said to Ernie, as they ran in behind the witch.

"Right?" said Ernie, smiling broadly, and punched Peter in the shoulder.

"You're still going to need to blend in," said the wizard.

They found the witch and wizard by the snack counter. The witch was holding a silvery bag that was wriggling wildly, left and right. People were taking notice, glancing at the bag and whispering to each other.

"This is bad, Ernie," Peter whispered.

"What's in there?" asked the witch, her eyes wide with alarm.

"Not something I've ever seen before or ever expected to see," said the other witch as she carefully folded back the long bag so that the lead witch could get a better look.

"No," she gasped, the color draining from her face. "How is this possible?"

Twisting wildly in the middle of the bag, a long black tentacle tried to escape.

"Stop!" yelled the witch holding the bag as the tentacle swarmed to the opening, reaching for her with its suction cups.

Before she could shut the bag, the tentacle wrapped itself around her neck in one fluid motion, and started drawing tighter like a noose, the suction cups planting themselves firmly on her skin.

"Ga," was the only sound she was able to make.

The lead witch whipped out her wand and said loudly, "Into the fire!"

Purple flames appeared around the tentacle, which only made it squeeze harder. The witch gasped for air, trying to clutch at her throat. The wizard held her hands back.

Peter could smell burning seafood as the tentacle started to glow purple from the flames. The witch fell back into the wizard's arms. The tentacle darkened and turned to ash, a small cloud of soot drifting across the front of her blue velour jacket.

"Is she breathing?" Ernie asked, trembling.

The wizard passed his hand over the witch's face, gently puffing air. The witch's chest rose and fell with each gentle puff until she finally took a breath on her own and her eyes popped open.

He helped her stand, saying to Ernie and Peter, "Much gentler than mouth to mouth."

"Everyone all right?" The manager of the bowling alley, a large fellow with wisps of air on the top of his head and a bushy greying moustache was hustling toward them. "Your friend need an ambulance?" he said, looking concerned.

The head witch looked around and saw that every face was turned toward them. More than one person had their cell phone out and was filming the whole thing.

Peter stepped back, his eyes wide, as the witch drew out her wand in full view of everyone and held it high in the air.

"Never was, never will be," she intoned. Rays poured out of her wand in widening shafts of white light that were so bright Peter expected them to hurt his eyes. Instead, a growing sense of peace filled him as the light caressed the entire bowling alley, even seeking out the kitchen and the rest rooms till everything within the four main walls was bathed in the light.

All the humans looked around, dazed, with goofy, lopsided grins on their faces. A large man dropped the bowling ball in his hands, giggling as he watched it slowly roll down the gutter.

The light hummed and grew steadily louder until it ended with a sharp snap and disappeared. Everyone froze, suspended in time.

"This will only last a few minutes, so we need to make this count. Help her out of here. Both of you are coming with us," she said, pushing them toward the door.

"What just happened?" said a dazed Ernie.

"What about them?" Peter pointed at a small group in one of

the middle lanes who were all still moving, nodding to the witches and wizards.

"A group of Arpaks, most likely," said the wizard, holding up his phone. "Yeah, I was right." Peter looked at the screen on his phone and could see a silhouette of the people in front of them, but they appeared to have grown large wings. He looked back and forth between the average looking people standing in the lane and the image on the small screen.

"Arpaks always blend in so easily," said the wizard. "They'll follow the usual protocol and play along. The spell took out the last thirty minutes of memory. All the humans will take up where their memory's left off. Some will think they need to pee again or go get something to eat and then just change their minds when they realize they must be wrong."

"Does this happen all the time?" Peter asked, helping to get the injured witch to the door.

"That is going to leave a mark." Ernie winced looking at the red welts on the witch's neck. They were starting to swell. "Is that normal?" He gingerly pointed to the large bubbles growing on her skin.

The lead witch turned around and gasped before catching herself.

"Hurry," she said.

The wizard said to Ernie, "There's no way for us to know what that thing could do. That kind of dark magic hasn't been seen for six hundred years. I've seen a tentacle or two in my day but not one that can do that."

"It's supposed to all be under lock and key!" said the lead witch as they went out the doors. "Under lock and key on an entirely different planet!"

"It's getting worse," Ernie said, wrinkling his nose. "It's starting to smell like rotted fish."

The welts on the witch's neck were starting to bubble and creep up toward her face.

"What's happening?" pleaded the injured witch, as the wizard once again stopped her from touching the pulsing wounds around her neck.

"There's no time to waste. We have only seconds left. I can't even alert them we're coming," said the head witch, as she waved her wand in a large circle and golden sparks started to spit out of thin air, creating a large hole in the air, right there in front of the bowling alley.

"A fucking portal," said Peter, drawing closer. "That's Oriceran." He peered through, his mouth hanging open. "My Nana told me all about it."

They were high atop a cliff with a view that went on for miles. Strange birds flew nearby.

Ernie pulled back, inching away from the portal. The witch grabbed him by the arm and dragged him back.

"We'll have to explain once we're there," said the tall wizard.

"Agreed," said the wounded witch's partner as he picked her up in his arms and stepped through the portal. The other wizard followed quickly.

"Come on, come on. There's only a couple of minutes left before time starts again. Get in here. That's an order!"

Peter snapped to and dutifully stepped through, grabbing Ernie's hand and dragging him. He felt an odd tug as he passed through to Oriceran and felt Ernie's hand slip out of his.

The last thing he heard before the portal zipped shut, sparks shooting everywhere, was a short plaintive cry. "What the hell?"

Ernie had hesitated a moment too long and slipped, out of Peter's grasp into the world in between.

"No!" cried the lead witch. She raised her wand, but it was too late. They were safely in Oriceran and the portal was closed. Ernie was lost.

"Where did he go?" Peter shouted, frantic.

"The world in between," one of the wizards gasped. His voice was angry as he spit out, "This was all handled badly. Where he is, that's worse than death! Trapped for eternity with other lost souls. The living and the dead!"

"What the fuck? No, I'm not leaving this spot till you tell me how we get him out of there. He'll never survive it!"

"I don't have time to baby you," said the lead witch, taking Peter by the arm, "so I'm going to tell you the facts, as much as we know. He'll survive it and that's the problem. The world in between seems to be some kind of waystation between Earth and Oriceran and whatever afterlife there is. He can see us and sometimes, maybe, we will be able to see him."

Peter's look of fear was turning to horror and he tried to sit down.

"Not just here, Peter. Ernie will be able to travel through the realm he's in and hear everything in both worlds. Even communicate sometimes but that's about it. Right now, we don't know any more than that. I can't do anything else for him but if you don't come with me, and quickly, my friend here will die."

The boils along the witch's neck spread and were turning black. The veins in her arms were also a deep, dark black.

"This magic is beyond me. It's beyond all of us here. Our only hope for her is one of the healers on this side of the world who is old enough to remember the old ways when they had to fight Rhazdon's cult. Now get off your ass and move!" she shouted and slapped him hard across the face. There were tears in her eyes.

"You are an elite member of the Silver Griffins," she shouted into his face. "We serve to protect all magical beings and sometimes we die doing that, or worse! You've been given an order and I expect you to follow it. If you can't be trusted to do that, there's no place for you in the Order of the Silver Griffins."

"I'm going," said the wizard carrying the witch. He put her down and waved his wand over her. She rose into the air in front of him and they disappeared in a swirl of wind and dust.

"Don't you understand yet? Dark magic is trying to return to this world. It's the very reason we were created. To make sure it can never come back. If it has then we have failed that part of our mission. But for the sake of all living things we cannot fail the more important part. To stop it by any means necessary," said the witch as she swirled her wand around the three remaining figures.

They disappeared into the wind.

CHAPTER TWENTY-FOUR

"What the hell was that about?" Leira yelled as they barreled down the streets, gunning the motor.

"You were seen performing magic. It's a crime to do so on Earth punishable by prison or even death," said Correk, forming a ball of red pulsing light.

"You did see it! Wait, what the fuck are you doing?" she asked, looking over at him.

"Seen performing magic is the key word." He quickly created an energy ball. His eyes glowed in the darkness of the car.

He rolled down the window and released the ball into the night air where it split into a thousand little sparks of light that looked like so many fireflies taking flight.

"What is that supposed to accomplish?" asked Leira. "You're sending up a smoke signal."

"That's a crude way of putting it, but yes. I need to get a message to the king before the Silver Griffins beat me to it. We were able to get out of there before they had a chance to identify you and I'm counting on the loyalty of the Pin Pushers back there to not give away any further information. But they'll make a report anyway and a hunt will be on unless I can get the king to somehow intercede and tell them to call it off."

Leira made it back to Rainey Street in record time. It was the first time she was the one being pursued instead of the detective on a case.

There was nothing about it that she liked.

"I haven't done anything wrong," she said defiantly. She found a parking space right next door and got out quickly, running for the gate without looking back to see what Correk was doing.

Correk hesitated at the sidewalk looking around to see if anyone had noticed them screeching to a halt and leaping out of the car. He still had the unsettled feeling that something magical and dark was following him.

"Is everything alright?" asked a twenty-something girl with a handful of friends. They all looked a little tipsy, dressed up in short skirts and tops with thin straps They stood close together, using the proximity to hold each other up as they wobbled on stiletto heels.

"Yes, routine call." Correk stood up straighter doing his best imitation of a police officer.

"You're kind of cute," said a girl with teased blonde hair that added several inches to her height. She pointed a painted mauve fingernail at Correk. "Are you really a stripper?" She gave him a smile that was more of a leer.

"Earthlings," muttered Correk under his breath.

"Ooh, that's kind of cute," said another girl. "Take me to your leader," she said, and licked her lips suggestively.

"You're a tall drink of water. Where's the party, Robin Hood?"

"Thank you, ladies," said Correk, exasperated. "There's no party. There's no stripper. Please move along. There's nothing to see here."

He walked away from them sensing that nothing good could be gained from continuing the conversation.

They would have followed him except one of them suddenly

fell off her heels crashing into the grass. They surrounded the fallen friend oohing and aahing, overly concerned with her well-being.

"Crap! I think I got a grass stain on my skirt." She frowned and rolled over to take a look. Her mood brightened when she noticed she didn't spell a drop of her drink.

"Nice," she smiled. Her friends pulled her to her feet, and she slipped her foot back into her shoe.

By then, Correk was briskly walking through the crowd at Estelle's, ignoring the shouts from the bar asking how the team was doing at the bowling alley.

"Is the tournament already over? Did we win?" people yelled from the outdoor bar.

"Estelle on her way back?" asked the bartender who was filling in for her. Correk ignored them all.

Leira was nowhere in sight.

He walked into the guesthouse and quietly shut the door behind him. There was already enough drama and slamming a door would've brought people asking what was wrong. Leira was changed back into a more typical outfit, a pale green shirt and black pants, and had slipped on her leather jacket. She was ready to roll. Her service weapon was strapped under her shoulder.

She was paying no attention to Correk and he could see that her mind was made up.

"In the short amount of time that I've known you I already realize that trying to change your mind is useless and a waste of time," said Correk.

"Good. Then I won't have to work so hard actively ignoring you," she said angrily.

Correk stripped off the blue pin pushers bowling shirt and tossed it on the couch, revealing ripped muscles and a well-defined torso. Leira caught herself taking a second look and her face warmed.

"Damn," she whispered, surprising herself.

Correk raised an eyebrow at her. "You have many different layers, Leira Berens. There may be hope for your magical abilities yet," he said, putting his own shirt back on.

"No, no, no." Leira waved her hand at the shirt he was trying to button up.

"It's a little indelicate that you're trying to get me to take my shirt off again," he said, still buttoning it up.

"Don't get your hopes up." She pulled out an old t-shirt that read, 'Keep Austin Weird 5K' with an old hippie truckin' across top of the words, a big foot in a floppy sandal stretched out in front of him.

"This is left over from some 5K I ran a while ago. They had run out of every size but large by the time I got there. It should do fine. You can't go around in this medieval costume everywhere we go. It gets old after a while and harder to explain. Put it on."

Correk slipped out of the white shirt, glancing over at Leira before turning his back to pull the t-shirt over his head. Leira couldn't resist and took one last look at his back muscles rippling when he pulled the shirt down over his shoulders.

She shook her head, clearing her mind. "Too much to do," she muttered.

She felt a new sensation running up through her chest and out through her arms. "I've already been through puberty," she whispered, embarrassed.

Suddenly her fingertips began to glow

"No!" she shouted, shaking her hands violently, trying to will it away.

Correk whipped around, his eyes widening as he saw the source of her distress.

"That won't help!" he shouted. Correk's eyes glowed briefly and symbols appeared on his arms. He scowled in frustration.

The glow in Leira's fingertips spread up her arms and

symbols appeared under her skin, giving her the same warm feeling that was now spreading to her bones.

"It's clear you have no idea who you really are," said Correk, trying to get his emotions under control.

Leira's training as a homicide detective kicked in and she steeled herself, taking a deep breath and assessing the situation. It never failed her. She was damned determined it wouldn't fail her now.

The symbols slowly faded from Leira's skin, a hum lingering that she felt all the way to her lips.

"You're getting better at this," Correk said. "You're a fast study. But common sense says we should wait until morning to leave when we have the Mustang back. Your friend will want his car and I'm not sure it will carry us the entire way to our destination."

Leira sat down heavily on the red velvet chair. "You have a point. But first light and I'm checking on the car."

"Deal."

True to her word, as the sun rose the next morning, Leira reached for her phone.

"I figured you'd be getting anxious." It was Ralph. "She's all ready. You speared the radiator just like I thought, but it's all taken care of."

"What do I owe you?"

"Don't insult me with questions like that. Meet me at the station so I can get home to my wife. You know, she misses you too."

Leira hung up the phone and felt an unfamiliar pang in her chest. She realized she was letting herself feel something. The troll let out a small whimper. She shook her head, hard. "Enough of that. Shelve it all till later," she said, hoping it was possible.

"Ready to go?" Correk stood in the doorway, already dressed. He was holding the CVS bags of snacks he bought for the road. "You can get the troll. He's not as fond of me as he is of you and I'd hate to have to turn him into stone."

"That's it?" she asked, astonished, swinging her feet out over the side of her bed. "You're not going to try and get me to wait or talk more?"

"You're the one who said we needed to get going," said Correk reaching for the door handle. "We have a long ride ahead of us and hours of time to explain what's happening to you. I can explain now because it's become clear. Why you don't know is going to take a little detective work that will have to wait for another day."

Correk stopped with his hand on the doorknob. "I'm not making light of what's happening to you. Your life is in danger from more than one source and it's all because of who you are. But if I start this conversation here it will make it that much tougher to walk calmly through the patio, smile and wave to anyone who might be there as if nothing is happening, and get in the car as quickly as possible."

Leira was about to protest but Correk held up his hand without turning around and opened the door. There was no more to say till they picked up the car from Ralph. She scooped up the troll and his box and headed out the door.

"Thank you. I really will call." Leira accepted the car keys from Ralph.

"I know," Ralph said. "Be careful out on those roads. Never know when a sign will run out in front of you." He smiled and squeezed her shoulder.

Really have to do better at keeping in touch. She gave him a crooked smile. There was so much more she wanted to say.

Correk refused to answer any of Leira's questions until they got out onto the open highway beyond the city limits and the constant congestion on I35 that had become part of Austin. The sky was different shades of blue and purple behind the tall buildings downtown.

Leira tried to get Correk to answer at least one or two questions but he sat in stony silence watching the passing scenery, biding his time.

Leira bit her bottom lip, drumming her fingers on the steering wheel, counting blue cars, one of the least popular colors. She managed to get all the way to five before Correk finally spoke.

"I would think it would be obvious by now," he said.

"Obvious has to be based on past experience and that hasn't worked for me since you and his majesty showed up in a hole in the world and pulled me back through it," Leira said.

"That must've been the trigger," he said, clearly trying to make sense of it all. "You are, young lady, at least half Light Elf, and from the look I got of the symbols that appeared on your arms, you have an ancestor of royal blood. You are a very powerful elf."

"That's ridiculous. I'm twenty-five years old. You don't think I would've shown some sign by now? No one has ever mentioned anything like this to me."

"Who would have known enough to have explained it to you?" he asked.

"My mother." She bit off the words. "Don't say anything. Not about that. Not yet when I can't do anything about it."

"Fair enough." Correk's head was down as he dug through the bag of snacks, pulling out the Cheetos. There was a trill from the box resting between them and the sound of sniffing around the edges.

"I'm not planning to share," said Correk.

"You may have to. I already introduced him to that delicacy. But you can't start digging into the food just yet. It's a well-known rule of road trips that you have to wait at least two hours after you get outside of the city limits before you start. On longer road trips like this one, you wait till you're out of the state."

"I'm not from this world. Your rules don't apply and besides Texas is far too big a state for me to wait that long. I'm hungry." Correk pulled the bag open and sniffed. "Reminds me of an aged cheddar but there's something else I can't identify."

"We call those preservatives and other five syllable words we can't pronounce but are glad to ignore," said Leira.

Correk took a cheese doodle out of the bag and gave it a lick. "Not bad."

"This is how we indoctrinate you. We slow you down with our fast food till you can't think for yourself anymore. Correk, if you can pull your attention away from the faux food, my mind is getting blown over here."

Correk gingerly lifted the top of the box and quickly threw in a few Cheetos. The troll nipped at his finger and hungrily took them, pushing them one by one into his mouth till his cheeks bulged, chomping down till they were no more than mush. Correk shook his head and put the lid back on, letting out a sigh.

"Leira, I've watched your culture for years and learned a lot of your idioms. You're very fond of adding new ones all the time," he said, crunching down on a large doodle. He gave his orange fingers a quizzical look and started to brush his hands together.

"Rookie move," said Leira. "You'll spread the orange fairy dust everywhere and once it gets on your clothes it's kind of tough to get out. You either lick it off, wipe it off, or just keep eating. Look under that lid. I'll bet it's a wall of orange by now."

"No thanks." He stared at his fingers for a moment, incredulous. He seemed to make a decision and dove back into the bag.

"Yeah, that's the choice I would have made too." Leira glanced over at him and looked back at the room. "You have to make a mental decision ahead of time when you choose Cheetos that you're just going to eat most of the bag in one sitting. It's a commitment snack."

"Should we honor your little road trip rules and not talk about your newly evident magical skills until we're out of Texas?" His mouth was full of mashed Cheetos. "Or shall we just go rogue with all of it and start talking."

"That is not a good look on you," said Leira, looking at the orange that was getting all over Correk's face. "But you do look more like you belong right here in the good ol' USA."

Leira looked back at the road and cut around an eighteen-wheeler ambling down the middle lane. "Before all of this started it wouldn't have taken much to convince me I was losing my mind. I would've thought I was the only one seeing the symbols or that crazy warmth you get under your skin," she said, a warm shiver running through her. "My mother..."

"I see you're wearing the ring we helped you find when we first met. That's your mother's ring with the two blue sapphires. You've mentioned her more than once but from everything we've observed you have no contact with her."

"Okay. I can't avoid talking about her, it seems. I have no contact because my mother, Eireka Berens, has been locked up in a psychiatric facility for fifteen years, since I was ten years old. She started talking about strange men with pointed ears and an entirely different world where people could make things appear out of nowhere and castles that couldn't be seen and was diagnosed with an official stamp of crazy."

"Do we have something in the car to wipe this off with?" Correk was trying to lick the orange off his fingertips but it was proving resilient.

"Check the middle compartment. There's hand wipes in there that I saved just for this kind of occasion."

Correk pulled out one of the wet wipes, rubbing his hands against it and admiring how the orange kept its color and was never diluted. "That was amazing."

He turned his attention back to Leira. "I ate so many of them and I don't feel at all full. I'm not sure if that's good or bad. Okay, okay, how long ago did your mother start talking about elves and Oriceran?"

"About six months before they carted her off and I ended up with my grandmother."

"Where's your grandmother now?"

Leira grew quiet and didn't say anything for the next few miles. The troll whimpered from the underwear nest on the backseat, picking up on Leira's sadness.

Correk waited patiently for Leira to speak.

The brown and green cliffs of the Texas Hill country rolled past them. Correk looked out at the large mansions built into the sides of the cliffs.

"Human beings have no access to magic and yet you manage to do these amazing things," he said. "Technology for you has become a kind of magic. You can manipulate your environment in so many ways. I suppose the difference is our magic leaves nature alone, for the most part."

"My grandmother disappeared over four years ago. It's why I became a cop. I want to solve that mystery."

"You believe she was murdered," Correk said softly.

"I did... I'm not so sure now."

"That's something to think about," he said. "She may be on Oriceran and unable to relay a message to you. It explains some of why you knew nothing about your heritage. That was probably for the best. You haven't had to deal with getting your magic under control all these years. Emotions drive magic, and there has to be somebody around to teach you the right way. Magic out of control can quickly turn into dark magic."

"I need to get this case solved so that I can get my mother out of that damn hospital," she said, hitting the steering wheel. "She never belonged there in the first place. There's no telling what fifteen years in a psychiatric facility will do to someone."

"If your mother is the one who's in the Elven line then the magic will have helped her survive. I suspect, though, she does not know enough about how to use it, or the walls wouldn't have held her all this time."

Leira moved into the fast lane again and accelerated to eighty-five miles an hour. The Mustang was cruising down the road, the engine humming.

"I thought we were trying not to attract attention," said Correk.

"We need to get to Chicago. Time is running out and Bill Somers has been alone with that necklace for days. There's no telling what's happened. I'm catching on that magic is not very stable.

Correk thought a moment. "If we are planning to drive through the night then you will need assistance with the driving."

"When you get your own badge," Leira said evenly, drawing her lips into a thin line. "This is an official badass Austin police car. Besides, you don't even have a license. I didn't see a single engine of any kind on Oriceran. This isn't something you can pick up in a few minutes."

"I'm a fast learner," he said. "But I will let you do the driving for now."

"Big of you." She swung out from behind a large truck to pass it on the left.

Correk ignored Leira's comment. "To ensure that we both arrive safely and complete this mission," he said, "I'm going to teach you how to access the Elven side. It's not even magic, really. If you can lock into this feeling of determination and belief in this mission, then you can summon the Elven blood that will keep you awake and alert for as long as you need."

"How do I do that?" Leira kept taking quick looks over at him.

"You have to feel it." he replied without a thought.

She made a face. "Then we're fucked," she told him, "and I'll have to use the human method of gallons of coffee."

CHAPTER TWENTY-FIVE

Correk thought about his response to her answer before trying another time. "Leira, you have Royal Elven blood flowing through your veins. It elevates your magic to an entirely new level. You're more than capable of this. Come on, you're telling me that you're backing away from a challenge?"

Leira gripped the steering wheel, her knuckles whitening. "Point taken." God, she wanted the coffee. "Give me the first lesson."

Correk turned in his seat to face her and tapped the center of his chest with his fingers. "You have to feel it in here. Draw on the feeling as if it is a living, breathing, being within you, because it is. Name something that you already believe without question."

Leira's eyebrows drew together, running through the possibilities. "I believe in my own ability to survive all this shit."

He made a twisting maybe sort of motion with his hand. "Reach for something more. Something positive."

"I believe… I believe that the people who hang out at Estelle's care about me."

It was the first time she had ever acknowledged it to herself. "They've done a decent job of being a family to me. A smoking,

MARTHA CARR & MICHAEL ANDERLE

drinking, bowling family. I know if I needed them, any one of them would drop everything to come and help."

Leira felt the growing warmth in the center of her chest. A surge of energy that felt solid, felt real.

He nodded. "Draw on that belief," said Correk. "It is the belief in others, the connections you have that matter most that will be the most powerful. Now, pull that belief into the idea that you need to be alert, focused and able to sustain this energy for the next few days. It won't stop you from sleeping when you choose to, but the choice will become yours. It is a power of the Light Elves and for a Royal Elf is immutable."

Leira felt the energy wash over her like she was taking a drug. She was able to think with speed and clarity.

"Oricerans have apparently been coming over to Earth for quite some time, if my magical lineage is to be believed." She flashed her lights to catch the attention of the slow Impala in front of her. Thankfully, they slid aside as she barreled past them. "No wonder there's a need for the Silver Griffins."

"It's a little more complicated than that. Our two worlds have a unique connection that has gone on for many millennia. Every twenty-five thousand eight hundred years gates open and stay open. They're like the portal you went through but larger and very public. Anyone can walk right through them at any time."

"Are we getting close to one of those years?" she asked. They came over a rise and from the top she could quickly see what pattern she would need to take through the miles of cars ahead of her in order to make the fastest time. She wove in and out of traffic easily, missing bumpers by mere inches and maneuvering her way out of a snarl of slow-moving traffic.

"We are only decades from when the process starts. A little under sixty-five hundred years till it hits its peak and crests."

"That means the last one was about nineteen-thousand three hundred years ago." Leira attempted to do the math in her head.

242

"I think." Why is it always a problem to subtract fives, threes and eights in my head?

"Frankly, residents of Oriceran have lived on Earth forever. Every time the portals have started to close some humans chose to stay behind on Oriceran for the magic, and some magical species chose to live on Earth for their own reasons. Technology has its own allure too. Some were also fugitives from Oriceran law, and some formed relationships with a human and were unwilling to leave."

"What you're telling me is that there are magical people all around the world," Leira said. "My world."

"Yes, entire magical communities and many of them live in plain sight. There are even many different types, too many to name."

"Even Light Elves?"

"A full-blooded Light Elf is pretty hard to hide." Correk tapped his ear. "The points are a dead giveaway. Early American settlers kept referring to us as demons and that was a problem. Magic never did go over very well with the Puritans."

"Were those distant relatives who got burned at the stake in old Salem?" asked Leira.

"No, even a human being with a small percentage of Elven blood would have easily been able to confuse and persuade the simpletons of old Salem. Those were most likely innocent human beings. But if you know where to look it gets easier and easier to spot your distant cousins. You knew a half Elf as Elvis Presley. His mother had a sense of humor and gave him a first name as a clue."

"I can see that," said Leira. "He has a certain luck. That explains the singing."

"And the dancing. Oh yes," said Correk, "we know how to dance but it's something normally only shared with your partner. It's considered intimate."

"Those rockin' hips." Leira smiled despite how she felt. It was one of her best defense mechanisms. She knew how to compartmentalize her feelings and put them aside altogether if there was a job to be done. It helped make her a good homicide detective. But she could sense things were changing and being able to intertwine her emotions in with her thoughts was becoming essential. The magic within her was waking up.

They drove all night, making only occasional stops to put more gas in the car or use the bathroom. Correk had his first soda, choosing a Dr. Pepper. He took a sip, screwed up his face, commented on the bubbles, swallowed and did it all over again till the bottle was drained.

"It's like watching National Geographic," Leira said. She poured some from her soda into a cup and put it in the box. The troll dove into the cup, drinking as he sank to the bottom. "You're both like wild animals around any kind of snack," muttered Leira. "Wait till you find out about double-stuffed Oreos."

The lid lifted and the troll's head poked out to look at her.

Correk was still thumping his chest with his fist to get out the remaining bubbles but he stopped for a moment. "What's a double stuffed...?"

"Oreo," said Leira, giving him a crooked smile. "So much left to find out," she said with a snort.

It was just around breakfast time the next day when they arrived in Chicago. They pulled in the parking lot of one of the no-tell motels along part of Lincoln Avenue still known as Route forty-one that dated back to when the road was the main state thoroughfare. It was replaced long ago by bigger highways and the motels were mostly ignored by everybody except those who wanted to use it by the hour to play or were trying to hide.

Before getting out of the car she waved her hand over the shoe box. "Nesturnium," she said. "I'll be back to get you." She heard scratching in the box but no real protest. She looked at Correk. "Let me handle this part, okay? It'll go easier."

Leira went into the small office to rent the room and the clerk behind the counter looked lazily up, glancing at Correk still waiting in the car. "Double occupancy, I take it," he said. "You want it for the night?"

"We'll need the room through the weekend," she said, giving him a cold hard look. She was tempted to flash her badge, but she was operating outside of the rules. Getting caught on a case that wasn't assigned to her outside of her jurisdiction was breaking the law. She resisted the urge and instead remembered what Correk had said to her.

She stared at the clerk coolly, summoning the feeling of belief within her that all was well, and they would succeed. A calm settled over her that she was sure the clerk could see, evidenced by the change in his personality. He suddenly became more amiable.

"Room two oh two on the second floor. It's one of our better rooms. The maid's been in that one today and the comforter hasn't been used, well, that much." He held up his thumb and forefinger an inch apart. "Ice machine will be halfway down outside this door and there's plenty of fast food restaurants everywhere you look. Welcome to Chicago and Lincoln Square."

She got back to the car and found Correk chewing a piece of beef jerky. He was beginning to look a little nauseous.

She opened her door and leaned in. "I have the room key, but I don't feel good about leaving our stuff there. We should really get some real food in you before this gets ugly.".

"This is your world, what do you suggest? And no more Chee-tos." He gingerly put a hand on his stomach.

"Yeah, that's phase two of eating too many Cheetos, and throwing in corn nuts and beef jerky on top of it with a Dr. Pepper. You have to work up to that. This is a marathon, Correk, not a sprint. Let's see, we're in Chicago. We need to go find Lou

Malnati's deep dish pizza. It'll either fill you up or kill you off, but either way you'll be out of your faux food misery."

"What's a pizza?" he asked.

"How is it possible in all of your eavesdropping you didn't pick up on so many barely-edible delights? Lou Malnati's is a thick crust followed by a ton of melted, gooey cheese, with homemade tomato sauce on top. More toppings are optional."

"Anything you'd call a vegetable?"

"You can get a mushroom or a green pepper thrown on there if you need to. Try a slice and then we'll head out to locate Bill Somers." Leira found the restaurant easily as if she was following an old memory in her head.

"How did you know where to go without a map?" asked Correk.

"Not sure, really. My grandmother used to take me on road trips a lot when I was younger. We'd go to Santa Monica, upstate New York, Chicago. She always said we needed to recharge. Wait, that's what that girl at Enchanted Rock said. What? I saw that," she said, as they walked into the restaurant. "What does it mean?"

"I'll explain later," he said.

They drove to the parking lot of the restaurant and Leira lifted the lid on the box, repeating the spell. "I promise you a large slice and I never break my word. You're connected to me. You have to know that about me by now."

Yumfuck let out a sigh and sat back. "A big piece," he squeaked.

"Covered in melted cheese," said Leira.

The troll drooled and smacked his lips as Leira put the lid back on, leaving it a little askew.

They walked up to the diner and made their way in, stopping at the hostess station.

"Can we have a table near the front window?" Leira asked.

"Right this way," said the waitress. She showed them to a booth and set down two tall plastic menus in front of them.

Correk took one look at the menu and winced, looking up at the waitress and asking, "Do you have anything smaller, you know, thinner?" He was pointing at the picture of the three-inch deep pizza.

The waitress and Leira gaped at him.

"We don't really do thin crust here, honey," the waitress said. "You're in the wrong city. Try New York. How about a nice green salad for you? You look like you might need it."

"We'll get a small deep dish and maybe a salad on the side," said Leira.

"And a Dr. Pepper," said Correk, with a little too much enthusiasm.

The waitress tapped the side of her forehead behind Correk's back with her eyebrows raised, asking Leira a question. Leira ignored her.

She returned with a paper placemat and a small box of crayons and set them off to the side. "I'll just leave those here, in case there's an artist in the family."

Leira laughed, and then glanced out the window toward the car to see if the troll was awake. No movement.

"Tell me what that look was about when I mentioned the road trips," said Leira.

"The locations you traveled to with your grandmother. She must have known there was Elven blood in your family. It's common for the magical communities here on Earth to live near what are known as kemana or green sectors. They are locations on Earth that have large amounts of quartz imbued with magical energy. It was done before the portals closed the last time. They're used as a kind of charging station so that Oricerans can maintain at least a minimum of magical ability. They've also become a way for different species to find each other. Like a community bulletin board."

The waitress came back with their pizza and a stand to set it on and Correk got quiet.

"Here, let me help you, honey," said the waitress. She was determined to help him get his slice. She put it on a plate for him and stepped back. "Try a knife and fork. It'll be okay."

Correk looked at Leira for some help to get rid of her but Leira was enjoying it too much to say anything. The waitress wouldn't leave until he tried a bite and assured her that he liked it.

"Now that's what I call service," said Leira, after the waitress finally bustled away to tend to someone else.

"She's treating me like I'm a child."

Leira nodded. "I think you hit the nail on the head."

"You know, this really is delicious, but I have a feeling I'm only making matters worse."

"Now you're catching on to the American diet." Leira grinned as she bit into her pizza. Memories of sitting here with her grandmother came flooding back to her. Just enjoy it Leira. More answers will come soon enough.

Correk insisted on taking a slice to go, earning him a hug from the waitress. Leira asked for another one, thinking of the troll, and noticed that the waitress had tucked a placemat and crayons into the bag. Correk seemed startled by the hug but was gracious enough to just let her do it.

"Humans are very odd," Correk observed as they left the restaurant and walked to the car.

"Agreed." Leira got in and the top of the box immediately popped off, the troll standing up and smelling the air. "Can you help him while I drive?"

"He bites."

"Then move faster." She grimaced watching Correk try to fit a slice of deep-dish pizza into a paper shoe box, wondering when it would all spill over onto the leather seat. But Yumfuck moved through the middle with ease, sauce pushing its way up his nose, and came chomping around the edges before anything had a chance to get very far.

Correk pulled his hand back just in time before the troll had a chance to mistake a finger for the crust. "Too close."

Leira kept watching the whole thing in amazement as she drove them to the motel. "Dinner and a show," she said, wondering what lay ahead.

They tracked Bill Somers all over Chicago for the next two days. At the university, they found Dean Muston who said, "Professor Somers has taken a short break from work." Both Correk and Leira noticed how relieved the Dean looked when he told them. "I'm sorry, but we're getting ready for our Centennial celebration of the school. I really don't have time to help you reunite with Bill Somers."

At his small, cramped apartment they found evidence of Oriceran, a clump of tall grasses that had fallen limp. Correk wrapped them gently in a small square of cloth and tucked them in his pocket.

"No evidence should be left behind," he said.

But there was no sign of Bill Somers.

The troll crawled out of Leira's pocket and climbed onto Correk's shoulder to get a better view of the room. He stretched his arms overhead, letting go of a wide yawn, smacking his lips together, and then running back down Correk's arm to go and explore. Leira took note but decided to say nothing. What could he break in this place?

"Do you think he knows someone is looking for him?" Correk asked.

"It would appear that way," said Leira, studying the papers on his desk. "Look at this," she said. "It's a receipt for a handmade tuxedo. That's a lot of money for someone who lives like this. From the little I know of the man, style and fashion doesn't seem to be high on his list of priorities. He's getting dressed for a special occasion."

The troll ran by unnoticed, ducking into the bedroom.

Leira looked down at a piece of paper on the wobbly folding table that served as his dining room table. It was a memo from Somers' department about what to expect at the celebration.

"This Centennial is on the same day that you said the energy will transfer from the necklace to whoever has it," she said, tapping the paper.

"We're going to the Centennial, aren't we?"

"Seems like our best chance to find Bill Somers and the necklace all in one place. The trick will be to find him before he tries whatever it is he's going to try. Right now, he's in the wind and I don't have my usual tools to find where he might be hiding out. He might be smart enough to stay off the grid until tomorrow and the celebration. Looks like you're going to need a monkey suit."

"Why would I want to dress like a monkey?"

"It's our cute way of saying a tux," said Leira.

"We have far more sentient beings on Oriceran than there are on Earth and yet we managed to find only one unique word for everything."

There was a loud rustling from under the couch that made Leira furrow her brow. "I hope that's the troll."

Correk nodded, his hands on his hips. "And not a cousin of a Willen."

"A what?"

"An oversized rodent that likes to steal and pass along secrets for barter."

Leira stared at him for a moment. "Oriceran has large talking rats. Wow." The couch scooted forward a few inches, scraping along the wood floor. "Please just be the Yumfuck. He's going to look like an oversized dust bunny when he crawls out of there."

"Yumfuck?"

"Yumfuck Tiberius Troll. He has a name now. I think it suits him. Don't roll your eyes. Come on, you can comfort yourself with more deep-dish pizza. Eat too much of that though, and you'll need a cummerbund to hide the middle."

"What are you going to wear?"

"That's a very good question. Something that will hide a gun," said Leira, "and still let me blend in."

"I will need to return to Oriceran to recharge before the events tomorrow," said Correk.

"Won't one of the kemana suffice for now? There's a lot going on here and I could probably use your help."

"That's why I have to go back. I can recharge faster to full capacity in Oriceran and I can make sure the Order accepted what happened in the bowling alley."

He took a deep breath and his eyes started to glow. Symbols appeared on his arms and Leira noticed for the first time that they were different from the last time. Correk held out his hand and formed a ball of light, stretching the light in every direction, opening up a portal. Leira could feel the pull in the middle of her being, as well.

"I can feel it," she said, surprised.

"Inhabitants of Oriceran are always aware of when a portal is opening if they're anywhere nearby. It's just another sign of your Elven blood awakening inside of you." He put one foot through the portal, turning back to give her a stern look. "I won't be gone that long. Don't get into trouble," he said, stepping all the way through the portal. Leira could see deep woods on the other side.

"Trouble comes looking for me. You can direct where you come out to some degree can't you?"

The question was lost when the portal closed, and gold sparks showered, sputtering in the close air of the musty apartment.

Leira looked around at the dingy room and wondered if anything was safe to sit on. She noticed a metal folding chair and decided that was the best choice.

The troll emerged from behind a bookcase triumphantly holding up a broken ruler topped with a shiny Chunky candy wrapper taped around the top like an orb. He had found a black magic marker and had decorated his fur with stripes and symbols and placed yellow and orange post-it notes around his middle like a paper skirt.

"What the hell is going on here?" Leira bent over to get a better look and saw a trail of cockroaches lining up behind him, waiting patiently.

"I should have seen this coming. You've organized your own army. It's a miniaturized Lord of the Flies. Like a fucking diorama."

Yumfuck raised his broken ruler again and tilted his head back letting out a whoop. He turned around to face the roaches and yelled, "to the fort!" The bugs dispersed, running in formation behind the couch.

"Do I even want to know what's back there?"

Yumfuck answered with a jab in the air and a full-throated yell. "Defend Fort Fuck Off!"

"Fort Fuck Off. You really are bonded with me," Leira said, arching an eyebrow. She put a knee on the couch and cautiously peered over the back. Pillows from the bed had been pulled back there, along with a towel from the bathroom that was draped between them, making a fort. "You work fast." Leira wrinkled her nose at the sight of the roaches entering the fort. "Talking rat cousins, organized roaches. What's next?"

She saw something coming straight at her head and leaned back just in time to miss getting hit with a Cheetos that had been chewed into the shape of an arrow. It was quickly followed by two more that bounced off the top of the couch and fell behind it, landing amid the cockroach army, which quickly devoured the remains.

She leaned back off the couch and looked at the troll, her hands on her hips. "Nicely done, my furry friend," said Leira with a crooked smile. "It's been a long time since I've let go even for a minute. Even in the middle of chaos." The troll smiled back at her, showing all his sharp, pointed teeth. "You can feel it too, can't you," she said. "You knew I needed this. Although your idea of fun..." Another Cheetos arrow came zipping past her leaving a trail of orange dust.

She looked around for something to throw back at the troll but couldn't find anything. "I'm going to regret this," she said, hurriedly burrowing her hand into the couch cushions. She came out with a handful of stale raisins and laughed, hurling them at the troll who expertly caught each one in his mouth, swallowing them whole.

"Hey! That has to be against the rules. At least the rules of basic hygiene."

The troll responded by pulling out a tiny trebuchet from just behind an old chair. The homemade catapult was made from an old eraser, rubber bands, a pencil and the cup from an old Dayquil bottle. In the cup was a malt ball.

"Hey, did you raid the road trip snacks? That is low, my friend."

Yumfuck pulled back on the pencil, creating tension in the rubber bands. "Let 'er rip!" he yelled, letting go. The malt ball pinged off Leira's arm, just as the troll launched another and another. "Leira put up her hands, laughing, catching a few of them. "Okay, I give, I give. You and your cockroach army win." She caught sight of herself in a mirror hanging on the far wall and was surprised to see how happy she looked. It was as if she had forgotten everything for just a moment. Her mother, her grandmother, searching for the killer of the prince.

Suddenly she felt tired all over and sat down hard on the couch as the troll pull off his post-it notes and came to sit in the crook of her arm, curling into a ball. Leira absently rubbed the top of his furry head, chewing on one of the malt balls, gently falling into a light sleep.

She didn't know how much time has passed before she heard a fizzing and cracking from the small bathroom.

She heard a crash and the sound of a shower curtain being torn down as she rushed into the room. Correk was crawling out of the bathtub, looking sheepish.

"Are you hurt? I thought you had a better handle on this portal thing."

"A portal was opened here recently," he said, an edge to his voice. "Very recently. That affects the opening of the next portal and draws the energy toward it. It's certain. Bill Somers has been back to Oriceran."

"Are you fully recharged?"

"You're not going to ask about the Order?" asked Correk.

"If it's good news I don't need to know and if it's bad news I don't want to know. Come on, we have things to do. You can tell me what you've learned while we get a jump on Bill Somers. Maybe we'll get lucky and find him and the necklace before the big party."

"There's only a day left to pull that off."

"Stranger things are happening every day," she said.

CHAPTER TWENTY-SIX

The prophets on the council met in the hidden room at the back of the vast Oriceran post office. The mood was somber and the Kilomea's representative was banging his oversized thorny fist on the table, leaving small holes in the hardwood. "Things have gotten too far out of hand," he said. He was wearing a deep red cloak over his leather and armor. No one had bothered to put on the familiar blue robe of the prophets.

The Kilomeas were a brutish species. In the past, they were more interested in war than group consensus.

"Let me guess," said the Mystic Dryad, a tree nymph from the far north, beyond the mountains. "You want to restore order by any means necessary." She stared at him defiantly even though she was only a quarter of his size and he could have swatted her like a pesky bug. That is, if he was fast enough. Dryads were known to flit so quickly, their wings beating too fast to be seen, they seemed to vanish from sight.

An Azrakan stood up, its great horns encircling its head like an organic crown of bone. "We are getting ahead of ourselves. First things first," he said in a deep, booming baritone.

"The intelligent elk has spoken," said the Kilomea. The

Azrakan opened his mouth and unfurled a long, thin forked tongue, hissing at the Kilomea.

"I call this meeting to order," said an elderly underground Gnome whose people lived in the old mines underneath the Dragon mountain chain. They were cousins to the Gnomes who looked after the Light Elves' library and were rarely seen outside of the mines. They were also known to live for hundreds of years, perhaps longer. No one was sure. They weren't big on socializing with anyone else.

"Put your differences aside," said the Gnome in the deep, rich baritone they were known for, even the females and children. It was only the difference in costume that made it possible for many outside of the Gnome world to tell the difference between the men and the women.

"Take your seat now," said the Gnome, picking up an oversize gavel and banging it on the table in front of him. "There is far too much at stake here for petty jealousies or old disputes. Take them up later. Right now, we have more important things to discuss. We have put things in motion…"

A clamor of voices rose as the prophets started arguing amongst themselves.

The Gnome raised the gavel over his head and smashed it down on the table. A loud crack echoed off the nearby walls.

"Enough! It no longer matters who came up with the idea, we all discussed it, and voted on it. It was unanimous, as I recall," he said, leveling his gaze at everyone in the room. "Now is the time for us to rise to the occasion. We did what we did for the best of reasons. Oriceran must be put first. That is our mandate, from which we must not shy. Our followers depend on that. The seer, Tessa, accurately predicted everything that has happened in the history of Oriceran to this day. Thousands of accurate predictions. We all know what her last quatrain said. The destruction of our beloved planet. Our only hope is to migrate to Earth. We had to take action."

"We are responsible for the killer being set loose in the Light Elves royal palace," said Kyomi, hanging his head.

"We should never have trusted a human," said the Crystal prophet, plumes of frosted air flowing out of his mouth as he spoke. "We've all seen how they treat each other on their planet. One species and they have never been able to live side-by-side peacefully for very long. Each one always looking for the advantage."

"They have also shown themselves to be able to rise to the occasion in the most tragic of times and come together as a species," said the Wood Elf sitting in the back row. "And like it or not, we will need to trust them, soon enough when the prophesy comes to pass."

"Whatever we did, we did it together for the sake of the bigger picture," said the Mystic Dryad. "To save our people. Mistakes were made but now we have to decide what we're going to do about it, if anything. We are all to blame and if this succeeds, we have all done our duty well. It was to be expected that there would be problems," she said, putting her hand Kyomi's shoulder.

The Gnome held up his short sturdy arms, waving his hands to calm everyone down. "The Light Elves have hired a human homicide detective from Earth to track down the killer. If she is successful it's possible more beings on Oriceran will find out what we have done."

"What do you suggest we do?" asked the Mystic Dryad. "We have no reason to interfere."

"All is not lost," said the Gnome. "The very survival of Oriceran depends on what we do. We must set aside niceties to ensure our population will not only survive on Earth, but thrive. Nothing must get in the way of that edict. The seer Tessa made it very clear in her last quatrain. Once the portals are fully open again, the Oriceran way of life will be no more," said the Gnome. "We will continue to keep our secret."

"It's a betrayal!" said Kyomi, his eyes glowing with fury. "We have become what we hate so much about the human species. We do what we want to do, and we justify our actions later. Consequences mean nothing as long as we get what we want."

"We all agreed that we had to find a way to build a bridge to the humans so that by the time our people were crossing through the gates in greater numbers they would have become accustomed to us. All of us," said the Gnome.

The Light Elf stood, gnashing his teeth, his eyes like two burning embers, fiery symbols raced up both of his arms and he lashed out, sending a fireball smashing into the opposite wall. The Kilomea raised his heavy sword, ready for any trouble.

"Weapons are forbidden within this chamber," the Wood Elf said sharply. "Are we now picking and choosing which of our rules we will abide by?"

Kyomi stormed between the rows of tables and waved his arm, opening a door in the back of the room. The woods beyond the post office could be seen through the magical opening and a gust of wind blew in, ruffling papers. He walked out, leaving smoldering footsteps burned into the floor behind him.

The Wood Elf followed him, yelling over his shoulder, "This is not over!"

The remaining prophets sat in stunned silence. In the millennia since they had formed the movement there had never been such discord.

The prophets gathered their things, most leaving by a hidden corridor, their usual path. Some made their own exits in the wall, erasing the openings behind them.

No one noticed that the old Gnome lingered until the chamber was empty.

A smile crossed his face as he stood in the center of the room, taking in all that he had accomplished. He waited till he was sure no one would come back for a lost object or to ask a question. When enough time had passed, he raised his arm and said, "Close them all," sealing every exit, making it impossible even for a spell to reopen them.

He carefully took off all his garments and stood naked in the middle of the room.

"Transformalia," he said with force. He held his arms out and began to shiver violently. It started at the top of his head and rippled slowly down toward his feet. The sound of bones crunching echoed off the walls of the chamber as his skin began to stretch and grow and his height doubled. Bulges bubbled and moved under his skin as his skeleton reformed.

Pain flashed across his face and he doubled over for a moment. Long black tentacles sprouted from his head until they hung down like long, oceanic hair.

When it was done, the ancient Atlantean, Rhazdon stood there, naked and for once her truest self, a woman. Not only did the world not know that she lived, no one had ever known she was a woman, standing in their midst.

"Too bad about the old Gnome," she sneered, remembering when she slayed him long before he could make the journey to the Light Elves realm. "Nasty little people."

It had taken her years to find the right dark potion to transform herself into the Gnome. It was only right. After all, their cousins had stolen her treasure of dark magic that she had carefully gathered so many years ago.

Her face twisted into a snarl at the memory. "I will take back what is mine," she said, clenching her fists.

Dark magic had long ago twisted Rhazdon's mind, even as it gave her the ability to live on for hundreds of years.

"The only time I can be myself," she said, rubbing the smooth, perfect skin of her arms. "Even if it's just for a few minutes."

She stretched her arms over her head as high as she could, running her hands over the tentacles on her head as they coiled around her fingers. She plucked one from her head and held it out, giving it instructions.

"Find the mouthy Willen and tell me where he is," she said, laying the tentacle on the ground. Another one quickly grew in its place.

"Intransformalia," she said, reversing the process. Once again, the room was filled with the hideous sounds of the transformation.

The old Gnome slowly reappeared. He was the only prophet that wouldn't routinely have a fellow Gnome travel to check on him. None of their kind would leave the dark confines of their home in the mines. And he would not be expected to make many friends. The perfect disguise.

He wearily took up the clothes and put them back on again, retrieving the tentacle, calmly going about his business. "I've already waited six hundred years for my revenge. A little longer is no matter. Everything is coming together nicely."

He lumbered to the far wall.

"Open the way," he said, waving his arm, calling on the dark magic that flowed through him. A doorway just tall enough for the Gnome opened in the back of the room. He walked out into the sunshine and put the tentacle on the grass, watching it slither away. "I can be patient."

He found a human with a horse and cart from a nearby village and offered him a few coins to give him a ride to the open-air bazaar, a vast market on the edge of all the kingdoms this side of the mountains. Beyond was the road toward the mountains and the dark forest.

The journey to the bazaar was rough and shook the old Gnome in the back of the cart continuously, rattling his teeth every time a wheel rolled over a deep rut in the road. The entire cart smelled of hogs and dung, but it was a much faster way to get to his destination, especially on his short legs.

"Drop me off here, he said, as they approached the bazaar.

He waited until the cart came to standstill before he scooted off the edge and dropped to the ground. "Thank you," he said, waving to the man. The old prophet knew it paid to keep up appearances. Everyone would expect the current leader of the prophets to be a diplomat with everyone he came across.

The bazaar was a series of colorful tents, each one stretching across an acre of land. A huge open-air market teeming with activity. Booths were crammed into every inch of space leaving only narrow pathways winding in and out among the peddlers in a maze.

Hawkers yelled out about their wares, promising the finest woven baskets or the freshest fruit. The Gnome passed one stand that was full of household items, some of them far too nice for the Light Elf who was selling them.

The Gnome knew the Light Elf must have bargained with a Willen.

They were a nuisance the palace tolerated. They stopped just short of going too far and they were a constant source of the best gossip.

The Gnome pushed aside colorful drapes of fabric in every texture and color, working his way through another narrow path, avoiding pointed elbows from taller Oricerans busy bargaining on every side, trying to get the best deal.

At last he got to a far corner of the market to a booth that was closed with heavy velvet draperies and a large Kilomea standing guard in front of them. He nodded at the Kilomea who barely looked in his direction. He held back just enough of the curtain for the Gnome to pass through but not enough to let anyone else see what was going on inside.

Inside, some of the highest-ranking members of the Oriceran society were busy negotiating on a thriving black market, trading technology brought over illegally from Earth.

They all eyed the old Gnome. They were careful to stay in his favor. The prophet's followers numbered in the thousands across Oriceran.

If it were to come out that politicians and business owners

were giving themselves better deals than they offered the rest of Oriceran, it would damage their reputations forever and threaten their livelihood. It helped the Gnome bend them to his will.

Several of them tracked his movements carefully, watching and waiting to see what happened next. He stepped over to a table where several Wood Elves had laid out the latest smartphones and were explaining their use to a couple of Light Elf brothers who served in the royal palace.

The black market had existed since the turn of the twentieth century when Earth started to have any technology worth stealing. Ever since then, prominent Oricerans watched with fascination and envy as the humans figured out how to make their world work for them in ways that Oricerans never imagined possible. Their cleverness and determination never ceased to amaze the Oricerans.

It didn't take long before an enterprising Wood Elf figured out how to combine the organic with the new technology they were gathering, creating hybrids on Oriceran that were more powerful than their original design. Insects were turned into drones that could gather information without being noticed, and small engines could replace the hearts of the Oriceran version of a horse. Most were a much larger beast than the variety found on Earth. They lived far longer and with the new engine were able to run for hours without needing a break. It was said, the engines were more effective than magic, especially for those with lesser skills.

All of it, of course, was illegal on Oriceran and sometimes it failed miserably. It was still a new idea on Oriceran.

It was a well-known fact among the elite that the well-connected Gnome was willing to look the other way as long as he received his share of the new technology. He made sure others looked away as well.

There was a special liaison assigned to make sure some piece of everything that came in went to the Gnome. That way, everyone got what they wanted.

There were good deals to be found for anyone enterprising enough and willing to take the necessary risks. Death or prison or even worse, the world in between.

The old Gnome encouraged all of it. The black market created a behind the scenes kind of chaos that was creating cracks in the society of Oriceran. So many different people keeping secrets from each other, damaging the trust between the species, teaching an entire generation of leaders to take what was theirs rather than share for the good of all.

It was exactly what he wanted. If he was to exact revenge for what happened six hundred years ago, then he would have to unravel Oriceran one thread at a time until it was too late, and dissent would be normal once again.

The old Gnome made a point of shaking hands and saying hello to a few key people before gathering the rucksack with his share. He paid a Mystic Dryad missing a wing a coin to carry the bundle for him back through the tangled jungle of the bustling market.

At the other end of the market, when he finally got back to the road, the regular stagecoach was arriving, making its usual stop.

The old Gnome went to stand at the back of the line, waiting to get on the stagecoach. Several recognized him and tried to wave him to the front, but he refused.

He knew he would soon have every luxury he ever dreamed of for over six hundred years. He could afford to sit up with the driver a few more times.

The rucksack was tied securely to the top of the stagecoach where the Gnome could keep an eye on it on the ride back to town.

When they arrived at his stop, the driver hopped down and waited for the Gnome, holding out his hand. The Gnome detested needing help but as long as this was his disguise, this was part of his character. He took the hand and jumped awkwardly down to the next step, almost falling to the ground, catching himself at the last moment. The other riders looked away in embarrassment for him, angering him further.

But he hid it all.

He waited patiently for the rucksack to be untied and held out his arms as the driver placed the bag in his arms. It overwhelmed him with its size. The driver looked like he wanted to say something but thought better of it.

"Have a good evening," he said.

"Always do," the Gnome replied. He walked slowly back along the road, around the bend, working his way to the woods. No one to see what he was doing but the beasts of the forest.

He was well into the known part of the woods before he made a sharp turn into the dark forest where no one ever roamed.

"Fleet of foot," he said, "Pedibusque fugaces," casting an old spell, long forgotten by others. The dark magic came rumbling to life inside of him.

Birds scattered overhead, flying off in every direction.

He was able to run through the dark forest at an incredible speed, carrying the heavy load easily. Deep into the dark forest to the old oak, where he had built his lair.

"Things are progressing nicely," he said, satisfied, when he was finally settled at home and the new mechanical bits and pieces were laid out. "Let's see what we can do with all of this. More will be revealed, in due time."

CHAPTER TWENTY-SEVEN

Bill Somers could feel the sweat under his new tuxedo. Not a good sign. He was never very good under pressure. It wasn't going to be easy setting up his reveal under the nose of Dean Muston. The man was everywhere that night, checking all the details and Somers was sure he had seen him once or twice casting a wary glance in his direction. A couple of times he saw the dean talking to someone, while looking over at him.

Somers half expected to see someone following him for most of the night like an academic babysitter. Clearly the dean saw him as a liability. It only made Somers want to pull this off that much more.

He'd been staying at Richard Randolph's apartment, only slightly better than the one he had abandoned after he was ripped through a portal from his grimy bathroom.

Most of his time was spent studying old documents and working on the timing of wearing the necklace to open the portal. Everything he read that talked about doorways or openings to a better place said the same thing. It took a living host to access the energy in the artifact and stream it outward to open the portal.

He was still tempted to wear the necklace again, if only to calm his nerves. He patted the front of his jacket, checking that it was still safe inside his pocket. "Wait, just wait," he muttered. "Nothing can go wrong."

Besides, there was no telling where the portal would open up this time and he didn't want to risk running into any more large beasts that could rip his throat out.

"Soon enough," he said quietly, wiping his face with a small cocktail napkin embossed with a shiny gold 'one hundred'. He ran the checklist through his head again. He had been doing it all day, finding a small amount of comfort in it.

Mingle with others for the first part of the party. Wait until a few minutes before Muston's speech and put on the necklace in the men's room. Go back to mingling and work his way slowly toward the podium on the stage up front. Give himself the time to let the energy flow through him again. Maybe even make some points with his charm, for once. Let others, like the dean see his easygoing, positive side, even if it was enhanced.

Just as Muston was winding things up, Somers planned to slip backstage where the two plants were hidden and stride out onto the stage. The plants would be a small sideshow after the main event.

He closed his eyes and imagined the looks on everyone's faces, especially Dean Muston, when it turned out Somers had been right all along, and the dean was a close-minded fool.

"You have everything ready?" Randolph was practically leaning against him, whispering in his ear, his hot breath against his face. Somers jumped, sloshing the drink in his hand.

"Don't sneak up on me," he hissed, a flood of anxiety pouring over him. "There's too much at stake here!"

"You mean your career," said Randolph, taking a step back. "People are going to freak when they see you disappear. You're an intergalactic Houdini!"

"Those were sleight of hand. Stupid magic tricks," snapped

Somers. "This one night will finally reset the world's history and everyone will remember I was the one who showed them the way. Like Moses."

"You think he could have been from Oriceran?" asked Randolph, stopping a waiter to scoop several hot crab balls off the tray, popping them into his mouth. "Hot, hot, hot." He held his head back, his mouth wide open.

"Sometimes I have to wonder why we're friends," said Somers.

Randolph grabbed a half empty glass of champagne off a nearby table that an older woman was reaching for.

"Sorry," he said, throwing it back. "Medical emergency. Ate too fast."

Somers took the glass from Randolph's hand, putting it back down. "Sorry, sorry," he said in the direction of the scowling woman, and he pulled Randolph away.

He looked around for the dean and saw him chatting away with a small circle of men and women, using the charming laugh he reserved for large donors. He pulled Randolph behind a pillar, keeping his eye on the dean.

"You want to get us kicked out before we even get the chance to show everyone? Please tell me you have everything ready," he demanded.

"I do, I swear I do." Randolph bit down on the last crab ball. "Man, I never get to eat like this," he said, looking around for a napkin. "Okay, okay, yes, I did what you asked. I paid the guy doing the lights for the stage the fifty bucks like you said to keep the spotlight on you, no matter what."

"And?" he prompted, pulling the details out of Randolph.

"And I'll be near the sound system to make sure no one cuts off the microphone till your big reveal. You really think this will work? You know, it's not the worst thing in the world if it doesn't. I mean, like, doesn't work tonight. There are other days. You just have to have an audience. We could do that over and over again. Take it on the road even."

"It's not a Vegas act. This is science," said Somers sternly. "Besides, you have no idea what I've gone through to show everyone," he said. Not my fault. His stomach twisted into a knot. "When I pull this off tonight it will make up for all of it. Sometimes, sacrifices are made in the name of advancement. It's an age old saying for a reason. People will look back and say, it was tragic but necessary. Besides, he wasn't even from this planet!"

"What are you talking about? What exactly did you do on that planet? Are there some kind of intergalactic police after you?"

Somers went pale when he realized he'd said too much. "No, no," he said, shaking his head. He grabbed Randolph by the shoulders. "Look, it was an accident."

"What was an accident?"

"It happened so fast. I…"

"Somers!" Dean Muston stood next to them, frowning. "Staying out of the way over here. Probably for the best." He fingered the lapel of Somers' tuxedo. "Very nice, Somers. If I didn't know how much you make, I'd swear this was handmade. Glad to see you take something seriously, even if it's not your work," he sneered. "Randolph, are you in a wedding later?"

"I take my work very seriously," he said quietly, his jaw clenched.

"What's that? Couldn't make out the words. Speak up. Oh, Mrs. Jarvis, so nice to see you," he said, distracted by a large woman with a small dog in her purse. The dean was gone without waiting for an answer. There was a small, oval grease stain on Somers' lapel where the dean had touched it.

"It's time," said Somers, clenching his fists at his side.

"But you said you wanted to wait till Muston gave his speech. Had everyone settled down and bored to death so they'd pay attention. Not miss a thing!"

"I'm tired of waiting," he said, his voice carrying. Several heads nearby turned to look. Somers gave a nervous smile and a small wave. "I've waited long enough. Hell, a giant hole in the very air around them should attract enough attention. Give me fifteen minutes to rev this thing up and I'll be good to go."

"Should we do a hand thing or a high five for good luck?" Randolph held his hand up in the air. "Fist bump?" he asked, "No? Nothing? Okay, then," he said, "ready to go. On three." Somers turned, scanning the crowd and walked away, ignoring Randolph.

"Not even that. Hard to feel like I'm on a mission without some kind of official sendoff," he said. "One, two, three, you can do this, Randolph. Hey, how are you? Nice to see you," he said to the couple passing by. "Nice night. Hard to change the world these days. Hey, Bobby, we on target?" he asked, flagging down the man in charge of the spotlight.

Somers made his way to the men's room, holding open the door for someone leaving, the door blocking him from view as Correk and Leira entered the hall.

"Invitation," said the large man in a tuxedo straining against his oversized biceps. A small woman in a long red dress stood next to him, checking off names. They both looked first at Correk and then to Leira.

Correk's eyes glowed for only a moment.

"Nastratium," he said softly. The pair blinked their eyes, glanced at each other and smiled at Correk and Leira.

"Welcome," said the young woman.

"Enjoy yourself," said the overdressed guard. "Ticket," he said to the couple behind them.

"Nice move. How much energy did that cost you?" asked Leira.

"Child's trick. A five-year-old knows how to do that one to convince a parent to let them stay up late. Even the Silver Griffins will ignore a trace of magic that small."

"The Silver Griffins. We'll need to straighten that out later. Giving back the necklace should go a long way with them."

"We may be okay." Correk hesitated. "The necklace is here." He took in a deep breath, letting it out slowly. "I can feel it."

"Is that what that is?" Leira put her hand on her stomach, feeling the energy pulsing through her.

Correk looked down at Leira, dressed in a dark green velvet ballgown. "I believe there is a saying here. You clean up well," he said, taking in the curves that had emerged in the form-fitting sleeveless dress.

"Good thing we spotted that costume shop. Right out of Beauty and the Beast." She gave him a crooked smile. "Aren't we cousins or something? Eyes up here," she said, pointing at her face. "You can rock a hat. Lucky break, men sporting man buns, satchels, and hats indoors these days. Don't know how we would have hidden your ears."

"There's a spell I found in an old book from the library but I want to avoid using the energy."

"So you can save it for Somers."

"Besides, satchels are quite common on Oriceran," said Correk.

"Mmm, not a newsflash," said Leira. "Let's move around the room and see if we can ferret out Bill Somers and hopefully, the necklace. Maybe this will work like a kind of magic GPS."

"You may be right. The rules are not proving to be exactly the same for magic here in your world as they are on Oriceran."

"Unsettling to know," she said, scanning the room. "I don't see him. He has to be here."

"He's here. The necklace is growing more unstable and the presence of magical people is only making that worse."

"We're making things worse. Great. Is there some kind of app that will give me all of your magical rules?"

"We learn them as children. You'll have to pick them up as we go along. There's too many to stop and try to tell you. And, it's not just us," said Correk. "Believe it or not, you brush up against people whose family is originally from Oriceran all the time. We've been here for thousands of years."

Leira saw a woman fanning herself with one of the programs listing tonight's events. She looked flushed and confused. Here and there, around the room were different people, tugging at their collars or drinking down a glass of water.

"Hidden in plain sight," said Leira. Her scalp prickled with the slowly growing heat from the energy already seeping out of the artifact. "There!" she pointed.

Bill Somers was leaving the men's room, his face red and splotchy, making his way toward the steps that led up to the stage.

"You take the left side," said Leira, hiking up the front of the dress. Underneath she was wearing her running shoes.

Correk looked down, raising his eyebrows.

"I'm still on the job. My service weapon is under here, too. I'm not here for the party," she said, elbowing her way through the tight crowd.

"Young lady! Young lady!" Dean Muston was shouting over the crowd at Leira. "Where do you think you're going?"

Somers looked back to see what the dean was yelling about and saw Correk first. Even with a tuxedo and hat, it was clear to Somers that he was a Light Elf. He swung around and spotted Leira, who had pulled her badge out of the top of her dress and was flashing it at Somers.

"Stop right there!" she shouted.

"Somers!" shouted the dean. "What have you done?"

"Now!" said Randolph, signaling Bobby. The spotlight switched on and shone directly on Somers, blinding him. He staggered backward, not sure what to do next.

The necklace burned against his skin, and his confidence surged.

"This is my time," he said, holding his arms out like a showman. "Screw the plants. I can show them later." He closed his eyes and willed himself to feel the energy course through every particle of his being.

Leira reached out to grab his arm, followed closely by Dean Muston who had scrambled up the front skirt of the stage. He wanted to be sure to fire Somers before he was carted away.

Somers' skin turned a deep red and a calm, deeper than anything he'd ever experienced, enveloped him. "It was just an accident," he said. There was loud humming in his ears that made it difficult to hear all the shouting that was going on right in front of him.

Correk watched in horror as steam poured out of Somers' collar, soaking his new suit.

"Welcome to Oriceran," Somers shouted, opening his eyes. He looked confused and surprised looking out at the audience, turning in a circle as if he was expecting to see something else.

"No!" shouted Correk. "It's too late. Something has gone wrong."

"Got you," said Leira, reaching for Somers. Correk yanked her arm away, lifting her off her feet. "What the hell?" She didn't have the chance to say anything else.

Correk threw her as far as he could, knocking over several people who were watching the fight on the stage. She instinctively tucked and rolled, one hand on the front of her dress, the other reaching for the gun strapped to her thigh.

She stood and turned in time to see Correk leaping through the air, trying to pull the dean with him. At the last moment, Somers opened his eyes and saw the dean, grabbing him in a tight embrace.

Correk rolled over in mid-air, stretching out his arms toward the stage, his eyes glowing like embers and his entire body glowing with fiery symbols. "Hoomanna protector," he yelled, throwing up an invisible wall of protection.

On the stage, a swirl of light started around Somers feet, encircling the dean as well, as it wound higher around them, faster and faster, until it was hard to see the two of them through the solid, pulsing light.

"Crack!" The sound was sharp and loud, and a rolling wave of clear energy spread out from the two men on stage, so powerful it pushed against the magical protection, bowing it in the center, sending shivers of blue electricity rippling through it, and knocking everyone to the floor.

Leira fell backward, her head hitting the wooden floor, making her squeeze her eyes shut for a moment. The impact knocked her breath out, making her gasp for air.

"Dammit," she said, clenching her teeth against the pain. She made herself open her eyes and looked down to see if she was hurt. Her gun was still in her hand. She rolled over and saw Correk flat on his belly, starting to stir. The hat had flown off his head and his long hair was neatly pulled back, exposing his pointed ears.

"No time to worry about that one, right now." Leira grimaced as she stood up, helping a woman nearby to her feet.

A man next to her was reaching for his glasses, the frames slightly bent in the blast but the glass still intact.

She made her way toward Correk and knelt next to him.

"You okay?" she asked, touching his shoulder. It was hard for Leira to hear over the ringing in her ears. Everything was muffled. She gave him a thumbs up with a questioning look and he nodded, pulling himself upright.

Leira ran for the stage.

All that remained was two piles of ash where Somers and the dean had been standing only seconds ago. Everything was incinerated.

"It's all gone. Even the necklace," Leira said to Correk as he rushed up next to her.

"Impossible," he said, digging through the ashes with his bare hands. "That artifact by its nature would not destroy itself. It has to be here somewhere."

"Where's Bill?" asked a confused Randolph, staring at the ashes. Correk spread them out all over the floor, searching for the necklace. "That's not…" Randolph said in horror.

"It's gone!" Correk said, standing to get a better view of the crowd. He turned his attention to the back of the stage and found an exit to the alley.

Leira followed, looking in both directions, but there was nothing.

"I take it this is bad," said Leira, "for many reasons."

"Your assessment is on point. Somers was a full-blooded human being and his being couldn't handle the surge of energy. He had no idea he was supposed to take it in small doses and store it or channel it. That crack you heard was the speed of light being passed as the energy surged forward."

"That was a lot of magic back there. Our suspect has evaporated and the necklace is lost. Plus, you lit up like a Christmas tree and threw down with a magical shield." Leira looked pensive.

"That about sums it up. We've exposed magic on a grand scale."

A minivan pulled into the alley spitting gravel as it pulled to a stop right next to Leira and Correk. The side door slid open and out piled three wizards and a witch, their wands already out in front of them. They were all dressed in some form of workout clothes.

They nodded to Correk and Leira and rushed into the hall through the back door. The red exit sign glowed in the darkness.

The passenger side door opened and a witch with long dark hair and bangs said, "Get in and stay put." She pushed her glasses back up her nose. "We'll take it from here. We've been tracking you." The witch jumped out of the car and followed the others.

Leira hesitated and went after her.

"This is my world," she said. "Damned if I'll turn over everything to out of town cops."

"You're from out of town," said Correk, right behind her.

"I outrank anyone not from this planet."

"You're not..."

"Okay, I get it," she snapped.

Inside, the wizards and witches stood in a tight circle, their backs to each other, as they held out their wands and chanted in unison, "Never was, never will be," freezing everyone where they stood.

"What did you do?" Leira asked, waving her hand in front of a man frozen in mid-sentence. "Are they all right?"

"What, you're still moving?" The wizard was startled. "You must be Leira. We heard about your elven blood. It must be strong in you. Let the others know we've located her," he said into his phone. "The detective is safe and sound."

"It's that obvious," said Leira. "The elven blood."

"Quite. Royal Elven blood is hard to hide. Come on," said one of the witches. "If you're going to interfere at least help us get everyone back up in normal party poses. We only bought ourselves an extra few minutes doing the spell as a group."

"Aren't you here to arrest us?"

"Arrest you? We've been assigned to help you, dearie. The network has been keeping track of you, just in case you needed our assistance. Didn't you get the memo? We lost you in the bowling alley but picked up on you again once you got to Chicago."

"You were the ones tracking us," said Leira.

"We were one group. Someone else was keeping an eye on your whereabouts but we were never able to determine who. Come on, there's no time to stand around and chat. Help me with this big fellow."

Leira helped the witch get a heavyset man back into a chair, and moved on to pose two waiters nearby, scooping up the spilled cheese puffs back onto his tray.

"Check the restroom," said one of the witches. "Go on," she said to the wizard. "I had to do it last time. It's your turn."

"Fuck me," he said, but ran for the men's room.

"Messy piece of business. Never know what you'll find and have to get it all straight in a hurry," she said, wrinkling her nose.

Another wizard used a portable vacuum cleaner and sucked up what remained of Bill Somers and Dean Muston.

"That's going to confound the police for some time," the witch observed, pushing up her glasses again. "Nothing to be done about that," she told Leira. "There are a few of our kind on the Chicago police force. We gravitate to this line of work. That should help."

"Okay, that just about does it. We all need to get out of here. They won't remember the last thirty minutes of their lives and that should erase every memory of the two of you. That way when the police question everyone here about the men's' disappearance, no one will describe you two."

"We think Somers had an accomplice," said Leira.

"It won't matter. All he can do is talk about magic and portals. If he's not careful, whoever he is, he'll find himself in a padded room. Don't worry," she said, smiling at Leira. "We'll keep watch. This kind of thing happens more than you realize. Not usually on this grand a scale," she admitted, "but close."

"Time to go," said one of the wizards, breathing hard. He was posing a large man, making him look like he was laughing at someone's joke.

"You can make their faces do that." Leira pushed the sides of someone's mouth into a smile to test it out.

"Sure can," said the witch. "We find it helps them ignore the momentary disorientation if they think they're having a good time.

"This is not your first time," she said to Correk, watching him deftly pose a woman. She looked like she was whispering something into another woman's ear.

Leira looked out over the room and saw that everyone was smiling or laughing. One man was even bent over in laughter.

"I had a hard time getting him to stand up straight," said a wizard, sheepishly. "Had to go with this."

"Only about ten seconds left. We need to be gone like the wind," said a witch.

The witch took one last look around the room and then ushered everyone quickly out the way they came in, piling into the minivan, shoving Leira and Correk into the middle seat.

"What just happened back there?" Leira asked jerking a thumb over her shoulder.

"The prince's death was avenged, granted, in an unexpected and unconventional manner and the necklace is still lost," responded Correk, concern written on his face. "Someone beat us to it."

"That will have to be for another day," said the witch from the front seat.

"Agreed," said Correk. "The necklace has lost most of its power."

"Still, even with only half it's a powerful artifact," said a wizard.

"We'll send out a description through the magical world here on Earth," said the witch. "If it turns up, we'll hear about it. The Order thanks you for your service. We'll file a report and for the time being, this matter is closed."

"We've done all we can for now and there are other matters for us to get to." said Correk, looking around.

"Like my mother." She nodded her head. "You're right. She's waited long enough and so have I."

The story is far from over. Leira's adventure continues in
RELEASE OF MAGIC.

Get sneak peeks, exclusive giveaways, behind the scenes content, and more. PLUS you'll be notified of special **one day only fan pricing** on new releases.

Sign up today to get free stories.

Visit: https://marthacarr.com/read-free-stories/

AUTHOR NOTES - MARTHA CARR
UPDATED MAY 28, 2020

Here we are almost three years later. Wow! It's hard to believe so much time has passed and so much has changed. For starters, Yumfuck helped me buy a dream house and I finally quite the day job.

By now, Michael and I have collaborated on almost 200 books and 21 different series and are still going strong. The Oriceran Universe has grown to include a lot more characters and a school and so many adventures. But this is the series that started it all.

With a twist...

We've added more story (an entirely new plot line runs through the books and explains more about some of your favorite characters – and yes, there's some more Yumfuck.) Plus, there are entirely new books coming that takes their stories even further. You'll see... No spoilers.

Another great change is that all of you are in the Fan Groups and we chat all the time. I've even met a lot of you at fan events and for now – we've been meeting on Zoom for lunch every Friday. I had no idea when this all started just how wonderful life was about to get. Makes me wonder what the next three years hold.

Enjoy reading about your favorite characters all over again and finding out things you may have wondered about – along with a few new surprises. Still more adventures to follow.

Original Notes: August 2, 2017: I'm not sure, I am struggling with it right now.

It was even one of *you* who had to point that rare thing out to me because I never expected to see it.

It was my first time – *I didn't know to look!*

But there it was. A little orange flag that reads, 'BEST SELLER'! And if that wasn't enough, then all of you wrote in, left reviews, sent messages that said how much you love Leira Berens, you love the characters, you love the story – you love the ENTIRE UNIVERSE!

You were even asking, where's the next one? How much *longer*?

Boy, is this a lot of fun, and well worth the wait. Everything happens in its own time.

Monday was an all-around amazing day!

Then the grown offspring, Louie called right after I noticed and I had to take a few breaths so I wouldn't cry on the phone. He said "great" and then wanted to tell me about his day.

Ha! This is why offspring are very useful. Back to reality, get back to work. Be a fellow among fellows.

And he's right. There are stories to weave and magic spells to create and some adventures to go on...

Plus, there are FOUR MORE AUTHORS coming along behind me. (SM Boyce, Abby-Lynn Knorr, Flint Maxwell, Sarah Noffke).

Lots to do to build this universe, as well as get to know all of you better too. So much fun...

But this result for me was thirty years in the making – just one more look back.

I made a wish as a kid the first time I walked into the Philadelphia library and my dad said, "If you can carry the books, you can check them out."

I was stunned.

We were pretty poor and I was a preacher's kid - #4 in a line of 5 kids. The idea of unlimited anything really didn't happen for us.

And books... wonderful, magical, take-you-anywhere books. I devoured the stories and kept going back for more. I made that wish that someday *I* could do the same thing and write a magical story that would take someone else on a ride and let them know, the world is a lot bigger place than they ever imagined.

Tell them, *Go for it – I believe in your dreams!*

Well, yesterday, all of you helped me get to that place.

I will *never* forget and I will be *forever* grateful to each and every one of you.

I'm telling you, it was a magical day all the way around. Dreams do come true – and sometimes they take just a little collaboration and a lot of other wonderful readers – exactly like you. So, thank you from the bottom of my heart.

One last thing... If you've read this far, you know the troll's real name – and we read how much you LOVE, LOVE, LOVE the troll too. So... if you want a little somethin, somethin for yourself go to: https://society6.com/product/yt-troll-revelations-of-oriceran-c_mug#s6-7392665p30a27v200. I already got some for myself (coffee mug) and more creatures are coming!

Make it so... (Yeah, I had to go there. ;))

<Edit by Michael - Martha didn't know I added the Yumfuck's store when she wrote these Author Notes... I left the link in on purpose. Why? Because I desperately want to see Yumfuck t-shirts and stuff out in the real world.>

AUTHOR NOTES - MICHAEL ANDERLE
UPDATED JUNE 23, 2020

Ok, so some things have changed a LOT since the original author notes (below) were written. Some things, not so much.

On the things which have changed? Lot's of new books, the Unbelievable Mr. Brownstone series was started, he had a little girl that went off to school and the whole series finished since the first version of this book was released.

On the side of things which haven't changed?

I'm still writing these authors notes the night before they are due. You can note the difference between the dates Martha wrote her notes and I wrote mine. Now, Martha has mentioned I needed to get going (at least twice), Grace has mentioned it a few times and so has Steve.

I'm still doing them the night before.

Like I said, some things never change!

Oh, and something else that has changed is we are on our third iteration of these covers. Our first were practically hand painted.

A lot has happened, folks... Except me doing this the night before.

Procrastination: The Art Michael Anderle Perfected.

Original Author Notes, August 8, 2017

I'm sitting on the same couch, thinking about *Waking Magic* and *The Revelations of Oriceran*.

And I'm so damned surprised and happy.

Each time another one of my collaborations comes out, I fear I have failed my collaborator some how, some way. Did we dream up the right story to explain the Universe? Are the fans going to like this weird set of characters we put together this time?

How about the fact that we took on a whole new universe?

One of our reviewers said it best and I'll do them the fair shake of clipping the first part of the review, before I comment (from Amazon.co.uk)

A great introduction to a new universe that leaves you wanting more

By Mr P McLean on 1 Aug. 2017

Format: Kindle Edition

I have read all of the Kurtherian Gambit and all of the expanded Universe books so was highly expectant of this new venture into the Oriceran Universe. You must have been really nervous to open up this whole new world to an established voracious fan base. Well done! Totally worth it. I immediately felt myself being drawn into the worlds and characters without wondering about what would BA do in this situation? ... (more follows.)

Mr. P. McLean is absolutely right. I was INCREDIBLY nervous to start a second Universe with a very successful first universe in play. First, the two universes are dissimilar to some degree, but not so far apart that fans of one, won't like the other.

However, the bigger fear was born of the comments about how music artists or bands usually have an incredibly tough time with their sophomore album and THAT is where my desire to chew my nails down to the bone came from.

While we only have the first book (the introduction) out, and this book (Waking Magic) is the next test, it seems we have some amazing fans who have clapped us on the back and said 'Well done, well done indeed...Now, hurry up with the next book!' and to you and those who bought and read, I say THANK YOU.

I have about as much success in Indie Publishing as I should ever hope to wish for, and then some more after that. In my early days in Nov-Dec of 2015, my goal was to be a one percenter. You know, top 1% of Amazon's 200,000+ authors meant I was hoping to jump into the top 2,000 authors on Amazon.

Now, through you amazing fans, a lady by the name of Bethany Anne and some amazing collaborations, I'm a top 100 Amazon Author.

It still feel's SO damned cool to type that...Just saying ;-)

I set out in early 2016 to help other Indie Authors just because I could, and I didn't care about how it was 'done before me.'

That effort became 20Booksto50k.

Then, the people in that group kept saying 'why don't we have a conference?' and Craig Martelle (yes, THAT Craig Martelle of Terry Henry Walton Chronicles fame) said 'I'll do it' and by God, he has! (One Indie authors conference in Vegas in November 2017, one in London in February, 2018.)

Next, I wanted to see if I could help teach a new way of story telling (basically, was I a special Unicorn (that isn't a compliment, by the way), or could others learn a new way of writing ... could I share my style?) so in late 2017, we started the Age's in Kurtherian Gambit and I'm super happy to say "HELL YEAH" they are very successful and the fans have (by and large, not everyone) loved the different authors and their stories...

Then, as I mentioned last book... I wanted to play with another idea and Oriceran was born.

But, could I do it? Could I create a new Universe and take

what I thought I learned from the readers and the fans and deliver another cool experience?

Or, once again, was I just fortunate with The Kurtherian Gambit.

It seems, so far, the response has been... "Shut up about your worries already, when is the next book coming out?"

And that is the BEST response you fans can give us.

So, thank you!

Michael

THE MAGIC COMPASS

If smart phones and GPS rule the world - why am I hunting a magic compass to save the planet?

Austin Detective Maggie Parker has seen some weird things in her day, but finding a surly gnome rooting through her garage beats all.

Her world is about to be turned upside down in a frantic search for 4 Elementals.

Each one has an artifact that can keep the Earth humming along, but they need her to unite them first.

Unless the forces against her get there first.

<u>AVAILABLE ON AMAZON AND IN KINDLE UNLIMITED!</u>

OTHER SERIES IN THE ORICERAN
UNIVERSE

SOUL STONE MAGE

THE KACY CHRONICLES

MIDWEST MAGIC CHRONICLES

THE FAIRHAVEN CHRONICLES

I FEAR NO EVIL

THE DANIEL CODEX SERIES

SCHOOL OF NECESSARY MAGIC

SCHOOL OF NECESSARY MAGIC: RAINE CAMPBELL

ALISON BROWNSTONE

FEDERAL AGENTS OF MAGIC

SCIONS OF MAGIC

THE UNBELIEVABLE MR. BROWNSTONE

OTHER BOOKS BY JUDITH BERENS

OTHER BOOKS BY MARTHA CARR

JOIN THE ORICERAN UNIVERSE FAN GROUP ON FACEBOOK!

BOOKS BY MICHAEL ANDERLE

For a complete list of books by Michael Anderle, please visit:

www.lmbpn.com/ma-books/

All LMBPN Audiobooks are Available at Audible.com and iTunes. For a complete list of audiobooks visit:

www.lmbpn.com/audible

CONNECT WITH THE AUTHORS

Martha Carr Social

Website: http://www.marthacarr.com

Facebook: https://www.facebook.com/groups/MarthaCarrFans/

Michael Anderle Social

Michael Anderle Social
Website:
http://www.lmbpn.com

Email List:
http://lmbpn.com/email/

Facebook Here: https://www.
facebook.com/TheKurtherianGambitBooks/